In Italy, the best attractions are always off the beaten path . . .

Mamie Weber doesn't know why she survived that terrible car accident five years ago. Physically, she has only a slight reminder—but emotionally, the pain is still fresh. Deep down she knows her husband would have wanted her to embrace life again. Now she has an opportunity to do just that, spending two weeks in Tuscany reviewing a tour company for her employer's popular travel guide series. The warmth of the sun, the centuries-old art, a villa on the Umbrian border—it could be just the adventure she needs.

But with adventure comes the unexpected . . . like discovering that her entire tour group is made up of aging ex-hippies reminiscing about their Woodstock days. Or finding herself drawn to the guide, Julian, who is secretly haunted by a tragedy of his own, and seems to disapprove any time she tries something remotely risky—like an impromptu scooter ride with a local man.

As they explore the hilltop towns of Tuscany, Mamie knows that when this blissful excursion is over, she'll have to return to reality. But when you let yourself wander, life can take some interesting detours . . .

Books by Sharon Struth

Blue Moon Lake Series
Share the Moon
Twelve Nights
Harvest Moon
Bella Luna

The Sweet Life
The Sweet Life

Published by Kensington Publishing Corporation

The Sweet Life

The Sweet Life

Sharon Struth

LYRICAL PRESS
Kensington Publishing Corp.
www.kensingtonbooks.com

Lyrical Press books are published by
Kensington Publishing Corp. 119 West 40th Street New York, NY 10018

All Kensington titles, imprints, and distributed lines are available at special quantity discounts for bulk purchases for sales promotion, premiums, fund-raising, and educational or institutional use.

Special book excerpts or customized printings can also be created to fit specific needs. For details, write or phone the office of the Kensington Special Sales Manager:
Kensington Publishing Corp.
119 West 40th Street
New York, NY 10018
Attn. Special Sales Department. Phone: 1-800-221-2647.

First Electronic Edition: September 2017
eISBN-13: 978-1-5161-0355-3
eISBN-10: 11-5161-0355-6

First Print Edition: September 2017
ISBN-13: 978-1-5161-0358-4
ISBN-10: 1-5161-0358-0

Printed in the United States of America

To Bill, who first introduced me to the wonders of Italy...

Acknowledgements

I'd like to thank the readers of my books, who often tell me they get lost in the worlds I create and wish they'd never end. Knowing others join me on this journey is the icing on the cake of each book I write.

Thanks also to Paige Christian, editor extraordinaire, my agent Dawn Dowdle, and the staff at Kensington Publishing, a place that feels like family.

Special thanks to all my writer friends, because without you who would I talk to about writing?

To my husband and beautiful daughters—you guys are everything to me.

To my wonderfully supportive mother, thank you for giving out so many of my business cards. I'm pretty we alone keep Vistaprint stock prices up.

And to my friends, your support is immeasurable. I love you guys!

Chapter 1

Mamie Weber's hands trembled as she shoved aside piles of neatly stacked clothes inside her luggage. Beneath her underwear, she found the well-worn Yankees cap, tossed it on to cover her unwashed hair, and tugged her ponytail through the back opening. She left her luggage on the bed and hurried to the hotel room door, officially fifteen minutes late. She inhaled a deep breath to steady her nerves and hoped the bus hadn't left without her.

One step into the hallway, she stopped. A room key. She propped the door open with her hip and slipped off her backpack. Halfway through her search of the pockets, she remembered seeing it on the nightstand after waking from the nap that now made her late.

She hurried inside, swiped the plastic key card off the nightstand and ran back to the door. As her hand fell on the knob, the shrill ring of the phone made her pause.

For half a second, urgency made her ignore the call and she turned the knob. Her boss had said she might call, but so soon? What if it was an emergency at home, like her parents?

She let the knob go and hurried to phone. "Hello?"

After seconds of silence, a man with a deep voice and American accent said, "Uh, hello. Wanderlust Excursions here. I'm looking for Felix Carrol, room 324?"

"Felix is..." Crap. Hadn't anybody called the tour company to tell them she'd be taking Felix's place?

"This is Julian Gregory. Tour director for a group who is expecting him." He paused, as if he expected her to say something. She debated between lying about the change in plans until she got downstairs or telling him the truth now. "Is this Mr. Carrol's room?" He sounded annoyed now. "We have a bus full of people waiting to leave and he's the only one missing. So—"

"He'll be right down." She hung up and hurried out to the hallway. Explanations like this were better face-to-face and she was determined to get on that bus.

At the elevator, she caught a glimpse of herself in a mirror on the nearby wall. Wrinkled peasant blouse and the same yoga pants she'd worn on the plane. Not exactly the Italian high fashion she'd seen in photos. An outfit that screamed to the world she didn't care enough to even tidy up her appearance. Exactly how she'd felt since that damn car accident.

She slapped the elevator button again, afraid she'd slip into the despair that almost stopped her from accepting this assignment in the first place. As she glanced around the elevator alcove, she saw a sign for the staircase and headed for it.

Each quick step aggravated her sore hip, but she worked hard to concentrate on the bigger problem of getting on this bus, not the accident.

Like how should she deal with the tour director. He expected Felix. Even though she'd packed all his documents, including a faxed note transferring the ticketing paperwork ownership to her, Mamie assumed Felix had called to confirm the change.

Felix Carrol, a.k.a. The Covert Critic, was Mamie's favorite author to edit for in her job at Atlas Publishing. He traveled the globe incognito while reviewing tours for his bestselling series with the same pseudonym. One month he'd be on a safari in Kenya, the next swimming with the sharks in Bora Bora, another mingling with the rich in St. Tropez. And now Mamie had agreed to stand in for him when he canceled last minute.

She entered the marble-floored lobby, glancing around for someone from the tour. Outside the glass doors was a gold mini-bus parked with the words *Wanderlust Excursions* emblazoned on the side. As she pushed through the doors, the hot July air blasted like a slap across the face. She stood on the sidewalk staring at the full bus, prepared to make a case worthy of Clarence Darrow if the paperwork she carried wasn't good enough.

This trip was for work, but it also would test the waters of the life she'd been wasting. Inhaling a breath, Mamie slipped the long strap of her purse across her chest and rushed to the open bus door.

In the driver's seat sat a square-faced man with a full Romanesque nose and short, dark hair. He greeted her with a wide smile. "Ciao, bella."

She climbed the steps and smiled back. "Hello. I mean, Ciao. Sorry I'm late."

Before the nice man in the driver's seat could respond, a man standing about halfway down the aisle said, "I'm sorry, miss. You've got the wrong bus."

Whoever he was, his cargo shorts and faded Led Zeppelin T-shirt didn't carry any authority. But he held a clipboard, and his tone suggested he meant business. His Gaelic-looking face carried a slight boyish quality, hardened into a manly appearance due to his trimly cut mustache and beard. Wavy hair the color of cognac peeked out from beneath a gold cap with orange and blue lettering reading *Wanderlust Excursions.*

"I'm sure the hotel front desk can help you find the right tour." He gave her a now-hurry-along smile and turned back to the man he'd been talking to.

"Did I just talk to you on the phone?"

He lifted his chin and raised a brow. "We're waiting for Felix." His gaze traveled her from top to bottom then he looked her in the eyes. "I'm pretty sure you're not Felix?"

"No, but..." Mamie became aware of the silence and scanned the passengers.

Everyone in the full bus stared back. Quiet. Curious. She squirmed and her gaze drifted back to the man who seemed to be in charge.

"No. I'm not Felix, but if this is Wanderlust Excursions, it's where I'm supposed to be."

He squinted. "Wait. Are you the woman who answered Felix's phone?"

"Yes. I'm taking his place on the tour."

He snorted. A short, patronizing laugh. "I don't think so."

"Why not?"

"Because you're clearly not Felix."

"But he transferred his vouchers to me."

"Nobody told me. Our company rules state that purchased seats are not transferrable without prior home office approval." He frowned and studied her again. "Besides, this is a specialized tour and you're not a member of this group. Felix is."

"How do you know I'm not?"

His lip curled into a little smirk. "Did you attend Woodstock?"

"The concert?"

"Is there another one?"

"Well, no, but..." Mamie scanned the other passengers more carefully. Other than the guide—everyone else was probably over fifty-five. Maybe even over sixty. "What group are they part of?"

"They are"—the guide, whose company sponsored tag read *Julian*, glanced at his clipboard—"the Woodstock Wanderers."

"Felix may not have been part of it either." Mamie never heard him mention them before.

"Are you kidding? Felix was one of our founder members." A man with thinning white hair, dark-rimmed glasses, and a full white beard sitting in the front seat winked at Mamie. "Bernie" in capital letters sat square in the center of a nametag with a tie-dyed background. Beneath his name it said, "Favorite Woodstock Song: 'Let's Go Get Stoned,' Joe Cocker."

Mamie would've never put Bernie together with that song, but... The bus's silence and everyone watching her jarred her back to the problem at hand. "Felix never mentioned your group to me."

Guess she *knew* Felix but didn't *know* him. The truth about how she and Felix knew each other, though, wasn't something she could share.

So she did the only thing she could do. Staring Julian square in the eye, she said, "Uncle Felix wanted me to take this trip. I'm his niece. He insisted I go in his place."

"His niece, huh?" The tour director rubbed the back of his neck and considered her again. He shook his head. "I'm sorry he's decided not to come, but on the transfer, I can't budge. Rules are rules."

A thin gentleman sitting a couple rows behind Bernie, with salt-and-pepper patches of hair above his ears, piped in. "Julian. Dude. Can't you just go with the flow? She looks harmless. Let her come."

Mamie squinted. His tag read *Bob*, but before she could read more, the others joined in with choruses of "yeahs," and she looked away.

"You know what they say, Julian." A woman with curly brown hair, peace sign earrings, and a pretty smile said, "Don't sweat the small stuff."

Mamie noted her nametag read *Martha* and her favorite Woodstock song was "Suite Judy Blue Eyes" by Crosby, Still, and Nash.

Julian pursed his lips. "All due respect Martha, me losing my job isn't exactly small stuff."

Martha grinned slyly and winked. "We promise to keep it a secret from the boss." She glanced around. "Right everybody?"

Another chorus of loud "yeahs" filled the bus.

One slim man with thinning hair who sat in the last row fist bumped the air. "We aren't afraid of the man."

The passengers murmured and nodded, complete agreement on that one. Mamie loved this solidarity. Though she'd never considered herself a hippie—more like a loner—she had an incredible urge to be part of this group.

Julian watched them, frowning. He refocused his attention on Mamie. "Sorry. I'm going to have to ask you to step out so we can start. We're already running late."

Normally, Mamie respected timeliness, schedules, and rules. But she had a job to do. A mission to accomplish.

"Please. My uncle, he *really* wanted me to go and—"

Julian took several swift steps to the front of the bus and stopped close to her. He dropped his voice. "Listen, this isn't personal. The last thing I need is to lose this job. Do me a solid and go see if you can get any of your money back."

She quietly replied, "You don't understand. I *need* to go on this tour."

He narrowed his hard green eyes, but before he could say a thing, a chant filled the air.

"Let her stay. Let her stay. Let her stay."

A blond-haired woman with a cherub face who sat at Bernie's side spoke up over the chant. "Doesn't she remind you of Tracy, Bern?" Her nametag read *Sandra* and her favorite Woodstock song was "Amazing Grace" by Arlo Guthrie. She patted Julian's arm in a very maternal way. "Tracy's our daughter. We'd love having some young energy around. Tracy's just too busy working to spend any time with us."

Julian's lower lip dropped. He drew in a deep breath, looked at Mamie, and motioned to the door. "Let's talk outside."

She turned and headed off the bus. Little did he know, she wasn't about to back down. Nothing would stop her from getting on this bus or making the most of this adventure. Two very good reasons existed for fighting the good fight.

The memory of her husband and daughter.

* * * *

Julian grabbed his satchel off his seat and stopped near Beppe. "Keep the bus running."

"Don't be hasty," the driver said, his smile almost a leer. "There's no ring on her finger, *sì amico*?"

The passengers up front laughed, adding to Julian's annoyance. For a man with a wife and two kids, Beppe never missed a chance to ogle a nice-looking woman. "Head in the game, Beppe. We're working."

He lifted his dark brows, clearly surprised. Julian's childhood friend, who'd found him this job, knew him better than most. Normally a cute, single female would've captured Julian's attention. Not today.

He hurried down the steps. Holding it together since this morning hadn't been easy. An old friend from the show had called him at breakfast with a warning. Seemed Gary Simon was considering asking him back to the show. The shrewd producer was getting pounded by audiences who wanted more of *Exploring the World with Eddie*, not the replacement host they'd found.

But Eddie was dead—at least in Julian's mind.

Julian's television alter ego, Eddie Morrison, was the thrill-seeking adventurer and former star of *Exploring the World with Eddie*. Nobody knew Julian Gregory, but a wide audience around the globe knew his fake persona.

Eddie feared nothing, lived dangerously, and mocked the word *risk*. Julian hated Eddie. Perhaps even more than he hated himself these days.

He stepped onto the sidewalk, stopping at a bench. The woman waited near the hotel doors and searched through her purse, a very determined gleam in her eyes. Over the years, he'd handled bigger problems than a stubborn female. A black caiman alligator in the rainforest. A run-in with Hezbollah militants in Lebanon. One persistent passenger would be easy.

He placed his satchel onto the bench and looked inside for his employee handbook. Other directors for Wanderlust Excursions, including his roommate, had told him the tour company owner had no sympathy for employees who didn't follow her rules. Julian kept this with him at all times. He located the book and opened to the page listing five simple rules Claudia expected her staff to follow.

No deviating from the predefined tour schedule or route.

Only previously authorized passengers can board our buses. Transfers of tickets on site are not allowed.

All stories guides share with our travelers must be true. We encourage passing along appropriate stories of your own travels.

No kickbacks from local merchants, who will often bribe you in order to lure your guests into their stores.

No fraternizing with the passengers off tour.

Before Julian had watched Carlos Lopez die in a wing suit jumping accident, he'd have scoffed at those rules. Anybody's rules.

Now, he desperately needed to live within the constraints of them.

Fear and guilt trapped him daily for the last twelve months. He could've stopped the jump that day. But he hadn't. What had Carlos called the winds? Questionable? Self-hatred pounded at Julian's head. What an idiot. A self-absorbed idiot.

Bravado that once led him to take on the show's challenges disappeared after that moment, the reason he was fired. This tour company provided the perfect hideaway to his shameful existence. Its strict policies helped him regain control of the life he'd forfeited when he'd encouraged Carlos to jump.

Footsteps nearby drew him back to the problem at hand. The woman clutched an envelope and lifted her chin as she neared, her legs long and frame lithe. She had a slight limp, a fact he hadn't picked up on until now. Yet it didn't undercut the bull-like determination in her gaze.

"Now listen," he said before she could speak. Best to keep an unpredictable bull grounded. "I'm not an unreasonable guy."

Her large brown eyes softened. "Did I say you were? It's just that the others don't seem to care if I'm on this bus or not. Bernie and Sandra, they'd even feel like they have their daughter along. It obviously means a lot to them. Wouldn't my presence make them happier travelers?"

"I told you. Rules are big in this outfit. Look." He offered her the handbook, opened to the rule page. While she scanned them, he said, "If it was my company, I might let you stay. But as you can see, miss—"

"Mamie." She looked up from the book. "Mamie Weber."

Julian found himself drawn to the innocence in her eyes, hiding behind her tough facade. "My problem is that you've come out of nowhere and want a seat on my bus. I don't have one piece of paper telling me I shouldn't still be waiting for this Felix Carrol."

She opened the envelope in her hands, pulled out some papers, and thrust them in Julian's hands. "I have the entire trip itinerary, with Felix's name on it. And a faxed note from Felix saying he's transferring the trip to me. The hotel gave me the room."

He flipped past the itinerary to the faxed note. "Anybody could've written that letter. If the passenger who booked the trip didn't take the time to call it in, well..." He worked hard to think of an excuse as a bead of sweat dribbled past his ear. Julian batted away the moisture, not sure when it got so hot outside.

"Excuse me?"

He glanced up to find her staring at him.

"Do I look dishonest?"

Of course she didn't. He reread the note from the original passenger. The package contained the full itinerary. Everything seemed legit. He removed his phone to call Claudia.

"Who are you calling?"

"The boss."

She frowned. "But if she says no, then I can't go."

"She probably will."

As he dialed the phone, he could see her lips pressed tight and she started to pace. Finally, Nicola, Claudia's assistant, answered. Julian explained his problem.

After a minute of searching the office, Nicola returned to the phone. "*Nein*. Nobody contacted us regarding a transfer on that passenger."

Damn. "Nothing, huh?" He glanced up at Mamie and caught her eyes watering. "Okay. Thanks."

A sadness Julian hadn't expected took him by surprise, overpowering him with the idea this trip of hers was about something more. "Why are you really so eager to go on this trip?"

"I told you. My uncle wanted me to..." She stopped. "Why are you shaking your head?"

"The truth. It'll go a long way with me."

She wouldn't meet his gaze for a long moment, but then she glanced up. Dark circles that he hadn't noticed before hung beneath her eyes. "This trip is a chance of a lifetime. I may never get here again." She drew in a breath and, he swore, she trembled. "It took everything for me to board the plane and fly here." She rested her soft hand on his forearm, the effect cracking a piece of him that always stayed tough. Or maybe that strong facade had been broken this year and made vulnerable to more damage.

"Please don't ask me to explain why, but doing this means *everything* to me." She dropped her hand from his arm, adding, "Everything."

The rules flashed like a warning, but his softened resistance buckled at the knees. He could only think of one reason this trip meant so much to her.

There was a chance she was sick, especially considering the limp. What if she was so sick this was her last chance to travel the Tuscan countryside?

She lifted a hand to wipe away a tear, drawing him to her high cheekbones and ivory skin, with a few faded freckles near her nose. Simple and pretty. But tired. He wanted to ask if it was her health, but to do so seemed invasive.

He glanced in the bus's direction. Inside, the passengers watched from the windows with expectant expressions. He didn't want to face their disappointment.

Julian rubbed the back of his neck and dragged his gaze away only to have it collide with Mamie's doleful eyes. Damn it! Every ounce of common sense said to end this now. Only he couldn't. Each time he glanced her way, a pain in the far recesses of her eyes mirrored his own sadness...or was he imagining it?

"Do you have a passport?" he asked.

She tipped her head. "How do you think I got into the country?

"Can I see it?"

She dug into the bag and pulled out a navy-blue US passport and handed it over.

It had been issued eight years ago. In the photo, her face looked fuller and eyes brighter. From her birthdate, he worked the figures. Thirty-nine. Further snooping showed she was born in New York. He flipped through the pages used for immigration stamps. "You haven't used this once."

She shrugged. "Like I said, taking this trip—it's a big deal for me."

Guilt sucker punched him. Damn rules! No wonder he'd ignored them most of his life. A quick risk calculation on a visit from Claudia was low. During his employment here, the home office only got good feedback on Julian's tours—so he'd been told.

If he did this one little thing, how would she know?

He looked again at the bus. Several occupants gave him eager nods. When he looked to Mamie, she watched him.

He kicked a stray stone gently off the curb. "If I say yes, will you promise to be low key?"

"Low key. Of course."

"I'd like to keep this letter from your uncle. For my records, in case my boss finds out your uncle transferred his paperwork to you."

"So, I can go?"

"Yup."

Twirling to face the bus, she flashed a thumb in the air. A loud cheer erupted from inside. She slowly turned back to him and smiled sweetly, the relief in her eyes a reward he wasn't sure he deserved. "Thank you. You won't regret this."

He motioned to the bus before he changed his mind. "Get on. We're behind schedule."

As she took a seat toward the front, the other riders whooped loudly. With any luck, he'd skate by without Claudia finding out.

How much could go wrong with a bus full of people over sixty-five and a thirty-nine-year-old who'd never left the US?

Chapter 2

From her seat in the bus's third row, Mamie admired the patchwork countryside. She wished the driver, who'd been introduced to the passengers as Beppe, would slow down and allow her to breathe it all in.

A minute later, she got her wish when he zipped off a highway exit ramp, causing the bus to sway like a roller coaster ride. Mamie grabbed the seat back in front of her, where Bernie and Sandra leaned with the turn. Holding on for dear life was exactly like her cab ride from Pisa airport to the hotel in Siena. But Italian driving speeds were part of the adventure, and she made a mental note to write about it later.

Her mission here was top secret. Ten years ago, when she started editing for Felix, she signed an agreement stating she'd never tell another living soul the Covert Critic's true identity. Now, as she filled in for him in the field, Felix had suggested she use a fake cover story about her life. She planned on telling people she was recently divorced, worked for a bank, and her dream was to write a novel set in Tuscany. That way her taking notes and pictures wouldn't look so odd. The one truth in her story was that she was now alone in life.

The bus moved more slowly now along a country road, passing verdant fields stretched out side-by-side and linked with golden wheat-colored patches. The ground-level view practically painted her into every picture of Tuscany she'd ever seen. An excited flutter tickled her belly.

I'm here. Really here.

She reached to the floor for her backpack, removed a journal brought along for taking notes, and flipped to the last page. On the plane ride over, she'd started a Travel Bucket List. One she hoped would make up for how she'd squandered the life she'd been spared in the accident and would honor Ted and Zoe. At the moment, only one item was listed: *Fly to Italy.* She put a check mark next to it, knowing more should be added to truly pay homage to them.

At last month's memorial service, to mark five years after losing them, she finally woke up to the way she'd tossed her own life aside like unwanted trash. The realization filled her with shame, so when this work opportunity came along, she took it as a sign. She wanted to believe they were both somewhere together in the spirit world, watching her fight her grief and rooting for her.

All the love she still possessed for her lost family surfaced, causing her chest to shiver with need. Some days, she could still feel her three-year-old snuggled in her lap, head resting on to Mamie's chest while Mamie stroked her soft cheek after she fell or had a nightmare. *Mommy is here. It'll be all right.* She missed the way Ted pulled her from her shell, at times still able to feel the power of his steady blue gaze watching her when he'd say, "Come on, Mame. Life is being on a wire, and everything else is just waiting." He'd loved the quote of Karl Wallenda's, which personified her husband's outlook on life.

The tour guide laughed and disrupted her memories. She looked across the aisle to the seat he occupied behind Beppe. Julian. He probably would hate her this whole tour after how they started off, with her late and unauthorized. He spoke on his cell phone in fluent Italian. A surprise because English sounded like his native language.

He hung up and stood in the aisle, holding onto a pole near the front of the bus that barely steadied him on the curvy road. "As I mentioned earlier, tonight we have a short excursion and dinner. I'll make sure we're not out too late. I'm sure you're all tired from traveling to get here."

"Tired?"

Mamie turned to a voice behind her. The man with a bald scalp and patches of hair above his ears—who'd been one of the first to convince their guide to let her stay— scratched his short, scraggly gray beard. He grinned at Julian. This time, she focused on his name tag, which read *Bob Leon* and "Volunteers" by Jefferson Airplane was his favorite Woodstock song.

"I'm worried about you keeping up with us, Julian." His larger-than-life red Hawaiian shirt suggested this was a man who liked fun. "We all survived Woodstock, you know?"

The other passengers laughed and so did Julian.

"I didn't forget, Mr. Leon. "

"Please, call me Bob."

"Well, Bob, *you* may not need rest, but I do." Julian smiled, then ducked his head low to see outside the front window. "Ahead is our destination. We're still in the province of Siena heading toward Colle Val d'Elsa. Tonight's stop is in Monteriggioni, one of the most important walled castles in the territory."

Mamie looked outside the window and almost gasped. Perched high on a hill and surrounded by lush fields, the medieval structure welcomed them. A self-contained city with a walkway surrounding it and tall towers jutting up at even intervals.

She pulled her notebook from her purse and scribbled notes about where they were headed.

"This commune," Julian continued, "has a perfect circular perimeter, but not because of artificial construction, rather it was created by just following the curves in the natural ground..."

Despite her earlier exhaustion, she soaked in details of the world they passed through. Words of poets and authors returned to her, but they barely did justice to the exhilaration stirring inside her chest.

Julian worked it like a travelogue host, and she scribbled furious notes. "The castle was built by the Sienese between 1213 and 1219 for defensive purposes; its strategic location atop a hill overlooking..."

Her hand slowed and she stopped writing. All this beauty and history. Ted would've loved it here. If only they'd travelled more...

Tears filled her eyes. She turned abruptly to the window, pretending to watch the blurred scenery.

Get a grip on yourself!

She counted to ten while forcing herself to tune into Julian's voice.

"We'll be parking soon at a lot at the bottom of the hill. There's a short climb to the village. Once we arrive, you'll be right in the village's center, called the Piazza di Roma. The church you'll see is the Church of Santa Maria Assunta, a beautiful example of Romanesque and Gothic style architecture."

Churches. There were so many in Italy. The car accident had deepened her disdain for a faith she once believed in. A church was the last place she wanted to visit, but they were unavoidable in this country, where they seemed engrained in the landscape. Besides, she had a job to do and a journey to take. Time to get over her issues. Fast.

She drew in a breath, stiffened her lip, and forced herself to turn around and face the tour director.

"Monteriggioni was cited by Dante Alighieri in his most famous work, *The Divine Comedy*—" Julian's gaze locked on hers and his brows furrowed.

Adjusting in the seat, she sat more upright and looked straight at him.

"Um...Dante..." Julian blinked a few times then looked at the paper in his hands. "I'd like to read a poem of his before we get off the bus."

He began to read, but she didn't listen. She reminded herself to stay strong and make sure nobody knew her real mission in Tuscany or her real story in life. Felix's offer for her to take his place was a gift, offering escape from the pity of well-meaning friends and family. An escape from the memories that kept her from living life. A chance to regain a semblance of her former self in a safe setting. Mamie inhaled and blew out a breath, feeling a little better.

Julian must've finished reading the Dante poem because now he faced the front, looking out the bus window. "Beppe will be staying on the bus if you decide to leave anything on your seat. We'll be here through dinner."

He turned around and, for a brief second, his gaze stopped on her. He parted his lips and she sensed he was about to say something. Only he closed his mouth and returned to his original position.

Mamie stared down at her hands to the empty bucket list. Ted and Zoe's bucket list. It needed filling up. From this point forward, she'd think like her husband. Do the things he'd have done if he were here. Even if it scared the hell out of her. Even if it pushed every single boundary she possessed.

The time had come to live again. In every way possible.

* * * *

"Here." Chef Saburo approached Julian, who'd been standing in the kitchen doorway and watching his passengers interact. "*L'antipasto* for the tour director."

Saburo smiled, showcasing the space of a missing tooth on the right side of his mouth. His splotched white apron covered his ample midsection, and he looked as if he'd lost a food fight with the simmering pots on the old gas stove in the restaurant's old kitchen.

As Saburo lowered the plate to a nearby counter, Julian's stomach growled. Salami, pecorino, bruschetta, and Tuscan crostini with chicken livers. "Saburo, you're always too good to me."

"Eh, it is no big deal. *Buon appetito*." He waved his hand in a simple Italian gesture that spoke to his modesty. On his way back to his stove, he asked, "Why you not out there with the others?"

"I usually don't eat with them at first. Gives them a chance to enjoy each other. Sometimes when I'm around, passengers feel like they need to talk to me about the trip."

The large man dipped a wooden spoon into a pot while nodding. "Ah, I see."

"How's Abriela?" Julian took a piece of pecorino and leaned against the counter.

"Keeping me busy." He rolled his eyes, but then softness filled his face with the love Julian understood Saburo had for his wife of many years. "She is good."

They chatted, as they'd always done since meeting a year ago, when Julian brought his first Wanderlust tour here for a meal. Like all the men Julian had grown up with in Italy, Saburo loved to talk. Life. Politics. The summer heat. The conversations reminded him of living in the homeland of his mother, at least when his parents weren't filming their show. While growing up, Julian had enjoyed being part of "The Wild Adventures of Allie and Alfred," yet he loved when the filming ended and they lived a more normal life even more. Back then, not only bloodlines, but also being a neighbor or friend defined family. Food always served as the glue bonding them together. His father's family in the US were almost strangers.

Julian reached for a crostini and leaned against the doorjamb, peering back out into the dining room. From this spot, he enjoyed a clear view of the woman who made him break Claudia's rules. What the hell had possessed him to say yes?

Sandra and Bernie Wallburg seemed to take her right under their wings. Kind of nice, actually. Maybe they sensed what Julian had, that Mamie seemed to need someone. Not because of her unkempt hair, with pieces of a sloppy ponytail sticking out from beneath a Yankees cap. Not because of those tired, albeit dark and mysterious eyes, that tugged at a more masculine side of him. Certainly not the subtle limp, because she carried herself like it wasn't a problem. No, she had an aura about her. One that said capable, but hurting.

Another passenger, whose name Julian didn't remember, loudly shared a joke. A roar of laugher rose above the table. Mamie's eyes brightened and full lips curled upward, softening the tension—or maybe pure sadness—he'd sensed earlier. What caused such misery in her wet eyes as they'd neared Monteriggioni? Was it an illness, as he suspected, or something else?

Once he finished reading the poem on the bus, Julian almost asked her if something was wrong. He'd stopped himself just in time. No sense in getting involved. He had enough problems of his own.

With the thought, hardness engrained in his heart since losing his parents wobbled and stole his emotional footing. Since watching Carlos die on that jump, the horrible hot air balloon fire that had taken his parents' lives twisted into his subconscious every single day. Helplessness and unsatisfied desire to save them had left Julian with lifelong regret, only compounded by the latest tragedy. Now, he could not stop thinking about them.

The food at his side lost all appeal as he wallowed in disgust for himself over the role he'd played in the loss of another life.

He again focused on the pretty stranger, taking a deep breath and exhaling to get rid of the negative thoughts pummeling him. Mamie. Unusual name, but it suited her. She smiled again at someone's remark and Julian breathed in her delight from across the room. Maybe he'd done one right thing by letting her join them. A small contribution toward helping whatever mysterious thing ailed her.

Julian left the doorway and pulled up a stool near the food. Only a fool would let this wonderful meal go to waste. He selected another crostini, better than thinking about his problems. "You've outdone yourself, Saburo."

"There's more to come."

Julian patted his gut. "You're killing me, you know that?"

"We need to fatten you up." The rotund chef grinned and patted his own extended belly. "Like me."

Julian's cell phone buzzed and he pulled it from his front shirt pocket. The display showed Josef's name.

"Hey, buddy." Julian's mood lifted at the call from one of his closest friends at Wanderlust Excursions. "Where are you this week?"

"Naples. I've got a lively group of forty singles that are in a chorus. The Singing Singles." Josef's German accent delivered the line rather straight, but Julian detected light sarcasm in his tone. "I swear, you can't make this shit up. We're headed north to the lakes over the next eight days. What about you?"

"Smaller group. Survivors of the famous Woodstock concert. They're pretty fun. We're doing Tuscany."

"I heard, from Claudia."

Julian had always suspected the German tour owner and Josef were closer than either let on. Since Claudia insisted everyone follow her rules, though, Julian wasn't surprised they were both quiet about it.

"My tour is scheduled to head north after Naples and we'll be in Siena for a couple days. Want to get a drink while I'm there?"

They worked out the details and were saying goodbye when a thought occurred to Julian. "Hey, question."

"*Ja?*"

"You know the company rule about transferring trip packages to other people?"

"The one Claudia fired a guy two years ago for abusing?"

Julian put down his fork, the food suddenly like lead weight in his gut. "Yeah, that one."

"Why?" Josef asked, saying the "w" sound with a "v."

"Just reviewing the rules."

"It's still a rule."

Julian should've kept his big mouth closed. "Thanks. I'd better run. Looking forward to that drink."

He hung up just as Saburo came over carrying a plate of thick pappardelle noodles covered with a meaty red sauce in one hand, a bottle of wine in the other.

"Here you go." He placed the dish in front of him. "A little red wine to go with it?" Saburo arched his thick dark brows.

Julian nodded as he eyed the Chianti, a surefire way to cure his woes. "Make it a large."

* * * *

Mamie tied her bathrobe tighter, crawled beneath the bed covers, and tucked a pillow behind her back. She sent a text to Allison, to let her boss know she'd arrived safely. No point in mentioning the problems on arrival since she'd worked them out on her own. She reached for a notebook and pen on the nightstand and started to write.

So far, Wanderlust Excursions got good grades. Julian proved to be knowledgeable and knew many locals. Beppe, though a fast driver, loved to joke and offered a smile to everyone. The Siena hotel decor pulled off contemporary and Tuscan in the same breath, and offered their guests million-dollar views of the countryside.

The restaurant where they'd eaten left her certain about one thing: Italian food back home would never be the same. The feast spread before them tonight was worthy of a meal for the Medici family—who once ruled the region in the fifteenth century, she'd learned. Wild boar ragu sauce over pappardelle noodles would live forever in her dreams.

She grunted as she leaned across the bed for her camera, her stomach so full she admitted she'd better pace herself with food on this trip. Flipping through the photos, she studied in more detail a vibrant hand-painted Tuscan countryside mural hanging in the main dining room, not far from the stone fireplace. Rustic goldenrod walls and flickering candlelight gave the room a certain romance. Almost a shame for her to have wasted the mood on a dinner with twenty-five people old enough to be her parents. But when she reached a group photo taken with her camera by the waiter, it struck her how she wouldn't change a thing about tonight.

She never wanted to forget these people. They'd welcomed her to their group, no questions asked. Reaching to the nightstand, she lifted the nametag Bernie had insisted she wear as an honorary member. Bob Leon, apparently the group's secretary at large, pressed her for her favorite Woodstock song as he wrote her name on a blank tag. She only knew a few, but one of them suited her life. Running a finger along the words, only she understood why Janis Joplin's "Piece of my Heart" held any meaning.

As she placed it on the bed to her side, she couldn't believe it had taken her this long in her life to visit Italy. A place rich in history, culture, and culinary treats.

She lowered the camera and lifted her notebook, going straight to her short bucket list. At dinner, while the others talked about sights they wanted to photograph on the group's free time, Mamie thought about how to fill this page.

Earlier, she'd considered asking Julian for some advice. The idea disappeared as quickly as it had arrived. Since he wasn't thrilled about her being on the bus in the first place, her more adventurous plans might cause him some mild hysteria.

Her cell phone rang. Allison's name flashed in the display and Mamie answered right away.

"Hope I didn't wake you. I couldn't remember if it was a five or six-hour time difference."

"I'm up. It's six hours I think, almost ten here."

"Thanks for the text letting me know you got to the hotel. Did you have any problems with the tour company?"

"I almost did. The guy in charge didn't want to let me join them." She explained about the communication problem. "I guess Felix never contacted them."

"So how'd you get on?"

"The tour is a bunch of former Woodstock concert attendees. I think their chants in my support may have tipped the scales."

Allison laughed. "Holy cow. That three-day concert sure toughened them up."

"Just like you want this trip to toughen me?"

"Nah, you're already tough. You're just rusty on how to use it. Is it beautiful there?"

"It's almost beyond words." It struck Mamie even after one day here any visitor could love this place. But she wanted to understand the mystery of Tuscany. What was really behind the charm that lured in so many unsuspecting visitors?

"Well, you'd better find some words. That's why we sent you."

"If not, another glass of Chianti will inspire me."

"That's the spirit. I'll shoot off an email to Felix to notify someone he transferred his ticket."

"Don't bother at this point." Mamie didn't want Julian to get in trouble for getting approval after letting her on board. "I think the director took care of it."

They said they'd be in contact later in the tour and hung up. Mamie reached for her laptop and jumped headfirst into a search for out-of-the-ordinary things to do in the region.

The search hit the jackpot. Her excitement mounted as she read about paragliding outside of Pisa, hot air balloon rides, cave exploration, and riding the countryside on scooters. Ted-worthy activities. She scribbled the ideas onto her list. A few, like the hot air balloon or paragliding, seemed terrifying. All the more reason to add them.

A half hour later, she stopped writing and admired the results. Ted would've loved this.

Once in the bathroom, she brushed her teeth and stared at her face in the mirror. Dark circles beneath her eyes belied the tremor of excitement making her pulse sail.

Less than forty-eight hours ago, fear gripped her over the notion of stepping foot on a plane. Now, after a full day in a foreign land, pride swelled inside her chest, something missing for five years. When she'd forgotten how to live and only existed.

A day of living a little sure felt damn good. Two weeks of this and maybe the fog of her life would finally clear.

Chapter 3

Julian entered the hotel restaurant. Coffee. With any luck, it would help wake him up. More damn nightmares had disrupted his sleep. Would they ever end? Considering the busy day planned in San Gimignano, lack of sleep was about the last thing he needed.

He nodded to a table where several people from the tour sat eating breakfast. At this early hour, he was glad to spot many of them already seated at the round tables covered with white linens.

He yawned on the way to a well-stocked breakfast buffet, tossed some cheese on a roll, and grabbed a coffee.

"Hey, Julian? Got a sec?"

He glanced over his shoulder to a table near the room's old brick wall. A man with short salt-and-pepper hair from the Wanderers waved him over. Across from him was the blond woman who sat at his side on the bus.

Julian glanced at their nametags, mentally remembered their names, and put on his best tour director smile. "Morning, Joel. Tina."

Joel jumped right in. "Listen, I enjoyed the short tour last night and am really looking forward to today. History is a bit of a hobby for me."

Tina raised one of her light brows and laughed. "Hobby? An understatement if there ever was one."

Joel affectionately grinned at her. "Okay, so history is a bit of an obsession."

"For me, too," Julian said. "Italy is *the* place for history. Listen, feel free to share anything I forget, or ask questions."

Tina cracked the shell on a hard-boiled egg while nodding to an empty chair. "Would you like to join us? You two can catch up on the fall of the Roman Empire or something."

Julian chuckled. "Much as I'd love to, I've got paperwork to finish before we leave. But we'll talk on the bus."

He headed through the lobby and up the stairs for the hotel rooftop, his thoughts drifting to last night in Monteriggioni. From his perch at the kitchen door, Julian had listened to the group's stories about Woodstock, keeping him far more entertained than he could remember in ages. His last tour, a group of morticians from the Northeast, had been a subdued group. The only time their energy picked up came during a visit to the Catacombs of Priscilla, Rome.

The Wanderers displayed a continued passion for peace, love, and rock n' roll after over fifty years. A purpose. The way he'd felt when doing the show, when each exploit became another important chapter in his book of life.

This past year, he finally recognized how those days were really spent adding empty content. Or as Jenny had said some four years ago when she'd handed him back his engagement ring, "Julian, you're emotionally vacant."

An uncomfortable sensation stirred inside him. Maybe Jenny's observation carried some truth.

While watching the group's antics last night, Julian couldn't take his eyes off Mamie. Her face would brighten like a hundred-watt bulb at each joke. Gone was the raw pain he'd spotted in her gaze on the bus. For some reason, her happiness made him glad. So maybe his ex-fiancée was wrong.

Halfway up the hotel stairs, Jenny's comment persisted, though. Truth was, the day his parents' died a part of himself had died, too. He'd seen it all. The descent. The landing cable getting caught in the helium tube. The blinding flash of light. And the explosion.

A chill ran down Julian's spine and he hurried up the steps before the pain that usually smothered overtook him. Bursting onto the rooftop patio, he sucked in a lungful of crisp morning air and took in fog-layered hills where the mist was beginning to rise. His state of mind slowly returned to normal.

A family sat at a table in one corner, so he went to the opposite side. As he took a seat, he spotted Mamie with her arms resting on the bricked rooftop surround, her face tilted to the morning sun. A soft smiled enhanced her lips. Pretty lips. Full and pink and complementing her dark, curious eyes.

Today, she'd brushed out her chestnut hair and it touched her shoulders. Cropped pants, a simple top, and white slip-on sneakers suggested a practical side—not a woman who'd attempt sightseeing in heels.

A gentle breeze blew her hair. She blinked, stood upright, and scanned the view one more time before turning around.

Her gaze landed on him. "Oh, hello. Or should I say...Ciao?" She frowned. He hoped it wasn't because it looked like he'd just gone to hell and back, but found himself relieved when she added, "There are too many ways to say hello in Italy."

"Buongiorno is what they say in the morning. Literally, it means good day. Enjoying the view?"

She stepped toward him. All the tiredness evident in her eyes yesterday had disappeared, replaced with a fresh, rested look. "It's magnificent."

He motioned to the chair across from him and took a bite of his roll.

She sat on the seat's edge. "You speak such good Italian, but I don't hear an accent in your English."

"Oh." He swallowed the food. "I have dual citizenship between here and the U.S. Growing up, we owned a house in Cinque Terre. The Italian Riviera."

"Wow. Sounds like quite the life."

"No complaints." He smiled and sipped his coffee, even though his answer wasn't completely true.

She glanced out to the hills along the horizon, her thoughts her own.

"Your empty passport needs some stamps. You've got a lot of catching up to do."

She glanced his way. "I suppose. This might be my only trip. It just sort of fell upon me. My uncle, offering it to me and all."

"Quite generous of him."

"Yes." She pursed her lips for a moment. "Exactly why I want to make the most of it. There were some excursions in the region that I wanted to check into."

"You'll enjoy our visits to the hilltop towns. There's even an organic vineyard tour in Chianti, a favorite with our passengers." God, he sounded like a recording. When had he stopped being...himself?

"Yes. Those sound nice. But I also saw parasailing just outside of Lucca, and hot air balloon rides." She spoke quickly and excitement brewed in her eyes. "Oh, and scooter rides in the country."

"Sorry, but we won't be doing those on our tour."

"I know. I figured I'd try them on my own time."

If she got hurt, Claudia would have his head for two reasons. "I'd rather you didn't. I don't need any problems."

"Like what?"

"Like an accident. Remember, I let you join the tour but it violates my employer's rules. If you get hurt, I'll need to report it to my boss. Then she'll know I let somebody on without her authorization."

She considered him for a moment. "They have guides. These things seem safe."

"Accidents happen." The words made Julian's gut tighten as the wing suit nightmare danced on the outskirts of his thoughts.

"I'll be careful."

Technically, he couldn't stop her. Hell, technically, he shouldn't have let her on the bus.

She stood before he could answer. "The Wallburgs invited me to join them for breakfast. I'm getting the full surrogate daughter treatment."

"Sandra and Bernie. Friendly couple."

She smiled, almost shyly. "They're sweet. Another reason to love it here." She turned toward the hills. A breeze lifted her dark hair, exposing her long neck. "This view...I simply can't get over it."

"It never gets old."

She twirled around and looked at him, her eyes glistening. Tears? "I'd better go eat. See you on the bus."

"Eight forty-five. Sharp."

"I won't be late. I swear." She raised her hand with the palm flat. "Scouts honor."

"Are you a scout?"

"Back in elementary school. I think using this still counts."

"Okay, then. I'm holding you to it." He grinned, feeling lighter than when he'd arrived on the rooftop.

She smiled and walked to the open door leading back inside the hotel.

"Hey," he yelled.

Mamie turned around.

"I've got something exciting you can do that you didn't mention."

"Oh?" Those pretty eyes of hers widened.

"How'd you like to climb a tower here in Siena with me one day before we leave for the villa? It's five hundred steps into the sky."

She laughed gently and the hard weight inside his chest lifted further. "It sounds enjoyable, but climbing a tower hardly qualifies as the type of excitement I'm seeking. Unless we're scaling the outside wall?" She raised a brow and her lips lifted in a playful smile.

"Oh, I see. Never mind." He lifted his mug and drank some coffee, but watched her over the lip.

Her hands slipped onto her hips and she narrowed her eyes. "You see what?"

He chewed and swallowed. "You're scared."

A dangerous grin crossed her lips and... There it was again. Another glimpse of the confidence she possessed that convinced him to let her join the tour.

She shook her head. "Reverse psychology? Are you kidding?"

"Nope."

"Okay, Mr. Tour Director. In fact, I'll bet you ten euros I beat you to the top."

"You're on."

She turned and disappeared down the hotel stairs. Mamie proved herself a walking and breathing conundrum; sadness mingled with bravado. What made her tick? Jesus, was he crazy for even wondering?

Probably. He sure didn't need a passenger who seemed hell-bent on doing things that could get him in trouble. Best to keep an eye on her. Losing this job was a chance he couldn't take, both for financial and personal reasons.

Would he ever be able to return to the job he once had?

* * * *

"This street is the Via S. Matteo." Julian walked backward on the cobblestone pavement, facing their group.

The flaps of his cotton button-down shirt hung on the outside of his jeans and his closed-toe leather sandals slapped the cobblestone. Who was this man? Sandy-brown curls brushed his neck and a handsome face hid behind a trimmed mustache and short beard. The appearance of a painter or craftsman, not quite what she'd have expected from their guide.

After their talk on the rooftop, she found herself curious. More than she wanted to be. He obsessed over the rules, and yet it didn't seem true to the man who stood before her. Just a feeling she got, confirmed by the way his eyes flickered when he'd said, "Accidents happen."

He stopped and motioned for them to gather round. "Shortly, I'll be giving you an hour and a half for lunch. You might want to return to this area to eat or check out the local wares. Then we'll be heading for the Duomo of San Gimignano. On the outside, it's a simple church, but the frescos inside shouldn't be missed. They were painted back in the middle ages."

Julian paused, as if he expected "oohs" and "ahs," but the tour members listened with half an ear. Most of them were either taking photos or gazing into shop windows.

"Anyway, if you decide against our afternoon plans and want to explore on your own, please tell me before lunch and make sure you return to the van by four."

Last night a church. Today another. There'd probably be one at each stop. If Ted were standing at her side, he'd say, "Mamie, honey. Let it go—this is about these beautiful paintings done on wet plaster during the Renaissance. Not your lost faith." His uncomplicated outlook on life made everything light and easy.

"Folks, listen up."

Mamie returned her attention to Julian, committed to the idea of visiting the church.

"After lunch we'll also climb the Torre Grossa—translated it means 'big tower.' It's the only one of fourteen remaining towers open to the public." He glanced around the group. "Climbing is optional."

"Julian, Julian," Bob piped in from the back of the crowd while shaking his head. His wife, a quiet woman named Carol, stood at his side watching her husband with an unreadable expression. "Don't worry. If you need a hand, you can get a little help from your new friends here." He winked. "Right, gang?"

Most nodded their agreement with smiles. Julian blurted out a laugh. His face softened, making the near-constant state of deep thought he carried vanish. "Ah, so you mean..." He raised a brow then cleared his throat. Using perfect pitch, he sang a line from the Beatles song about getting by with some help from his friends—not quite as good as Paul McCartney, but not bad either.

"Hey, Cocker did that at Woodstock," yelled a man from the back that Mamie didn't know well yet. Julian nodded but didn't stop singing.

Suddenly, the Wanderers joined him. Tourists, store clerks, and wait staff watched, some surprised, others amused. Mamie listened, but then Ted's voice whispered in her ear, "Have fun, join in," so she picked up at the chorus. When they finished, the spontaneous moment of song left her feeling strangely free.

They continued the tour, trudging up a hill. Tina came up from behind and fell in line with Mamie's steps.

A strand of thin blond hair fell loose from her low ponytail. "Little does Julian know, we seniors come prepared for anything. I'm wearing my Easy Spirits and brought along cream for my lower back. Nothing will stop me from enjoying this trip."

Mamie laughed. "First, you don't look like a senior. And second, I may need to borrow that cream."

"Hon, it's all yours."

They walked in comfortable silence. Mamie breathed in every sight and smell. Storefronts filled with cheeses, sweets, ceramics, and beautiful woodwork beckoned for her to return.

"So, you and Julian, you're getting along now?" Raised brows on Tina's sweet face gave away her curiosity.

"Sure. He was just worried about breaking the company rules when I arrived. Can't say I blame him."

"Funny." She twisted her nose, peeling from a little sunburn. "He doesn't strike me as the worrying type, and yet, he's a real mother hen." She laughed and motioned up front. "Oh, my Joel. Already glued to Julian's side. God, if only he hung on every word I said the way he does when someone's talking about history."

Mamie laughed, remembering that Ted used to do the same to her. "Men are funny like that. Before he—" She'd almost fumbled, forgetting her story in this world was a made-up one. "Before we divorced, my ex used to do it too."

"Mine too. I thought when I started dating Joel he wouldn't take on husband-like qualities. But after five years of living together, it's exactly the same."

For the first time since losing Ted, Mamie tried to imagine herself with another man. It wasn't easy, though.

After seeing two more sights, they stopped. Julian reiterated the afternoon plans, adding, "After lunch, we'll meet at the Piazza della Cisterna, the town square with the well in the center. Let's say at one-thirty." His gaze drifted to Mamie. "Sharp."

She pointed to her chest. "Are you talking to me?"

"Did I say your name?" Julian grinned as he glanced at the others. "Did I say her?"

"I hope not," Bernie chimed in. "She was on time this morning."

"Yes. I guess she was." Julian's eyes softened and warmth niggled inside her chest. She got the feeling in check, considering her job required she spy on his tour.

Tina turned to her. "Want to join us while we eat?"

"I think I'll wander around." She'd gone from days alone working in her condo to being set in the midst of a large crowd overnight. A bit of peace would be welcome. "But I'll see you at the church."

Mamie headed back to Via S. Matteo, her head held high. People would see her and think she was a woman who could walk around Italy alone, not someone who hated to leave her own house.

Soon she reached the cobblestone hill they'd been at earlier and passed by stores filled with trinkets, clothing, wine, and food, all begging for her to enter. Pausing at a bakery window, Mamie gazed at the delectable goodies and her stomach growled. She went inside and left with a cookie she ate while walking. A shop with beautiful Tuscan ceramics so pretty she wanted to buy them all drew her inside. She entered, popping the last piece of cookie in her mouth.

A dark-haired woman who appeared to be in her forties peeked up from the register and smiled. "*Buongiorno*. Let me know if I can help."

"*Grazie.*"

How easily she'd started to use some of her limited Italian. She wandered along the rows of gifts, committed to purchasing at least one memento from each town she visited. A shelf filled with smooth, opaque figurines caught her eye and she lifted one carved into an elephant.

"Those are made from alabaster," the shopkeeper said as she unpacked some new merchandise near the register. "A stone native to Tuscany, near Volterra."

"They're beautiful." She lowered the elephant and picked up a few other carvings.

At a basket filled with alabaster hearts, she lifted one. She ran a finger over the smooth stone. *Zoe would've loved these.* A permanent scab on her heart reopened, again leaving raw and fresh pain. Sometimes it was a TV show. Or a sound. A word. Even a scent. Always unanticipated, it would leave her momentarily numb with only her memories.

She clutched the cool stone in her palm, closing her eyes and embracing her sadness. Seconds passed then she inhaled, opened her eyes, and reached in the basket for a second heart. One for each of them.

She walked to the register, acting as if she hadn't almost been taken down. "I'm still shopping, but definitely getting these." She carefully placed the two hearts on the counter, refusing to let grief steal these first big steps on her own.

She spent five minutes admiring the ceramics, so pretty she almost forgot her problems. After deciding glass wouldn't travel well, she wandered to some stone items as the doorbell sounded.

"*Andiamo*, Lanzo!" A young girl entered, her head turned to look back over her shoulder.

"Emilia! Shhh." The woman behind the counter gave her a stern look.

"*Sì*, mamma."

Her dark hair was cut to her chin and she mimicked a fairy in white leggings and a puffy skirt. A stylish sort of fairy. A boy followed behind her, who Mamie guessed was Lanzo. They ran to the woman at the counter and emphatically kept asking her for something, while she only shook her head. Mamie didn't need to speak the language to understand that kids and parents were the same everywhere.

She focused on the girl, who couldn't have been more than eight or nine. About the age Zoe would've been now. Mamie rode the wave of grief, trying to concentrate on a display of necklaces made from round, flat pieces of gold while the feeling passed. Each medallion contained wording written in Italian and ended with a dash and the name *Dante.* Julian had shared something about Dante on the bus yesterday, but she couldn't remember what. Joel might remember.

After reaching into her purse for her phrase book, she dissected the quote by each word, starting with *bellezza.* According to the book, it meant beauty.

The woman appeared at her side. "You need me to translate?"

"*Sì. Grazie.* Can you tell me what this says?" Mamie handed her the medallion.

The doorbell tripped again, but the woman continued to study the medallion. "'*La bellezza risveglia l'anima ad agire.*' It means 'Beauty awakens the soul to act.'"

"Dante."

Mamie turned to the deep, heavily accented male voice. A man with perfectly combed black hair, a chiseled face, and rich, dark eyes studied her. He wore a dark suit jacket with a white dress shirt underneath and black slacks. Her cheeks flushed.

"Ah, my brother wants to sell jewelry today instead of run his restaurant?" The storeowner raised her thick dark eyebrows at him.

He laughed and replied to his sister, but Mamie didn't understand. As she handed Mamie back the medallion, he turned to Mamie and smiled. Something deep and magical sparkled in his dark eyes. "*Scusi.* I am a fan of the poet and philosopher. I could not help myself."

Loud giggling voices of the children carried from the back room, followed by a thud. The mother shook her head, excused herself, and headed towards the noise.

He watched his sister leave, then focused on Mamie. "Do you like Dante, too?"

"I'm just learning about him. So this says, 'Beauty awakens the soul to act'?"

"*Sì.* I suspect Dante meant this about the beauty of Tuscany." He shrugged. "It is unsurpassed."

"Indeed. It's the most beautiful place I've ever seen. You just made a sale."

His sister returned holding several large ceramic platters that she handed to her brother. "Your order came in."

"Ah, I had hoped." His gaze brushed over Mamie. "I own a restaurant around the corner. My sister, she gets me a good deal." He winked at his sister.

"Not that he deserves it," she teased.

"What? And to think, I may have made you a sale just now."

Mamie laughed. "He did. I'm taking this."

"See." He raised a brow at his sister, but then turned to Mamie with his hand out. "I am Paolo. Nice to meet you."

She took his hand. "Mamie. Tourist at large...as if you couldn't tell."

He laughed and followed her over to the register. While her purchases were rung up, they talked. At one point, the children came out, speaking in their native tongue. Mamie paid for her purchases, amused by their interactions.

As she tucked her purse away, he moved a little closer. "Have you eaten yet? My restaurant is close." He motioned to the two kids. "And these two monsters want to join us."

She thought about spending time with this handsome man and these two cute kids. "Well, I do need to eat before returning to my tour."

"*Perfetto*. Join us. My chef just made a Pappa al Pomodoro."

"What's that?"

"Stale Tuscan bread, tomatoes, garlic, and basil leaves. Simple and delicious. An area specialty."

She checked her watch. Just under an hour. This would also give her a chance to sample local cuisine, something she needed to do for her piece for the publisher.

But she didn't know this man and the detour might make her late getting back to the others... Was she looking for excuses? The invisible hand of Ted nearly shoved her from behind toward Paolo.

"Sounds like fun," she said and they left together, with the kids leading the way.

Chapter 4

Julian walked ahead of the others, trying to calm down. Most days, an organized group behind him gave him the satisfaction of a mother duck guiding her ducklings to safety.

But one of his chicks was missing.

Mamie had neither shown up after lunch nor told him she wouldn't be on the afternoon leg of their tour. Despite his specific request passengers let him know if they planned to skip the afternoon sights. Normally, he might chalk it up to forgetfulness. The glimpse of her he got during the lunch break, though, gave him good reason to have concerns about her absence.

Break time had started out with worries. Claudia left a message during the morning tour. He quickly called back, worried it was because she'd learned about the unauthorized passenger on the bus. It turned out to be a routine confirmation call about the tour's second week, when they would be staying at a villa near the Umbrian border.

After he'd hung up, he strolled back to the Via S. Matteo relieved and with a growling stomach. His appetite had vanished when Mamie exited a gift shop with a strange man.

Staying a distance behind, he'd followed them a few blocks. Given the stranger's dark good looks and smart style, Julian pegged him as a native to the area. They'd disappeared down an alley, behind two children. Julian jogged to catch up and peeked around the corner just in time to catch her vanishing into the alley entrance of a restaurant. The man guided her through with his hand on her back—a subtle and intimate gesture. Julian had used the same move enough times to know.

Over the years, Julian witnessed more than one vulnerable American woman fall under the snake-charmer seductiveness of an Italian man.

Hell, Julian occasionally approached American women in Rome bars by speaking the beautiful, romantic language first, though always admitted to his dual citizenship. But during the initial meeting, their bright eyes and eager attention would be evident.

Same as Mamie while talking with the stranger.

Damn her! If she didn't know how to tell time or judge men, he sure as hell didn't plan to handhold her every step of the way.

Who was he kidding? It was his job to keep an eye on her. Simple as that.

He tried to shake off this odd mix of worry and irritation over Mamie. So unlike him. People usually described him as a cavalier, brave, an adventurous soul. A man who'd visited a primitive tribe in the Amazon and didn't show one ounce of worry. Although the pain a tribe might have inflicted on him would be *nothing* compared to getting fired right now. This job demanded he get out of bed each day, not stay beneath the covers and drown in his shame.

They neared the church's wide steps, so he stopped to wave the group closer. "We're now at the Collegiata di San Gimignano, also known as the Duomo of San Gimignano. An example of twelfth-century Romanesque architecture." He started backing slowly up the steps leading to the main doors. "While the facade is plain, the treasures inside include a fully-frescoed church. The colors displayed are the original ones painted in the thirteen hundreds. Once inside, note their vividness and brightness. Not all frescoes look this good." He pulled the tickets from the front pocket of his satchel. "As you come through the door, you'll get your entrance ticket."

He scanned the square outside the church one last time, hoping Mamie might appear. Disappointed, he passed into the entrance foyer. The line went through. After he pressed one in Bernie's palm, he pocketed the only ticket left. A hand flashed out in front of him.

"One please." Mamie smiled back, her creamy cheeks flushing bright red and her breath short.

His relief at the sight of her annoyed him as much as her absence. "What happened to being on time?"

"You didn't see me in the back of the crowd?"

"You weren't..." He narrowed his eyes and handed her the ticket. "Just go in."

"Sorry I'm late." She grinned and hurried in behind the others.

Once inside, he offered some suggestions on significant artwork in the building, all while anger boiled beneath his skin over Mamie's relaxed attitude. "Enjoy your visit. In one hour, we'll meet outside."

Everyone dispersed in different directions, but he stood in the back of the church watching them, too annoyed to enjoy it like he usually did. Who was he really mad at? Her or himself, for even bothering to care?

Definitely himself. Over the past year, he'd been a model employee. This single mistake of letting Mamie on the bus stole the one thing he needed: control. When filming the show, he used to look forward to unpredictability. It always added a new element to the final product and played great to their audience. Now it was his Achilles' heel.

Julian left the quiet area and strolled the nave, glancing at the stunning wall paintings through a succession of black and white marble arches. Some visits, he'd walk close to them, study the intimate details of each scene with a close eye. This distance, though, gave the dramatic frescoes a different perspective. Yes, distance. Exactly what he needed with Mamie. Because the subtle pain often visible in her eyes revived his own.

Julian passed a painting of Judgment Day. Judgment was a funny thing. Nobody he spoke to blamed Julian for the accident where Carlos had died. Looking closely at the painting, Julian studied the grim expressions of those making the descent into hell, their agony brought to life. Pain bombarded his chest, reminding him he could never forgive himself for not standing up to Gary when Carlos shared doubts about making the jump.

Julian headed for the back of the church, wishing the heaviness weighing him down would disappear. As he approached the Chapel of Santa Fina, he spotted Mamie. She held a pamphlet, alternating between reading and examining the fresco inside the chapel.

Awe filled her expression. He stayed behind a pillar, where he could watch her covertly.

If he were to do his job, he might approach her and mention this spot was considered a jewel of Renaissance architecture, painting, and sculpture. How the people of San Gimignano dedicated this place to a young girl, Serafina. A child renowned for her piety who'd been orphaned at an early age, suffered a disease that rendered her an invalid, who then died at the age of fifteen.

That's what he *should* have done.

Instead, he silently watched. The ache in his chest faded, until suddenly she frowned and sadness overshadowed the joy of a moment ago. Bowing her head, she let the pamphlet slip from her fingers and lifted her hands to cover her face. Her shoulders began to shake.

Was she crying?

A second later, she pulled a tissue from her purse, blew her nose, then took off down the aisle and exited the building.

Julian's feet moved on their own, following in her footsteps. When he reached the propped open exit door, he paused and watched her in the piazza.

She pulled out a water bottle and took a long drink. Once finished, she just glanced around, no longer crying.

Why had he followed? Plans to keep a distance from her fell apart before they got started. The painting of Santa Fina, who lay on her deathbed, must've caused her reaction. His conclusion she might be sick, the reason her uncle forfeited his ticket, now carried some merit. He stepped outside as a million questions formed on the tip of his tongue. As he skipped down the steps, fully prepared to ask them, a shout echoed in the square.

"*Signora* Mamie!"

Two young children approached her carrying a package. Julian recognized them as the kids who went down the restaurant alley. He froze at the bottom step, close enough to hear.

"Hi, Emilia, Lanzo." Mamie's face brightened. "Oh! My bag."

"You left it at the restaurant," said the young girl.

"I was in such a rush to get back to the tour, I totally forgot about it."

"Uncle Paolo, he wanted to bring it tomorrow, but we told him we would find you."

"You're so sweet." Mamie smiled as the young child passed off the package. "*Grazie.*"

"*Prego. Ciao!*" The two kids skipped off.

Tomorrow? What was she doing tomorrow with Uncle Paolo?

He almost went straight over to have a little talk about men in this country and safety on his tour, but her smile vanished and he stopped. As she watched the children leave, a deeply sad and tender expression filled her eyes. One he'd seen before.

Mamie turned around and their gazes met. For several seconds, she stared at him before finally turning away and heading for the well centered in the small square.

Curiosity snaked through him. What were her secrets? Her problems? And just what the hell did she plan on doing with a man named Paolo tomorrow?

He must be crazy to even care about wanting to know more, but he did. In fact, the notion of helping her possessed him in the most unsettling way, for reasons he couldn't understand.

One thing held him back from questioning her, though. How the hell could he help her when he couldn't even help himself?

* * * *

Lorenzo's lanky frame wilted at the shoulders as he frowned and glanced around the table at Mamie, Bernie, and Sandra. "No more?" He pointed to the unopened bottle of wine that he held in his hand. "Are you certain? In Italy we say '*Due dita di vino e una pedata al medico*,' meaning 'a little wine kicks the doctor out the door.'"

Mamie laughed. The owner of Osteria Antica della Luna had a great sense of humor. "In the U.S. we say an apple a day keeps the doctor away."

"So apples, grapes." He shrugged. "They are the same? No?" Before they answered, his dark eyebrows lifted. "Ah, I get you a little grappa instead. On the house."

He smiled and hurried off.

"What's grappa?" Mamie glanced to her dinner companions.

"An after-dinner drink." Bernie shrugged. "You can't refuse a freebie, right?"

Lorenzo returned and filled small glasses with the beverage as he told them how grappa came from remnants of wine-grape pressings.

She sipped the strong drink and didn't love it, but to please the host she finished what he'd poured. Twenty minutes later, they walked out the door while Lorenzo and his family shouted familial goodbyes.

A surprising number of people filled Siena's streets near the Campo. Strolling after dinner appeared to be a custom shared by both tourists and locals alike. Bernie snapped photos as dusk settled in, while Sandra and Mamie window-shopped. A gelato shop display case filled with colorful offerings got everyone's attention.

Minutes later, armed with multi-flavored gelato cups, they wandered into the busy main square. Packed cafes served patrons late suppers at outdoor seating while those seated ate, drank, and people-watched. Mamie breathed in every sight and sound. A city that had been a stranger only two days ago already felt like home.

As they passed a shop, Sandra paused. "Oh, this place has exactly what I've been looking for." Sandra peered into a window that seemed to have the same assortment of tourist gifts as all the others. "Let's go in."

"I'll wait out here," said Mamie. "Finish my ice cream."

Sandra nodded and went inside, Bernie bringing up the rear in silent compliance. He seemed to do whatever Sandra wanted, her happiness becoming his. Mamie knew her father wouldn't have enjoyed the shopping aspect of this trip and would've said so.

Mamie strolled past a few stores, then stopped and leaned against a building's brick wall, quietly observing the campo activity.

A roar of laughter made her glance to a cafe not far away. Beneath an awning sat a group of ten or so, their conversation lively and spirited. They weren't tourists. Maybe it was their simple attire or comfortable attitudes. Hard to say. As she watched them, she was surprised to spot Julian at the table.

Observing him in his more natural setting gave her a teeny thrill. Not as a tour guide who worried about following rules, but himself. Because she couldn't quite figure him out.

Compared to the others at his table, he quietly listened, only speaking occasionally and always an attentive listener to whoever talked. At times, though, his eyes drifted away from his friends and seriousness took over his expression.

More laughter erupted from their table, but this time Julian didn't laugh with his friends. Instead, he scowled at his phone, pushed a button, and then shoved the phone into his pants pocket. He stared out into the square, seemingly unaware of the laughter around him.

She watched him, propelled mostly by curiosity. Seconds passed. His gaze unexpectedly drifted and their eyes locked. Tenseness on his face softened. The same interest that shadowed his expression when she'd caught him watching her take the package from Emilia now returned.

A family walked in between them, breaking her trance and snapping her back to reality. When the space between them cleared, he still stared at her. The famous Siena Campo's hypnotic buzz stirred around them, like magic dust cast by Roman gods. The grappa she'd had, after many glasses of wine, left her feeling lighthearted and bold. All activity around her dulled to a muted sound, drowned out by Julian's intense eyes. Kind eyes. And those reddish-brown curls made her fingers itch with a need to touch them.

Several people passed by, jarring her like a slap in the face. What was she doing? Reviewing Julian was her job. Anything between them could only create problems in her undercover mission to report on this outfit for her employer.

She quickly went inside the store where she found Bernie and Sandra at the register paying.

"What'd you get?" Mamie glanced over Sandra's shoulder, still flustered.

"Just some T-shirts, for us and our grandchildren."

"Good idea." Mamie went to the shelf, looked them over, and decided to buy one, too.

After paying, they stepped back outside. "How about we head back to the hotel this way?" She pointed in the opposite direction of where Julian sat.

They walked the quieter side streets. Mamie hung a few steps behind her new friends. The brief interaction with Julian lingered inside of her, igniting womanly awareness. Desire. A man's tender touch. All need for those vanished along with her husband. At this moment, though, she craved more. Mamie smiled to herself. A new item would be added to her bucket list...*Enjoy a man.*

Twice today her womanly urges sprouted after a long hibernation. Paolo's attention earlier gave her the same thrill. Back in the States, a guy like Paolo wouldn't make her pause. Over-confident and way too handsome, he could charm the pants off a woman sworn to a chastity vow. But in this enchanted land, an encounter with Paolo carried the appeal of an untasted Chianti; you might not care about it at home, but you'd want to try it in Tuscany.

Julian's rugged yet boyish looks and more subtle way of dealing with women were more to her tastes, but Julian wasn't on the table. Even if he sometimes threw her off kilter just by giving her a simple glance, he was the man whose tour she'd be reviewing. Period.

Still, there were plenty of men in Italy who could help her fulfill this new item.

Paolo's attention at least proved the beaten woman starting this trip no longer existed. After tomorrow's scooter outing with him, she might be able to cross one item off her list. And if it got casually romantic, then she could cross off two.

Chapter 5

Mamie approached the table where several of the Wanderers sat eating their breakfast. The small banquet room had thick navy carpeting and stiff white linens, and a row of windows letting in the bright morning sun.

Maggie stopped at an empty spot next to Tina. "Can I join you?"

"Please do." Tina wore loose gauze pants, a bright orange shirt, and had tied her thin blond strands back with a silky scarf.

Mamie's denim shorts and polo shirt screamed "plain Jane," but this type of outfit always suited her in-the-house wardrobe when home. Next to Tina, the attire felt drab and very old-Mamie. Perhaps new-Mamie needed to update her wardrobe.

She lowered her plate filled with two different cheeses, a hard-boiled egg, and a thick hunk of Italian bread she planned to douse with Nutella. Breakfast at home consisted of an egg and fruit. If she kept up this eating pace, a gym membership when she returned home might be in order.

Across the table Sandra used her spoon and plopped a dollop of the delicious hazelnut spread on a hunk of Italian bread. Bernie sat to her side. Both wore their new "I Love Siena" T-shirts.

Sandra smiled. "Good morning. How'd you sleep?"

"Best night's sleep since I got here."

Tina reached for her coffee. "Me too. It always takes a few days for my body to adjust. We were just talking about yesterday's trip to San Gimignano. What a lovely town."

Sandra moaned while biting into her bread.

Bernie shook his head. "Why don't you make sounds like that around me anymore?"

Sandra swallowed as her cheeks flushed bright pink. "Bernie!" She gently swatted him on the arm. "I can't help it if I love Nutella."

Joel sat on Tina's other side, quietly reading a travel guide. He looked up. "It is tasty, but not healthy like people think."

Bernie speared a sausage. "Okay, Dr. Joel. You've retired from your practice. Let the rest of us enjoy our vacation food."

Joel put down his book and reached for his half-eaten cup of yogurt. "Everything in life is moderation and balance, my friend. But you're right. Vacation is to be enjoyed."

Mamie took a piece of her cheese and bit into it just as Julian entered the dining room, pausing to talk to pretty waitress wearing a short dark skirt with an apron over it and plain white blouse. She'd been there each morning, keeping the buffet table in order. While she spoke, Julian listened quite intently. The way a woman liked to be listened to. She finished speaking and he smiled. As he responded, the charming smile seemed to captivate his audience of one.

Mamie studied the width of his chest and shoulders, the wind-tousled look of his brownish-red hair. The brief, intimate moment between them last night had stayed with her for hours, an eye-locking that caused a flurry of heat inside her belly. His sudden interest in her had to be her imagination. Perhaps she was giving off a vibe, fueled by her waking from a deep sleep caused by her sadness.

Julian hadn't even wanted to let her join the tour.

Mamie picked away at her food, onto better thoughts, like today's date with Paolo. An outing she hoped would fulfill her quest for action on this trip. His tender goodbye kiss yesterday as he walked her to the door of his restaurant was unexpected. A soft brush of his lips on hers. Maybe kissing people was a casual Italian thing and she shouldn't read into it. She couldn't deny how it left her craving intimacy but scared as a virginal bride on her wedding night. Five years without a man. Way too long.

His niece, Emilia, had been delightful during their lunch, but a haunting reminder of Zoe. The pretty young girl offered a living and breathing image of what Zoe might be like if she'd lived. A swift wave of pain pounced on her chest, but Mamie lifted her coffee and took a long, slow drink, letting the much-needed dose of caffeine dominate her thoughts.

The sound of a utensil tapping on a glass rang throughout the room. Julian stood in the room's center waiting for quiet. "Okay, Wanderers. I need your attention."

He sounded very official for a man wearing cargo pants and a slightly wrinkled Woodstock T-shirt that read "Three Days of Peace and Music."

When the group quieted, he cleared his throat. "Quick announcement. You guys have free time until three today. At three, our bus will leave for Chianti. We'll be visiting an organic vineyard for a tour and tasting. Then we'll have dinner at a place in town."

His intense green eyes drifted to Mamie. She froze, some part of her brain telling her she really ought to turn away. Except she couldn't.

He finally looked back to the others, much to her relief. "This morning is a great time to see the sights in Siena. Visit the duomo, climb the tower, shop. You may notice setup going on for the Palio, a horse race, one of great honor to the people of Siena. Seventeen *contrade*—areas of the city—race each other twice a year. If you walk around town today, keep an eye open for unique emblems and flags to represent each neighborhood."

Mamie marveled at how easily Julian spouted off facts. History had never been her strong suit, but Ted had taught the subject at a local college.

Julian glanced around. "Any questions?"

Nobody had any so they returned to their breakfasts. Mamie ate and listened while the others talked. Every so often, she'd glance up at Julian while he got his food at the breakfast bar.

"Want to join us around town, Mamie?" Bernie picked up his coffee. "We're going to the Siena cathedral."

"Thanks for asking, but I have plans. I'm going on a scooter ride with someone I met yesterday. But I'll be back for our trip into Chianti."

"A male or female friend?" Sandra raised her brows, her round face full of innuendo.

"Male." Mamie tried to sound casual, but she was excited to see Paolo again.

"You didn't tell me that at dinner last night." Sandra frowned.

Mamie almost felt bad she hadn't been more open. "It's with a man I met in a gift shop yesterday. Paolo. He's a friendly guy. No doubt all the American women he meets fall for him. He's very..." She paused. "... confident with strangers."

"A real charmer?" Sandra tipped her head and her silver chin-length hair tilted with it. "Like my Bernie?"

Bernie grunted as he speared a piece of melon. "Nobody appreciates your sarcasm this early in the day, Sandy."

She rested a gentle hand on his shoulder and softened her voice. "Who's being sarcastic?"

Bernie rolled his eyes, but a smile played on his lips.

Mamie adored their warm relationship, the kind of love that grew over the span of marriage. How many times had she and Ted talked about what they'd be like some forty years into their marriage? They'd never know now. Her heart ached for all the lost dreams.

"Hey, Julian!" another tour member yelled across the room, breaking Mamie's thoughts.

Mamie didn't know him, but he always sat toward the bus's back. He had a thick New York City accent and his slicked back salt-and-pepper hair made him look like he could own the local pizzeria.

Julian glanced over while slipping a mug under the stainless-steel coffee maker. "Yes, Mr. Bruno?"

"Please. Call me Frank. I've been thinking how you look familiar."

Julian pulled the lever to fill his mug, but his jawline tightened. "I'm pretty sure we haven't met."

"Ever live in the Bronx?"

He let the coffee lever go and turned around to face Frank. "Nope. Nowhere near it."

"Ah, well...guess these old eyes are failing me."

Julian chuckled with a few others as he walked toward a small table in the corner carrying his mug and plate. Frank continued to stare at him, though.

"I know!" Frank said, loudly. "Ever watch that show *Exploring the World with Eddie*?"

Several heads turned and looked toward Julian.

His smile stiffened. "Nope. Why?"

"You kinda look like Eddie." Frank squinted and jutted out his chin while he stared more closely. "Yup, that's it."

More people stopped eating and glanced Julian's way.

His starched-on smile didn't budge. "Well, they say everyone has a doppelganger. Eddie must be mine." He changed his direction and left the dining room.

"Huh," Joel said. "He does resemble the host, if the guy let himself go."

Mamie didn't watch much television and had never heard of the program. She turned to him. "What's the show about?"

"Another one of those cable adventure programs. We've seen it a few times. The guy is a real daredevil, explorer type. Travels the world, visiting places and doing things the rest of us are too chicken to do." Joel took a piece of bacon off Tina's plate and brought it close to his lips.

Bernie nodded. "I prefer my travel in an air-conditioned bus with three square meals. Where I have no worries about wild animals or natural disasters."

Tina excitedly jumped in. "He once did a show in Iceland while a volcano was erupting and the officials there almost threw him out of the country because he wouldn't stay out of harm's way. That doesn't sound at all like Julian."

Sandra pushed her nearly finished plate away from the spot in front of her. "Gosh, he almost didn't allow Mamie to use her uncle's tickets because it broke his company rules."

Mamie chuckled. "You're right. Julian doesn't act like a man who'd do those things."

And yet, he *had* reacted.

After breakfast, Mamie returned to her room. She had close to an hour before Paolo arrived to take her on a scooter tour so she grabbed her computer and checked her email.

When through, she searched the Internet for the show Frank Bruno had mentioned. Before she could look at the results, her phone rang so she answered.

"*Ciao*. It's Paolo."

"Oh hi. I mean ciao to you too."

"Be there in fifteen minutes. I'll pull up front. Parking is hard to find near the hotel."

"Sounds good. See you soon."

She hurried to the bathroom to brush her teeth. Later on, she'd see if she could find the show.

* * * *

Julian's view from the rooftop patio did little to improve his shitty mood. He pushed aside his plate and leaned back in the chair, drawing in a long breath.

He'd been looking forward to today, a chance to get in a run, take care of some administrative work. But Frank Bruno's connection between Julian and Eddie completely unnerved him.

Since Julian started with the tour company, only one other passenger had recognized him. It was before his facial hair had filled in and the short hair he had on the show had grown. He'd denied it then, just as he had today. Hopefully his response put Frank's ideas to rest and didn't get anybody else thinking the same.

Julian downed his coffee in one gulp and took his plates back downstairs. The dining area had emptied out other than two couples who weren't with the tour.

He mentally formed a list of things to get done, starting with confirming some upcoming reservations already made for the remainder of their trip, followed up by his run.

On his way through the lobby, he spotted Mamie. She clutched her backpack straps near her shoulders, and peered anxiously out the hotel front doors.

Oh right. How could he have forgotten her plans today with Uncle Paolo? Who the hell was this guy? A jab of irritation rushed at Julian. The idea he didn't know what they were doing or where they planned on going nagged at him. She should be hanging out with Sandra and Bernie, like he'd seen her do a few times.

He debated on going over, flat out asking about her plans. What if this guy was a serial killer? Julian would have no idea even where to send the police if she didn't return, other than the tie to San Gimignano.

He reached the elevator. As he swiped the button, he imagined the call he'd need to make to Claudia if Mamie went missing.

"I've lost a passenger, Claudia."

"What?" Claudia would say in her thick German accent. "Who?"

"Her name is Mamie Weber."

"I don't see a Mamie Weber on your tour documentation."

"Oh, you won't. She's here because she had someone else's ticket and I let her join us."

She'd fire him in an instant. Like a few others before him who hadn't taken the company's rules seriously.

The elevator door dinged open. Instead of going inside, he turned around and followed a straight line to Mamie. She shifted onto one knee and her denim shorts tightened on one side. He admired her absolutely worthy backside, especially in that pose. Not to mention those slender, long legs. He followed a trail up the curve of her waist and stopped at the tip of her ponytail, resting between her shoulder blades.

He stopped at the door a few feet away and pretended to look outside, too. "Beautiful day."

"It is."

A car sped by. Her head turned with it as it disappeared down the road. He cleared his throat, hoping she'd look at him. "What's going on?"

She glanced his way for only a split second before returning to her car-watching vigil. "I'm waiting for someone."

"Oh. Got some sightseeing plans?"

"Yup." She glanced at her watch then looked his way. "You must enjoy having a little time away from the group. Your job seems pretty demanding."

"I enjoy sharing my knowledge about places with others."

She nodded, gave him a quick smile. "You do a great job of it."

"Thanks." Another car passed, reminding him he'd better get to the point. "So, where you headed today?"

"A scooter ride in the country."

"Scooters?" Aw, Christ. His first scooter ride had been precarious, at best. "Italian's drive passionately, like they do everything else. An inexperienced scooter driver will have to deal with cars going well over the speed limit."

She stared at him, but said nothing.

"I mean, it's an accident waiting to happen. Whoever is taking you—"

"Someone I met yesterday. In San Gimignano."

"Oh? Is that the stranger you followed into an alley?"

Her cheeks reddened. "You were watching me?"

"I was nearby having lunch," he lied. No way would he admit why he'd been following her, even though he could chalk it up to tour safety. Problem was, deep down his reasons seemed to go beyond that. "You should be careful. Italian men have been known to take advantage of beautiful American tourists."

"Then I'm off the hook," she said with a sarcastic little snort and returned to staring outside the door, her jaw tight and lips pursed.

Did she not think she was beautiful? "I'm serious, Mamie. Those scooters aren't as safe as they look."

"What? They look fun. Like in *Roman Holiday*." Her rich brown eyes took on a nostalgic gleam. "In the movie, it was glamorous and exciting to see—"

"It's a movie."

Her brows furrowed. "I'm beginning to think you might be the oldest person on our tour."

She cracked a "gotcha" grin, but the dig hit him in the gut and he didn't laugh.

"Look..." She turned and faced him. "I plan on enjoying as much as Tuscany has to offer that I can. Not only the things you deem safe."

"Yes, but you're on *my* tour."

She sighed. "Not on my free time." Looking both ways out the glass doors, she mumbled under her breath, "Come on, Paolo."

"Ask Beppe about driving in this country. He drives our bus all day. Italians perceive their national traffic laws as a loose set of guidelines."

She laughed, a sarcastic little hoot. "You exaggerate."

"Not one bit. I almost had my knee taken out by a reckless car while riding a scooter." Okay, so he'd heard a friend talking about someone it happened to. "You have no idea how the Italians drive."

"Trust me. I've got an idea. My cab ride from the airport was like the chase scene in *The French Connection*. But I'll be on country roads." A piece of her chestnut hair slipped from her ponytail and she tucked it behind her ear. "Don't you think you might be overreacting? Just a little?"

He tried a new tack. "In this job, the responsibility falls on me to keep everyone safe."

"And I'm impressed you take your job to heart, but..." She paused and thought for a second, a wistful gaze in her eye. "Try to understand. This may be my only trip here." She shrugged her slender shoulders. "Doesn't that count for something?"

He kept his sympathy for her under lock and key this time. "Mamie, I stuck my neck out letting you join us. If you get hurt and Claudia finds out, my ass is on the line."

Her expression shifted. Finally, he might win this argument. A cranberry-red Alfa Romeo pulled up to the curb and all his hope withered. The handsome Italian who'd taken her to the restaurant sat in the driver's seat, flashing his pearly whites and waving.

"My ride's here. I'll be back in time for the Chianti tour." Mamie pushed open the door. Before stepping out, she glanced back over her shoulder. "I'll be careful. I promise."

Julian watched her get in. Paolo leaned over and gave her a kiss on the lips. What went on during lunch yesterday?

Pressure squeezed his chest. Jealousy? No, more annoyance that she hadn't stayed behind.

He glanced at his watch. Five hours until they left for Chianti. He'd be counting every minute of it, hoping she got back on time and in one piece.

* * * *

Freedom.

A warm summer breeze fondled Mamie's skin while she roared on the scooter past rolling hills, where elegant cypress trees leaned with a gentle gust and orderly fields of varying patterns seemed sketched by the hand of man. Cotton candy clouds as far as the eye could see mingled against a perfect blue sky. If nirvana existed, it was here.

The beauty of Tuscany through a car window didn't compare to the wonderment of racing past the fields in the open air. An awareness that pulled her into another world. She felt alive and—

Whoosh!!!

A small car whizzed past her, rattling the scooter with a blast of air. Mamie gripped the handles. This one cut it closer than the last few. God, were these people blind?

Julian hadn't been wrong about Italian drivers. Paolo's driving speeds on the way here gave her reason to be concerned. Italians never appeared to be in a rush, except when they stepped into a vehicle.

Mamie had asked Paolo to be mindful while they drove their scooters, this being her first time using one. He now rode up ahead, his speed fast but not terrifying. He glanced over his shoulder, motioned to the roadside, then pulled his bike there and stopped. She pulled alongside him.

"It's beautiful, yes?" Paolo flashed his bright smile.

No woman would ever tire of his accent or his looks. And that kiss in the car, so unexpected but certainly welcome. "*Sì*. It really is."

"In a few miles, we will stop and eat the lunch my chef packed. My speed, it is good?"

"Perfect."

He appeared satisfied and they continued. She kept one eye on the sights, another eye on the road. Paolo might be a bit of a player, but she liked how he worked overtime to make her comfortable. His friend owned the scooter company and had let them go out unguided. She almost wished for a guide, though. For safety reasons.

All her concern switched to irritation. This worry, it was Julian's fault. Here she'd been trying hard to embrace Ted's enthusiasm for life while Julian kept putting his stamp of disapproval on her ideas.

Maybe when he was a kid, his mother made him nervous about trying new things. Or he'd experienced too many setbacks himself. Although, he had put himself on the line by letting her on the bus that first day. A kind of bravery of its own.

She made a mental vow to be extra careful for Julian as she tried to complete her bucket list items.

Paolo motioned with his arm for her to make a right turn ahead. Behind her, a loud rumble neared. It got louder. And louder. Suddenly so close the menacing roar made her feel like a machine was chasing her. She signaled a turn with her hand then let up on the gas.

The bike slowed; however, the noisy vehicle rumbled louder with each passing second. She motioned with her hand signal more emphatically, daring to glance back. The driver of a small truck held a cell phone to his ear, seeming oblivious to her.

She faced the front and maneuvered her bike closer to the road's edge, lifted her arm again to signal for the turn—

Slam! Mamie sailed through the air.

Chapter 6

Julian used the back of his hand to wipe sweat from his brow, wishing now he'd brought a water bottle for his run. He turned down a shaded side street, finding some respite from the noonday sun.

At the street's end, a section of the magnificent main church of Siena became visible. He continued to the end, where the street opened to the large square housing the structure. Pausing for a moment, he took in the cathedral's gothic peaks, an edifice with majesty of its very own. Inside, artistic treasures by Pisano, Donatello, and Michelangelo awed visitors and he hoped some of his passengers visited her today.

The zipped pocket of his shorts vibrated from his phone's ring. He took it out, glanced at the display, and sent it straight into voice mail. A third call this week from Gary. Julian suspected it wouldn't be the last.

The *Exploring the World with Eddie* producer—and the person who'd fired him from the show—could be described in one word: relentless.

He continued his run, going past the cathedral and toward another street with shade. As he ran downhill, he passed arched doorways and splintered shutters. A car approached. Julian slowed and waited near several parked cars squeezed tightly together. The narrow thoroughfare would have been an unsuitable road for both cars and drivers most places in the world, but in Siena, pedestrians and cars competed for the same space like a game of chicken.

God, he loved this crazy country. Strange how fate pulled the rug out from beneath him, but landed him a job stationed in Rome to do tours of Italy. The one place that truly felt like home.

Fond memories. Their family home on the Italian coast. Holidays spent with his parents and sister, far from the TV show and their life of adventure. He last talked to Jenny about six months ago. His sister, so unlike him. Her quiet life in the States with her hard-working husband and two kids had never appealed to Julian, although lately he could admit the reasons he pushed away such a commitment came from a deep-rooted place. One blocked until the accident on his show...

He shook off the grief about to drag him down and jogged in the hotel's direction. Two blocks from the hotel, his cell phone rang again. Goddamn Gary! Julian's jaw tightened as he reached into his pocket to shut the phone off. Beppe's name stretched across the display, so he answered.

"*Abbiamo un problema....*" Beppe spoke fast and sounded upset.

"What kind of problem?"

He turned down a street and the phone went silent. "Hello? Hello?"

The phone showed no bars. Julian continued checking for better service as he ran faster, hoping to God Beppe made the call from the hotel.

He rounded a corner near the entrance. An Alfa Romeo just like the one Mamie left in this morning parked at an angle near the entrance, both the passenger's and driver's doors left open.

Images of scooters and crazy drivers flashed in his mind's eye. He shouldn't jump to conclusions. Maybe it was something else, another passenger or... Who was he kidding? It had to be her. Suddenly her safety mattered more than anything. All she'd been trying to do was enjoy herself, have the trip of a lifetime because for some reason he wished he understood, she needed that. His theory she'd come here because she was sick hadn't been disproven, but lately she seemed rested. Still, what could explain her sadness during moments he secretly watched her? Now if she got hurt...

He blew out a breath and pushed open the hotel's glass entrance doors. A blast of cool air slapped his damp, hot skin. Across the lobby, a small crowd stood gathered around one sofa. Beppe spotted Julian and waved.

He hurried over and the crowd parted. Mamie lay stretched out on the beige cushioned couch, Paolo kneeling at her side and wiping her dirt-stained face, arms, and legs. Blood oozed from a cut on her arm. Paolo's expression carried the worry Julian felt inside.

Her eyes lifted away from Paolo to Julian.

"What happened?" He tried to stay calm, but wanted to scream the question.

"My scooter got clipped by a truck. A small truck."

Paolo started babbling in half-English, half-Italian about a truck driver on his phone who hadn't seen her slowing down. His tan face tensed as he explained how the truck didn't even stop to help them out and he had been too upset to even get a license plate number.

The need to be right taunted Julian, making him want to shout reminders of why he hadn't wanted her to go. Instead, he asked, "How do you feel?"

"I'll be fine," Mamie said, even though her white cheeks suggested she lied.

Julian raised a brow. "Are you sure about that?"

She didn't answer right away. Her gaze trailed along his body, going from his sleeveless tank top to his Adidas running shorts. Her cheeks flushed pink as she looked at his face. "Yes. Don't gloat about being right."

"I'm not—"

"Here I am!" Joel rushed to Mamie, Tina right behind him carrying shopping bags. Both Julian and Paolo stepped aside and Joel kneeled at her side. "What happened?"

Julian couldn't take his eyes off her as she retold the details. Why hadn't he stopped her? Why should he even care this much?

"What hurts?" Joel asked.

"I've just got a few cuts."

"Mamie..." Paolo shook his head, frowning at her. "Tell him everything."

"My ankle hurts, but only a little."

Julian had to give Paolo some credit. He seemed to have more control over Mamie than Julian did.

Joel systematically checked Mamie, lifting her arms, rotating her wrists, and examining the cut on her arm. "We'll have to clean that cut and bandage it." He moved onto her legs.

Julian stood at the end of the couch, willing her to glance his way. An accident like this couldn't happen again, and they had many days of this trip ahead of them.

When she finally looked his way, he raised his brows.

Right away, she turned her head and avoided his eyes.

Nobody liked saying I told you so, but at some point, she needed to hear it. Easier to do than giving into a deeply buried urge to hold her in his arms and point out how doing crazy things not only could hurt her...it could hurt people who cared about her.

The admission struck him like a bolt of lightning.

On the day his parents died, he vowed never to let himself be hurt by losing a loved one again. On that day, he held in his tears. They'd bottled up inside his throat and chest, strangling him, making it hard to breathe. Then slowly his breath had returned, but only after he mentally squashed the vulnerability threatening to own him. One leaving a wide gap in his heart. A painful gap. Since that day, he'd never reached out for that feeling again. He couldn't, for too much was at risk.

Almost every relationship Julian ever had with a woman ended when he couldn't commit to the idea of love.

How have I not seen this before?

"Julian? What do you think?" Beppe's quiet voice fell near his ear.

He shook off the uncomfortable realization. "I'm sorry. What?"

"Should we call Claudia?"

"No." Shit. Claudia. "Not yet."

Joel examined Mamie, running his hands over her long legs, the movement showing the preciseness of a doctor who knew what to search for.

"Was there a tearing sensation? Or a popping or snapping sound?"

"No, it just hurts."

He drew her legs together and examined the ankles side by side.

"Tell me when it hurts." Joel moved his hands around her foot. As he neared the ankle area, she flinched.

"There."

Her pained expression made the rest of Julian's anger wither. He tried to shut out what he'd realized about his own feelings, but vulnerability owned him.

Joel put out his hand. "I'm going to ask you to try to stand on it."

Mamie nodded, lifting her chin. Yup. She was a brave soldier, of that Julian felt certain. She came here alone and with problems, yet despite them her determination glowed.

She took Joel's hand, carefully balanced herself while lowering the foot. She stood, a bit unsteady, but soon rested her weight on it.

"Okay. So it's not horrible." She shifted. "I can put some weight on it without it hurting." She tried a step and grimaced, working quickly to hide her pain. "I think I can walk."

Joel watched her as she took two uneasy steps. "It's a grade-one sprain. Let's find you some ice. You should stay off this the rest of today. By tomorrow, you could try some walking. But don't overwork yourself."

She dropped back down to the sofa, worry lines clouding her face. "Really? Isn't there something we can do? Maybe wrap it? I don't want to miss anything on our schedule."

"I wouldn't overdo it or you'll hurt it more." He glanced to Julian. "Is there a pharmacy around here? Where we could buy a support wrap and some ibuprofen?"

Beppe offered to go buy what they needed.

Joel glanced between Paolo and Julian. "If someone can help to her into bed, I'll find ice and be right up."

Julian nodded, although a quick image of getting her into bed did something unexpected to him below the belt. Not his usual needs of a purely sexual nature, but an awareness inside his heart and head offering the promise of more.

Julian shook off the thoughts, aware she'd been watching him. Before he could take a step, Paolo moved to Mamie's side.

He slipped an arm around her waist. "*Il mio amore*, let me help you up."

My love? Jesus, women didn't fall for that kind of...

Mamie's expression softened as Paolo helped her up from the seat. A foreign heaviness pooled in Julian's chest. Jealousy? Again? What the...

"I will help you into bed," Paolo crooned, helping her step away.

"I'll join you." Julian fell into line with their footsteps. "Mamie and I need to have a chat."

She glanced his way with a worried expression. "I know what you're going to say."

Paolo's cell phone rang. He hesitated.

"I'm fine, Paolo," Mamie said, even though her tired eyes suggested she was anything but fine. "Go ahead and take the call."

They stopped and Paolo pulled the phone from his pocket. While he spoke to someone in Italian, Julian listened, but Paolo's responses were vague.

He hung up. "Work emergency," he said to Mamie. "I need to return soon."

"I'll help you upstairs," Julian said, hearing the eagerness in his own voice and wishing he sounded less like it mattered.

She glanced at Julian with some reservation, then turned her smiling face to Paolo. "Thank you for today. I mean, it was fun before this happened."

Paolo flashed a charming grin and winked. "I will call later." He hurried from the lobby.

Julian looped his arm around her waist. She stiffened, and a second later reluctantly put her hand on his shoulder. "You really don't have to help me. I can do this on my own."

"I'll bet you can." He eased her toward the elevator, wishing she'd relax. Had he been so horrible she didn't even like him? He smiled. "Now I've got you where I want you..."

She drew in a breath and her eyes widened. "What do you mean?"

He gave a sinister laugh and grinned. "You're unable to move while we talk about my tour, the rules, and safety."

She frowned. "You win. Sounds like I'm about to hear a lecture."

"I'm afraid so." He reached up and wiped a little bit of dirt off her cheek. "But let's get you cleaned up first."

She leaned into him as he guided her to the elevator. Close enough a sweet floral fragrance drifted from her hair and clothes, reminding him he hadn't been with a woman in a while.

Beppe's question about reporting this to Claudia reeled inside his head. In short, he simply didn't want to tell her now. If she found out, she'd insist Mamie leave the tour. A notion that left him with more unease than the idea of her staying.

* * * *

Mamie's ankle throbbed as she pulled on a pair of light blue, elephant-patterned cotton pajama pants. Julian's muted voice carried from the other side of the locked bathroom door. He spoke on his cell phone in Italian, and the only part she got was when he said Beppe's name.

A minute later, someone knocked at the room door.

After she heard it open, Joel started talking. She had taken her time changing rather than be alone with Julian. Not out of fear. Rather the gentle way he'd touched her cheek to wipe off some dirt. And the way he watched her at times. Both left her feeling exposed, though why, she wasn't quite sure.

After pulling off her dirty polo shirt, she rinsed the spots under cold water and hung it on the shower rod to dry. Standing in front of the mirror, she slipped a white tank top over her bra and assessed her clean up. Dirt still smudged her cheek, so she washed it off then removed her hairband, letting her hair drop to her shoulders.

She stepped out and smiled at the two men. "Sorry to make you wait." Walking toward them, she tried to act as if her ankle wasn't pulsing with pain and her hip discomfort worse than usual.

Julian quickly propped up a few pillows near the headboard and patted the mattress. "Better get off that foot."

So much for her acting. She did as he asked, while Joel waited for her to get comfortable.

"Your treatment for this is easy," said Joel, his tone confident. "We call it RICE: rest, ice, compression, elevation."

He went into detail about each one, speaking in layman's terms, then got quiet for a second. "What happened to your hip?"

The question surprised Mamie, but why would she think people wouldn't notice? "A dislocated joint damaged some blood vessels."

He nodded. "Avascular necrosis. How?"

"A car accident." Mamie's face warmed and she avoided looking at Julian, but sensed him watching and listening.

Joel frowned. "A replacement of the injured bone can help with that."

She knew. Avoidance played a part in never having had it done. A fact she didn't want to discuss right now. "Yes. I've been told."

Joel patted her leg gently. "Rest. I'll check back after we return." He smiled, and something told Mamie he was the kind of doctor people stayed with for a lifetime.

Julian walked him to the door, the two whispering on their way over. About what, she could only imagine. The door clicked shut and he returned to the foot of her bed.

He ran a hand through his damp curls, a beam of sun from outside the window brightening the cinnamon tones in the light brown mess. He shifted his large frame and crossed his slightly freckled forearms in front of his sleeveless running shirt, making him a forbidding presence. A tightness in his jaw suggested his thoughts weren't sympathetic. Couldn't blame him, really. He had tried to warn her.

"Houston, we've got a problem," he finally said.

"Oh-oh. Lecture time." She reached for a bottle of hand lotion while smiling at him, hoping he might take it easy on her.

He shook his head and kept a serious expression. "I was straight with you when I let you on the bus. Did you forget about that?"

"No." She smoothed some lotion up her arm while thinking about her next words. She felt like a heel. "You're right. I'm sorry."

He moved closer, bringing with him the scent of sweat and man, an irresistible aroma. "And my problem right now is that all accidents must be reported to corporate."

"But I fell off the tour, at least technically. Surely they don't mean those types of accidents."

He frowned, clearly annoyed. "As long as you are part of this group, any problems must be reported. What can I tell you?" He shrugged. "My boss makes up the rules. I just follow."

"That's ridiculous. I have things to do on *my* vacation and what I do away from this ..." She stopped because he was shaking his head. "What?"

"You promised me if I let you join us, you'd make sure I didn't end up in trouble. Now I feel like you're hell-bent on getting me into trouble. Care to tell me what's so important that you'd violate that promise?"

She twirled a loose thread on her pant leg. "I guess I did promise. But..." She sighed. The list done in Ted's memory had filled her with more hope than she'd had in a long time. But now, she risked getting a decent man in trouble because of her personal goals. "You're right. I'll stop and behave. I just—never mind. You're right."

"I'm not trying to be right. I'm doing what I'm told by my employer. Oh, and since we're on the subject of safety, please be careful with guys like Paolo."

"You're joking."

"Do I look like I am?"

She studied his stern face, but something behind his eyes gave away that this was about something more. "Strangely enough, you don't."

"Listen, I know Italian men."

She grinned. "Well, good for you for coming out."

He frowned. "Ha-ha. Cute. You know what I mean. I've spent a lot of time in this country. Tourists, especially pretty ones, are perfect targets to men looking for a one-night stand."

This morning, he'd called her beautiful and now pretty? Still, his remark was annoying. "What makes you think a grown woman can't want that, too?"

He stared at her long enough she almost wished she hadn't said something so provocative. Julian's voice softened. "You should be careful."

Not once had she considered her safety. Paolo was charming, handsome, and very attentive. Amazing what a man's attention did to a woman, especially one who'd lived a near-hermit existence for five years.

He tilted his head and scrutinized her. "Why didn't you take a more adventurous tour?"

"Because, this is one my uncle gave me. Remember?"

"Oh, right." His jaw tensed and he walked over to her window.

Were the things she wanted to do silly? The activities she'd written down started to slip away. The same way Ted was yanked from her life without warning. She wanted to grab onto the stupid piece of paper and hold on for dear life. Panic squeezed her chest. Suddenly the idea of doing the things in her husband's honor mattered more than anything.

"Please," she said softly, hoping he'd hear the torment associated with her request. "I realize I said I'd give up the things I want to do but..."

He turned around, his expression serious. "But what?"

"I *need* to do them."

He arched a brow. "Care to explain?"

"This trip...it's more than a vacation. It's a second chance for me."

"How so?"

"I haven't been living life the way I should."

"Why not?"

She lifted the pillow at her side and hugged it against her chest. "Does it matter why? What matters is I've been handed an opportunity to change what I ignored." Her throat thickened unexpectedly and her eyes welled. She blinked away the blurriness. "I want to return home with no regrets. So I created a list."

"Of things you want to do?"

She nodded.

Julian reached up and scratched his beard. Sadness flittered inside his eyes then he quietly asked, "Why?"

The truth peeked around the corner, in the form of Ted and Zoe. Sharing with anybody about the angels on her shoulder was something she wouldn't do. Telling him would toss her back into a world where people pitied her. Hiding her problems had been a welcome change. The lump in her throat returned.

She shifted her body and the pillow under her foot fell to the floor.

He picked it up and came to her side. "Scoot over a little."

She inched further to the bed's center. He sat down on the edge and helped elevate her foot back in place. He rested his hand on the pillow, too.

"What's so important only a list can cure it?"

She blew out a breath. "I told you. It's my second chance."

"Then let me try to explain. This job, it would be my second chance. I did something. Totally fuc—screwed up my life. And here's a little truth. I've always broken the rules. Pushed the envelope further than most people would. Until one day..." His face hardened and eyes glistened. "One day I went too far." He tore his pain-filled gaze away from hers and stared straight ahead. "This job...these restrictions...I need to follow them."

Sadness hung between them like a cloud ready to burst. Whatever ghosts haunted Julian they seemed like fresh wounds, like a cut that hadn't yet healed. She felt horrible, adding to his problems. But his focus seemed to come from an inner place. Not only his boss.

An idea struck hard and fast, one so bizarre she almost nixed it right away. Only it wouldn't leave. Julian needed help. Coaxing him to break whatever held him back might help him face his demons. Doing so might help her, too, by allowing her to honor Ted without going behind Julian's back.

With her uninjured foot, she stretched her leg and poked his hip with her toe. He looked up and she smiled. "So, you broke some rules. Everyone does. The trick is to break them for the right reasons."

"Is there such a thing?"

"Sure there is." The wheels inside her head churned with a way to sell this half-thought-out plan. "I've got an idea, but I'm not sure you're going to like it."

"Why do you think that?"

"I just do. But hear me out first. By breaking a rule, maybe you can save a rule."

He chuckled. "I have no idea what the hell you're saying, but you've got me curious."

"I'd like help executing a few items on my list. If you can help me accomplish all the things I want to do, then you don't have to worry about me getting hurt."

"You could still get hurt."

She shook her head. "Nah. You're a wonderful guide. You won't let me."

A wave of sorrow flashed inside his eyes, but he recovered fast. "What's on this legendary list?"

She reached over to the nightstand for her book and opened to the first page. "Paragliding outside of Pisa. Hot air balloons. Exploring caves." She glanced up. He watched her with furrowed brows so she continued. "Riding scooters—which I can now cross off. Plus, hiking in Cinque Terre. Oh, and the Palio, I want to catch those trials you talked about..." She caught him smiling. A truly genuine smile. "What?"

"You are pretty damn excited to do this stuff, huh?"

"Hell yeah."

"But if I let you and Claudia finds out, she'll have me on two counts. We're not supposed to spend time with the passengers outside of the tour."

"But, you're keeping me from harm—thereby saving the overall game. In other words, what Claudia doesn't know won't hurt her."

He considered her words, looking like a man who'd been beaten and knew it. "Anything else on there?"

She glanced down. The only one she hadn't read was a fling. "Nope."

"Okay, Miss Weber. You've got yourself a deal. But only after a day of rest on that foot."

"I'm fine."

"Those are my conditions." His eyes grew hard, making it clear he was a man not willing to budge. "Take it or leave it."

"Okay. A day of rest." She extended her hand. "Deal."

He took her hand in his larger one and held it there. Warmth coursed through her body, the gesture simple but the heat of his softened eyes wielding an intense power.

His hand slipped away, and she immediately missed his touch. Warning bells clanged inside her skull, a reminder about her real mission in Italy.

Mamie debated for all of a split second then turned her back on all caution. She could do this! The trick was not allowing herself to become sidetracked by curiosity over a man she barely knew.

Chapter 7

Julian sat on a lawn area not far from where Beppe parked the bus. Marcello's voice carried in the air as he spoke loudly in broken English to the group about his vineyard's history while guiding them down a gravel path to the fields.

On the way here, Julian announced to the others what had happened to Mamie. Everyone showed concern, especially Sandra. It never ceased to amaze him how fast strangers could bond.

He picked a blade of grass and twirled it in his fingertips while replaying his conversation with Mamie. Although being her personal guide seemed like a great idea in the room, now uneasiness tugged at his gut. To fulfill his end of the bargain, he'd face physical feats that the old Julian would've embraced in a heartbeat. Not the hot air balloon ride, but the others wouldn't have made him flinch. Now, though, all the items served as a reminder of paralysis that cost him his job.

His parents embodied the word risk-takers. People who believed life was a game of chance. Once, the show's producer suggested a hot air balloon ride for their show. Julian said no. Bravery, a facade he wore as Eddie, did have boundaries. The idea of stepping into one of those things was his kryptonite, easily stealing his courage. Courage he'd possessed before watching a man die...

Shit! Where had his courage gone? Somewhere along the line, every morsel of his bravado disappeared. He tore the grass blade into tiny pieces and let them fall to the ground. Now a simple agreement with a pretty lady who wanted to do some ordinary, mild thrill-seeking activities caused him worry. Utterly ridiculous, yet, what if he panicked in front of her?

Agony tore at his gut, proving one thing; he definitely wasn't ready to return to the show. If he couldn't stomach the idea of taking part in a novice sport like paragliding, he might never again face the more challenging stunts done on the program.

Footsteps on the gravel driveway made him look up. Beppe returned from the restroom, shaking his head as he looked in the tour group's direction. "Marcello, he sure loves showing the tourists his fat truffle hunters."

The group had stopped halfway down the path near two enormous pigs wandering in a field.

Julian smiled. "He's proud of his pigs. Did you know they believe pigs were used as far back as the Roman Empire to find truffles?"

Beppe raised a brow. "I did not. See, I always say you got your father's Irish looks and your mother's Italian heart for this reason. Nobody else would care about that." Beppe pulled out a pack of cigarettes, lit one, and took a deep drag. "Now I test you. Why are pigs so good at finding truffles?"

"They went to Truffle Hunting University?"

Beppe laughed. "Not even close. The male pig's natural sex hormones are similar to the truffle scent."

"Now I can say I've heard it all. You should share that with the others on the way back to the hotel."

"You are the guide. Be my guest." Beppe shoved one hand in the pocket of his khaki pants, his cigarette dangling from the other. "I'm going to walk around. My legs are stiff. Want to come?"

"Go on. Maybe I'll catch up in a bit."

Julian probably should've walked with his friend, but he wanted to be alone. Beppe strolled toward the rows of grapes running along the hillside, but Julian kept watching the industrious pigs while still thinking about what Beppe just shared. Aromas that attract. He smiled. Swine weren't the only ones drawn to scents.

While Julian sat close to Mamie on her bed earlier, the way she smoothed the citrus-scented lotion on her graceful arms made him want to reach out and help. Aw, hell. If she'd asked, he would've massaged her sore foot and even skipped the afternoon tour to keep her company. All in the name of learning what made her tick.

Damned if she didn't leave him far too eager to learn about her background. There was no doubt she hid something deep. It registered quite clearly on her face.

For some strange reason, he'd easily offered her a piece of his past without much thought today. Being around her took an edge off him, encouraged him to think about something besides himself. She carried a quiet sensibility, tempered by a quick sense of humor and an oddly forced sense of adventure. And bravado quieter then the type he once possessed.

Most of all, there was something he liked better about himself when he was around her. She mystified him. Exactly what past relationships lacked. Relationships he never took any further, other than one impulsive proposal.

What had Mamie said? Maybe he took chances for the wrong reasons? What the hell did she mean?

Risk taking came naturally to him. But when had risk become so... routine? He wasn't like that as a child and yet a flip switched one day, causing his boldness to happen without thought. But when?

Think. Think. Think.

He stepped back in time and stopped at an obvious moment. Ah, yes. Right after his parents' accident.

At first, their loss owned him, choking him so tightly he wished he died with them. He'd never felt more alone in the world than in the days that followed, paralyzed with unimaginable fear. Every single time he shut his eyes, the death of his parents came to life. The parents he loved and admired, gone in a blink. A single, horrifying blink.

Lesson learned. Love could disappear in an instant. He'd gone through the motions of living with his aunt in Michigan. But only when he began to hang out with kids who rode dirt bikes had something inside him turned on again. He gravitated to the confident, adventurous group of teens. Every afternoon he joined them at a quarry to practice dangerous stunts. Julian acquired a strange comfort in living dangerously.

The thought numbed him even after all these years, but it also struck him how logic back then told him he couldn't possibly face anything more terrifying than what he'd already seen. Both love, life, and death had become surreal concepts, making it easy to pursue danger.

A pair of magpies landed nearby, their odd chirp pulling Julian back to the vineyard setting. His chest ached. Convoluted and detached thinking had guided him in life and love. All because his heart got stuck in a moment of loss. And life, well, he lived it on the edge with no regard for his own safety because doing so was easier than caring.

At least it was, until he witnessed Carlos slam into a bridge. The moment had ripped the seal secured around his heart.

The loud engine of a tour bus pulling into the lot's far side tore him from the powerful insights. He stood up and tried to shake off the discomfort inside of him by walking down the path to find Beppe.

So he'd been living life the wrong way.

And somehow an overeager tourist, with a wish list that seemed to mean everything in the world to her, loosened feelings that had pinned him down for ages. For that reason alone, doing everything she wanted might be a smart move. But he wasn't ready to go paragliding or sail off in a hot air balloon. Or pretty much any of the things she had listed.

So how would he balance the goal of ensuring her quest for adventure with his own insecurities?

He considered the itinerary ahead, the places they'd visit and how it related to her list. Not even close to the types of things desired by the adventurous Mamie. Yet, the places they would go were beautiful, with a type of thrill she wasn't thinking about.

His parents had shown him that, always pointing out how beauty could be found in the simple observation of life.

Their words returned to him this past year while working with the tour company. He enjoyed what he saw on the tours he guided. What if he tried to show Mamie there was more than one way to pursue excitement?

The day after tomorrow they'd visit Lucca, one of his favorite towns in Tuscany. If he could just get her away from the group for a few hours....

He picked up his phone and dialed.

At the third ring, Fabrizio picked up. "*Pronto.*"

"*Ciao*, buddy. It's Julian."

"Hey, Jules! How are you?"

"Good, good. This is last minute, but are you interested in doing a tour of Lucca two days from now?"

"Happens to be my day off at the store. Same price as always?"

Julian thought for a minute. "I'll up it since this is a last-minute call."

"Then you've got yourself a deal."

Julian hung up. The more he thought about his plans, the more excitement brewed inside of him. He'd show Mamie how the beauty of Tuscany could come in many forms.

* * * *

Knock, knock, knock.

Mamie tightened her bathrobe and opened the door. Sandra stood on the other side. Her silver pageboy hair looked freshly styled and she wore white slacks with a striped red and blue shirt. Very patriotic.

"Oh good. You're up." Sandra smiled. "I didn't want to knock on your door when we got back last night." She held up a small brown bag. "I bought you something at the farm in Chianti."

"Thank you. You're so sweet. Come on in." Mamie moved aside as Sandra entered. "You didn't have to do that."

"I wanted to." Sandra glanced in the direction of a room service tray on the table not far from Mamie's bed. "Oh, you've had breakfast?"

"Yeah, I'm supposed to take it easy today. Doctor's orders. How was Chianti?"

"Beautiful. You know, Julian said there's another vineyard near the villa where we'll be staying next. Maybe you can visit one then." She handed Mamie the bag. "We missed you."

"I missed you guys, too." Warmth settled inside her heart over Sandra's sweet gesture. She considered herself lucky to have found such nice people on this trip.

"Well, open the bag," Sandra said, her tone excited.

Mamie pulled out a tissue-wrapped item and opened it to find a rooster corkscrew. "It's so cute! Thank you." She hugged Sandra. "I'll think of you every time I use it."

"We learned that the rooster is a symbol of Tuscany. I'd tell you more but these days I can't remember a damn thing. But I'm sure Julian knows. He seems to know everything."

He sure knew Mamie could have an accident on a scooter, but she hadn't listened.

"I'd better go. Bernie's waiting for me to come down for breakfast. So I guess you'll miss the trip to Volterra today?"

"Julian would probably drag me off the bus if I tried to step on."

Sandra frowned and started toward the door. She reached for the knob, but paused before opening it. "On our bus ride to the vineyard, I could tell he was worried about you."

"Me?"

Sandra furrowed her brows. "Yes, dear. He told all of us on the bus how you got hurt and...well, I could just tell." She opened the door. "Rest up. I'll stop by when we return and tell you about the sights."

"I'd like that."

Mamie shut the door. She walked over to the bed and sat with her back to the headboard, lifted her notebook off the duvet cover. Last night, she'd jotted down more notes about the tour. Today would be a perfect time to get proper spellings on where they'd been in San Gimignano.

Several minutes into it, while revisiting the city on the Internet, her mind wandered to the cute store where she'd met Paolo. When he'd left in a hurry from the hotel lobby, he promised to call her later. At the time, she didn't think much of it. Now, sitting here alone, she wondered if he meant what he'd said.

She picked up her cell phone from the nightstand. No missed calls during her shower. Of course! At this early hour, he most likely slept after a late night at the restaurant. Maybe he'd call later.

She tried to get back to her work, but restlessness possessed her. How could she sit here all day while Tuscany waited right outside her window?

Rising from the bed, she walked to the window. The morning sun cast a spotlight on the countryside, each little pocket of buildings with terra-cotta roofs coming to life. People busied themselves outside their homes, some leaving in their cars, others watering flowers or tending to their gardens.

She wanted to be out in the world, hearing Italian voices, enjoying the delicious food. Lunch at Paolo's place left her taste buds begging for more of the simple, fresh ingredients. Having been served each dish by a good-looking man with a side plate of his charm didn't hurt.

Paolo might be nothing more than a vacation fling, but his attention awakened a desire in her for more than Tuscan food. The intent way he stared into her eyes when she talked made her feel as special as the food he hand delivered. His responses were always so alluring. Or was it the accent? No, the words he spoke made her feel alive.

So would it be bad to call him instead of waiting for his call? This was a new millennium, where woman didn't have to sit in the passenger seat and wait passively for things to happen in matters of romance. She lifted her cell phone and flipped through her call log for his number. As she did, an idea surfaced, unlike anything homebound Mamie would normally do. Yet the idea left her energized.

She'd surprise Paolo with a visit. Even use the visit there to shop in a few of those cute clothing stores she'd had to pass by due to time. Why envy Tina's style when she could improve on her own?

The plans started to falter right away. How could she get there? Without a car, her options were limited. Trains, according to the travel sites online, were the best way to go anywhere in Italy, but that would involve walking once she got to her destination. But there had to be cabs or private cars around for hire.

She went to the hotel phone on her nightstand and dialed zero.

"*Pronto.*"

"*Buongiorno.* This is Mamie Weber. I wanted to get to San Gimignano this morning but don't want to take a train. What are my options?"

The front desk clerk provided prices for both cabs and private cars, but said a private car would wait until she wanted to come home. She asked him to check availability. Fifteen minutes later, he called saying they'd found one. The steep hourly rate didn't deter her. This trip had been free so a little of her own cash on this extravagance didn't matter.

Mamie did her makeup and put on the only dress she'd brought along, a plain fuchsia sundress. A satisfied feeling settled over her. She'd just planned her own little adventure. So safe even Julian couldn't complain about it. She considered the agreement they'd shook on yesterday afternoon. Julian had promised her adventure.

Why, though?

She sensed he needed something, but whatever his secrets, he kept them closely guarded. Maybe while they were together, she'd figure him out. Today, though, was about a different kind of quest.

As she slipped on pearl drop earrings and flipped her hair into a bun, she admired herself in the mirror. For the first time in ages, she thought she looked pretty. Her skin glowed and no matter how hard she tried, she couldn't shake the genuine smile.

An hour later, she approached the walled city of San Gimignono in the back seat of a Mercedes sedan. After an hour of shopping for some new outfits, she gave the driver the restaurant address and he started the car. Her stomach knotted into a nervous mess. Would Paolo be happy to see her?

As the driver pulled to a corner not far from the restaurant, she said, "Can you stay nearby? I'm surprising someone and I want to make sure they're here."

She got out and went in the front entrance. Her eyes adjusted to the reduced lighting. Lunch service didn't start for another half hour. Voices carried from the bar area, so she walked over.

As she neared, a woman's soft giggle caught her attention. "Paolo, you're so sweet."

Mamie froze, close enough to see a blonde sitting on a tall stool with Paolo at her side, leaning close and playing with her hair. Her Southern accent gave her away as an American.

"No, *amore mio.* You're the sweet one." He kissed her neck. She faced him and he pressed his mouth to hers, a gentle kiss like the one he placed on Mamie's lips when he'd picked her up for their scooter ride. "Only you."

Mamie stood still as a stick. Charm obviously came naturally to Paolo. An American man would never presume to kiss a woman that casually. But now she'd seen Paolo do it twice.

"So, tonight," he crooned in a voice that could entice a corpse to sit up, "you will come back when I get through here and I will take you out in town? *Sì?*"

Mamie turned and quietly walked away, feeling every part the fool for traveling here today. She was nothing to this man. Just another easily manipulated tourist. That's all.

She hurried back to the sedan. Hopefully the driver wouldn't detect the embarrassment making her face feel hot, or notice the slightly inflated sense of self-worth she'd arrived with now slipping down the drain.

Chapter 8

Ping.

Mamie sifted through the bag of clothes she'd purchased yesterday and chose a pair of black overall shorts then rushed to the nightstand to find out who'd texted.

Are you there?

Allison again? Mamie glanced at the clock. Eight-thirty in Italy made it three-thirty AM in Manhattan. Late last night, Mamie had chosen to cry on her boss's shoulder after the surprise visit to Paolo went sour.

She returned to the shopping bag and put the phone down. After removing a black and white striped T-shirt, just like the mannequin at the store wore beneath the overalls, Mamie slipped it over her head. The outfit had been displayed with leather platform sandals, but Mamie could only take this new attempt at updating her looks so far. She shimmied into the overalls and slipped on flat white Keds.

The phone pinged again. This time she replied.

Yes. What are you doing up? It's the middle of the night in NY.

She hit send and tossed the cell phone onto the bed. Allison's consolations had helped eased some of the foolishness Mamie felt over visiting San Gimignano to see a man she hardly knew. Of course the thing with Paolo was never serious, only she never dreamed he'd have a lineup of American women.

She studied herself in the mirror, surprised by the improved reflection staring back at her. More stylish, but still casual enough. The phone pinged again.

Can't sleep. Lying here thinking about your thrill-seeking list and the idea of a fling. You know, sometimes we all need a good roll in the hay. Why don't you head for the hotel bar?

Mamie sat on the bed's edge deciding how to answer. Someone else had caught her attention, but not a stranger at the bar. Ever since she'd made the deal with Julian, spending time with him lurked in the back of her thoughts. Time not as the mysterious trip director, hell bent on taming her off-tour pursuits, but as... As what?

A persistent interest in him haunted her. What did he hide behind his close-cropped beard and longer-than-necessary hair? Was it camouflage to hide the story his piercing emerald eyes sometimes gave away? The short peek he'd offered her yesterday only fueled her appetite for more.

Under any other circumstances, she'd pronounce Julian as smart, interesting. So what if she wanted to feel that scruffy beard against her cheek while kissing? Once Ted had grown out his facial hair for a week. Mamie loved it, but Ted ended up shaving it off, preferring a cleaner look.

What was happening to her?

This short time in Italy somehow broke the lock off a door she'd shut on her emotions, and kept closed during those nights alone in her bed, missing Ted at her side. Now the door had cracked up and—lo and behold—a line waited outside to get in. Some advice right about now might be useful.

She started to type back about Julian but stopped and erased it. Allison might be her friend, but she was also her boss. Julian played a role in her review of Wanderlust, something Allison would see as affecting her objectivity.

A valid point, reminding Mamie how a fling with him would come with other drawbacks. The excursion still had another week after they left Siena. A week that might be pretty damn awkward if anything intimate happened and then fizzled.

She started typing again...

Thanks for the suggestion. The more important things on my list are the ones I can't do at home. There are still men in New York, right? Try to sleep and don't worry about me. Gotta run. We're heading out soon. Xx

Mamie tossed the phone into her backpack and left. As she came down the stairs, she thought she saw Julian dart into a lobby alcove with vending machines. Yesterday, Mamie went in there and purchased two bags of a treat called Biski, a cookie with chocolate filling.

She hit the last step and rushed past the alcove thinking about the delicious treat when he grabbed her arm and gently pulled her into the small room.

"Shhh." Julian stood close, looking down at her with a serious expression. He lowered his voice. "Do you trust me?"

Her heart pounded, partly from the shock of being pulled inside the hidden area, partly very aware of his hand still touching her arm. "Yes," she whispered. "I trust you."

His eyes softened and he let go. "Good. Because today we'll have our first adventure."

"Oh." She'd expected a little warning. "Am I dressed okay for it?"

His gaze trickled over her, more appreciatively then she'd seen him looking at her in the past. He grinned. "Perfect. Now listen. Follow my lead when we arrive in Lucca. No questions asked. Okay?"

She nodded, caught up in the scent of freshly showered man and the finer details of his trimmed beard. Again thinking how it would feel brushing her skin during a kiss or—

"And tell Sandra you're going to sneak away at the start of the tour," he added. "I don't want her—or anyone else—worrying about you. But don't tell her it's with me."

"Okay." *Sneak away?*

"See you on the bus." He winked and walked out, leaving her wanting for... What did she want?

And what exactly did he have planned? Yesterday in the lobby she'd taken some paragliding brochures, now inside her backpack. Maybe he'd found the same place just outside of Lucca, although she suspected her current outfit wasn't perfect for paragliding...

Whatever plan he'd concocted, anticipation wrapped her in its grip. Usually she didn't care for surprises, but right now she loved the idea.

* * * *

"Okay, folks. Can I have your attention?" Julian stood in the front of the bus, holding the back of Beppe's seat to steady himself as the vehicle made a turn.

He waited while the noise settled down. "Thank you. We're just outside of Lucca. This is one of my favorite places in Tuscany. Lucca is both charming and cosmopolitan. Though it hasn't been involved in a war since 1430, it is Italy's most impressive fortress city, encircled by a perfectly intact wall."

All eyes were on him, their faces curious as they listened intently to the wisdom of his travel experiences. Back when doing the show, Julian loved an audience, about the only thing he missed since leaving. A job allowing him to share his passion for exploring new places and cultures had been a true gift. Learning how much he enjoyed imparting his knowledge in a more personal way on these small tours was a surprise. On the show, he talked to a camera and any locals watching from the sidelines, but he rarely got to know anyone.

From her seat behind Bernie and Sandra, Mamie pulled out her notebook. She was always scribbling something. What did she write about today?

They hit a bump, sending him pitching to the left and grabbing Beppe's seat more securely to avoid falling. "There's an old Italian proverb my grandmother used to say to me, 'All things are difficult before they are easy.' One could say this about Lucca. It's not the easiest place to find your way around, but I promise, you won't remember all the times you got lost. It's a place untouched by time, so authentically Italian you'll think you are on the set of a 1940s Fellini film."

His gaze drifted to Mamie, who had stopped her note taking and smiled gently at him. He wished for her to love this city like he did, especially in light of his plans.

Standing close to her in the vending machine alcove earlier, taunted by her glistening lips and dark-chocolate eyes, Julian couldn't remember when a woman had caused his heart to beat so hard against his ribs. Her eyes sparkled, a sign she'd already gotten caught up in his mystery.

Today, he planned to turn the ordinary into the extraordinary. Television had taught him how to do it, starting with building suspense. His introduction to their day had been the kickoff.

Knowledge, he'd always found, carried some power. He'd channel his into something she wouldn't expect. Ordinary things with enough magic to make her believe she'd been on an adventure worthy of her list. All while doing nothing she actually had on her list.

He glanced up to find all eyes on him, waiting to hear more while he'd been off in la-la land. "Okay, so today I have a treat for you guys. One of my friends is a tour guide in Lucca. His name is Fabrizio and he knows this place better than the back of his hand. He's far more qualified than I am to share this city's secrets."

"Aw, we'll miss you," Bob Leon remarked from his seat in the back, making the others chuckle.

"Don't worry. I'm not leaving you for good." Julian smiled. "Question... anybody know the name of one of Lucca's most famous citizens?"

He expected Joel to answer, but he sat next to Tina with his nose buried in a book on Italian history. The other passengers shook their heads.

"The answer is Puccini." Mostly puzzled faces stared back. "Nobody? He didn't play at Woodstock, but some of you must've heard of him."

Bob's face brightened. "Oh wait. Isn't the the guy who wrote La Bohème?"

"Yes! Did you see it?"

"My first wife made me go see that for her birthday one year."

Bob's curly-haired current wife raised a brow, but remained typically quiet.

"What'd you think?" Julian asked.

"I think it made my wife happy." He laughed. "She got me there by telling me it was a tale of youth, love, and tragic loss. I told her for some that *would* describe Woodstock."

Julian enjoyed their laughter as he returned to his seat. Soon they neared the city wall. He looked over his shoulder, his gaze drifting to Mamie, who studied him through softly hooded lids and an ever-so-slight smile, her message so tempting it made his heart skip a little faster.

Beppe pulled into the lot and Julian tore himself from her gaze. The turmoil she caused still raged inside of him. What was it about her? So different from the women he usually gravitated toward. In fact, he might have walked right by while barhopping with friends in Rome.

Standing outside the bus door, he counted as each person stepped to the ground. As Mamie got off, their gazes met. She offered another smile as subtle as the Mona Lisa's. His neck warmed and his damn heart started jumping around again. "Don't forget what we talked about."

"I'm all set," she said casually, strolling to the others.

They stayed together while walking through throngs of tourists heading for the city gates. Julian talked about Lucca's history then added, "We'll meet our guide at the Piazza dell'Anfiteatro. This town square was once a Roman amphitheater. Make sure Fabrizio points out what remains from the original structure."

The group entered the city beneath an arched gate built into the city walls. Julian walked in silence, unable to help his own smile. He had so many fun things planned for Mamie today. He only hoped she enjoyed them as much as he did.

A few minutes later, they reached the amphitheater. He ushered them inside, inhaling a deep breath as he scanned the open area for his friend. The circle of buildings surrounding the main square carried a charm all its own, with uneven stucco houses painted in a spectrum of shades from bright gold to more muted pales, all with green shutters.

"This, folks, is the center of town. Once a place where the Romans held spectacles and gladiator games for up to ten thousand spectators. A humbling fact, isn't it?" He glanced around the tourist-filled amphitheater and this time found Fabrizio. Standing in the center, the tall, thin guide had dressed in dark suit pants and a white dress shirt. Almost out of place amongst the vacationers.

Julian waved and Fabrizio approached.

After a brief introduction to the passengers, Julian said, "I'm leaving you in very capable hands. We'll meet at this spot by three-thirty. During your lunch break, Fabrizio can recommend some great places." He waved a hand at the tour guide. "Take it away, my friend."

Fabrizio spoke English quite well. Julian watched for a few minutes as he engaged with the tour's passengers. He located Mamie in the group, standing alone near Bernie and Sandra.

Julian walked on the outskirts of the semicircle and went straight to Mamie's side. She glanced his way and he held his index finger to his lips.

A spark of excitement over the secrecy played in her eyes as she nodded.

He whispered, "Did you talk to Sandra?"

"Yes. She's covering for me. I didn't tell her I'd be with you."

"Perfect." Breaking another of Claudia's rules was one thing, but announcing it to the others on the tour could lead to more problems. "When the time is right, just follow my lead."

She nodded.

Fabrizio led the Wanderers toward an original Roman wall, one of several. The pack followed like a content herd of sheep. Mamie started to follow, but Julian took her hand and pulled her to his side, slowly walking backward as the gap between them and their tour widened. When everyone else's attention seemed focused on Fabrizio, Julian said, "Let's go."

Together they walked fast toward an arched opening leading out of the square. He slowed, reminded about her injury from the scooter accident, not to mention the slight limp she always had. When Joel had examined her after the scooter crash, she'd said the injury happened in an accident. Maybe he'd ask her about it.

They finally reached the archway and stopped inside, where he could no longer see the others. Her soft hand remained in his, but he let go. "How does your leg feel today?"

"Like new." She gave him a quick smile, then got serious. "Hold on. Before we start..." She slipped a small backpack off her shoulder and opened the front flap. "I got this from the desk last night." She handed him a brochure.

He studied the cover of a paragliding outfit, not far from the Lucca city limits.

She went to his side and peeked at the brochure. "I wasn't sure what you had in mind for today, but this caught my eye." She pointed at the cover. "Gorgeous views, huh?"

"So it's views you want?"

"I'd say that would be a decent start—"

"Perfect. The plans I have will give you some." He folded the brochure and stuck it in the pocket of his shorts. "Let's go."

They walked through the city and Julian stayed in his tour-director mode, pointing out landmarks, talking about the sights. Always easier than small talk. In the back of his mind, he worried. His plans didn't come close to paragliding. The idea of disappointing her nagged him like a pair of tight shoes.

He couldn't forget his end game, though... To show her adventure could come in many forms.

"Is it true there's a mummified body of a saint here in Lucca?" Mamie asked out of the blue.

He glanced her way, caught off guard by her pretty smile. He wished he could frame her happier expression. Not the sadness he'd caught her first few days with the tour. "Now that question is probably the last thing I'd have expected you to ask me."

"Sometimes I surprise people. I even surprise myself." She arched a brow. "Like agreeing to sneak away with you."

"Well, you're right. There is a mummified saint and she's known as the incorruptible St. Zita. She died in the thirteenth century. Her body was exhumed in 1580 and hadn't deteriorated, but rather mummified. Hence the incorruptible."

"Maybe she just wouldn't take a bribe."

He laughed. "Trying to rewrite history, are we?"

"Never." Mamie's eyes went wide as they took a corner and walked straight into an open-air market. She rushed to the first table, holding more antiques than a shopper might find in the whole of New England. "Can we look around?"

"How about later? You might need your hands free to do what I planned."

"Oh? Sounds like you *did* find me an adventure. Okay. I'll wait."

She smiled and walked at his side, the joy in her eyes so palpable he swore he could feel it. At this moment, breaking the rules felt strangely right and he just didn't care.

* * * *

Mamie was falling madly in love with Tuscany. Yes. It was definitely love.

She thought about a line written in her notebook last night and decided to try it out. "Want to know what I love about Tuscany?"

He glanced her way. "Of course."

"How each medieval hilltop town holds the adventure of a box of mixed chocolates...you don't know what you were getting until you take a bite, but are never disappointed."

He tipped his head and considered her for a moment. "That's great. Did you make that up?"

"In a way. It reminded me of the line Forrest Gump says in the movie."

Julian nodded. "Oh, right. About life. Well, I still like it. Sounds like you're a fan of chocolate, too?"

"A super fan."

"I'll do my best to find you the best in Italy, then."

Julian smiled and rather abruptly began to describe the sights. He remained quiet about what he had planned for them. The secrecy gave her a teeny thrill. Even telling Sandra she planned to sneak off had carried a decadent quality, like telling your mom you'd be with a friend, but instead were meeting a boy in the mall. Something she *never* would've done. Only new Mamie would.

Her gaze drifted to the top of a light tan stucco building. Between two second-story windows was a cracked fresco of baby Jesus and the Virgin Mary. Directly beneath, metal brackets held several lines of pants, shirts, and towels drying in the fresh morning air.

"Now see." She lifted her arm to the display. Julian looked up. "This is why I love Lucca already. It's so real, so lived in."

He nodded, but watched her with a satisfied glow in his eyes. "Same thing I like about it."

They started to walk again and she asked, "So, where are we headed?"

"Impatient, are we?" He squinted from the sun's glare and lowered the sunglasses tucked in his thick hair. "Shouldn't life be like a great book and save a few surprises for the end?"

She wanted to say no. Surprises didn't always come in good packages. Instead, she smiled. "You win. I'll be patient. Lead the way."

"We're almost there."

He led her down a maze of cobblestone streets lined with stucco buildings, the outsides painted faded salmon, creamy yellow, and gold. They entered an open area with cars and businesses and stopped in front of a business called Cicli Bizzarri. Several rows of bicycles parked in front of the establishment.

"Here we are." He walked up to the door. "You might want to have ID ready."

A sign stationed near the front door read *Noleggio Bicilette,* which meant nothing to Mamie, but next to it in English was written "Rent Bikes."

"We're bike riding? The other day I was like James Dean in the country and today...I don't know, Dorothy before she got swept away to Oz."

"This morning you said you trusted me." Shaking his head, he reached for the door and opened it, waving for her to enter first. "So short lived."

She walked past him to enter the store. "No. No. I still trust you. I just haven't ridden a bike in decades."

"See? It'll be an adventure."

She tipped her head and grinned. "Or a disaster."

Once inside, they approached a man who stood near a cash register. For several minutes, Julian negotiated in Italian with the older gentleman, who wore a shirt with gaping buttons near his navel. After some discussion, he made a deal. Together, they walked outside.

"Which ones?" the man asked, his accent strong and voice husky.

Mamie selected a white bike with a basket and Julian picked a dark navy one right next to it.

He unlocked them and moved the bikes out to the open area. The man disappeared inside the shop.

"Hop on, James Dean." Julian grinned. "You're in for the ride of your life."

"Ha-ha."

He studied her, the smile still on his face. "Come on. Be a believer."

"Yeah, yeah." She focused on putting her backpack in the bike's basket. When finished, she hopped on and lifted her eyes to him. "Where to?"

"We're headed to the Renaissance walls encircling Lucca." He motioned to a grassy area leading up a small hill. Beyond it was a long stretch of trees. "Up there is where we'll start."

She noted the city wall with a broad flat top and several pedestrians.

He lowered his hands on the handlebar grips. "Ready?"

She grinned. "I guess. Do you think I'll be able to handle all this excitement?"

He laughed. "Okay, Miss Sarcastic. When we're through biking, I'll happily accept your apology."

She readied herself, one foot on the pedal and hands on the grips. "Let's go. I hope I'm wrong."

They peddled just across the street, up a hill, and onto the elevated, tree-lined path. For a while they rode between the patches of sunlight streaming through the trees, neither saying a word.

While she felt he'd duped her into this tame outing, her disappointment didn't last long when the view opened up and she realized they were elevated above the rustic town. Passing the colorful stucco buildings she'd seen at ground level, she had a new appreciation for the clay roofs dotting the cityscape from this height. To her left, Mamie feasted on the countryside, an entirely different, more intimate vista than she'd had from her seat on the bus.

"You told me your parents owned homes in Italy and in the States. Is that how you learned so much about Tuscany?

"I suppose it didn't hurt." He quickly glanced her way. "We spent half our year here."

"What did your parents do for a living?"

"They were in the travel business, too." He pointed into the distance. "There's another church. Lucca is said to be the city of a hundred churches."

She couldn't tell if it was the tour guide in him reacting, or a man who didn't want to talk about his past. Pedaling slowly, she admired the shadowed mountain range in the distance. "What are those mountains?"

"The Apuan Alps."

"Ever been to them?"

"Yup."

They rode in comfortable silence, passing people walking dogs, couples strolling hand in hand, and others riding bikes. A motorcycle careened in the distance. A dog in a nearby building stood on the balcony and barked at no one in particular. A gentle symphony of movements and sounds performed for them as they rode atop the strong fortress guarding

Lucca, a buffer between the vast mountains and the realities of life found in the maze of streets.

Walls weren't new to her. A slow ache bubbled inside her chest. On the day she lost her family, the inside of her apartment became her own barricade. A place to hibernate from a world that showed her pity and where she stood alone—no longer with the ones she loved.

Her gaze traveled the majestic beauty surrounding this fortress. As she looked, a truth about her own life unexpectedly unveiled: by coming to Tuscany she'd found a beautiful world waiting for her. Maybe she had something in common with Lucca.

"Let's stop for a sec." Julian maneuvered off the path, to a spot beneath some trees.

She pulled alongside him and parked. He walked over to a low brick wall and she followed. For a minute, they stood side-by-side, staring into the city below.

"See that tower over there?" He motioned to an area. "Later we can climb it if you want. It's not as tall as the one in Siena, but you can't ever beat a bird's-eye glimpse of Tuscany."

"Will they be like the paragliding views?"

"No." He lifted his sunglasses to the top of his head and faced her. "But they're still breath-taking."

Julian's hopeful expression made her feel bad for making it sound like she didn't like what he'd chosen for them today. "I'm only teasing."

He smiled and pretended to wipe sweat from his forehead. "That's a relief." The smile slid from his face, replaced with a more solemn expression. "Seriously. Are you disappointed in today?"

His need for her approval caught her off guard. "No. Not even for a second. It's a spectacular way to see the sights."

"Okay. I'm glad." He turned and faced the town. They stood together, their shoulders nearly touching. Part of her was afraid to move because she kind of liked being this close to him. The other part wanted to run away, because their closeness felt right, almost necessary. A scary prospect.

Mamie broke the silence. "Why did you become a tour guide? I know you said your parents were in the travel business."

"I didn't plan on following in their footsteps, but I just fell into it. Mind if I ask you a question?"

"Ask away."

His phone rang. "Hang on."

He pulled it from the side pocket of his shorts. Glancing at it, he tensed. He tapped the button, ending the ring, and pocketed the phone. "So, what's the real reason you're in Italy?"

She wondered about the call, but now wasn't the time to ask. "Real reason?"

"I just get a feeling there's more to your story."

Lies had never sat well with her. Mamie wanted this man to know her real story. Her loves. Her losses. Even the job that brought her to Italy. Only legally she couldn't share about the job thanks to her publisher. Plus, the other passengers already knew her made-up personal tale, a welcome break from being with people who understood her losses. But with his comment, all she could do was tell partial truths.

"I recently went through a divorce. My uncle...he..." She squirmed inside. Lies and more lies. They needed a link to her reality. "Uncle Felix saw what I was going through afterward. I wasn't very happy. He knew I'd always wanted to see Tuscany, maybe even write a novel set here, so he offered me the spot on his trip."

"Oh. A divorce?"

She nodded, watching as he frowned and considered her explanation.

"So you weren't happy about the marriage ending?"

"Is anybody ever?" She tried to stare at him without showing any signs about the real way her marriage ended, so he wouldn't be suspicious of what she'd shared.

"Some people are." He tilted his head. "Why the adventurous list?"

"I'm trying to start living again."

Saying the words aloud gave them meaning and some power, even if she couldn't mention her dead husband. Her throat grew thick and the clay roofs blurred. "Without going into details, I haven't really been embracing life these days."

She blinked away the wetness and turned to him. He didn't say anything, but confusion marred his expression.

"Is something wrong?"

"No. I'm sorry about your marriage ending. I guess I'm kind of relieved, too. The day you arrived, I drew other conclusions."

"Like what?"

"That you were sick and, well, this might be your only chance to take a trip like this."

"Why would you think that?"

"You seemed so tired that day."

She laughed. "I was. I'd just taken a sleepless overnight flight. My health is fine. So you thought I might not live long enough to come again?"

"Something like that. I feel silly now."

"You shouldn't. Life can change on a dime." Julian must've been very worried about her, a very sweet thought. "Being here, I hope to have more chances to take full advantage of what life has to offer."

He studied her carefully. "You hungry?"

"For some reason lately, I feel like I'm always ready to eat."

"Italy will do that to you. Since you missed the organic farm and vineyard yesterday, there's one that's a short distance from town. We can finish the rampart then ride there, grab some lunch, take a tour, and get back in time to meet the gang for the afternoon stop in Pisa. Sound good?"

"It sounds great."

As they climbed back on their bikes, it struck her how much Ted would've loved this intimate way to learn about the city of Lucca. The kind of trip they could've made with Zoe, as she got a bit older. Maybe it didn't qualify as the type of adventure on her list. These centuries-old sights and incredible countryside offered stimulation of a gentler nature, but she was certain it would be an unforgettable day.

Chapter 9

The bus slowly chugged in a line of early morning rush hour traffic. Mamie stared out the window as they passed homes and a few industrial complexes. This more modern area hardly seemed like the place Etruscans lived or the Renaissance was born. A while later, they approached a road sign. *Firenze 3 km.* Florence, the city they would explore today.

Sandra sat beside Mamie reading a book. When they'd boarded, Bernie asked if Mamie minded sharing a seat with his wife so he could "spread out a little." The seating was close quarters, but having someone at her side on the bus ride was a nice change.

She scrolled through pictures taken yesterday in Lucca and Pisa. One photo with the famous leaning tower made her smile. Julian had insisted upon taking the photo and swiped the camera from her hands before she could say no.

"Hold out your arms," he'd said. "I'll take a picture so it seems like you're holding up the tower."

She'd hesitated. "I'll look silly."

But in a matter of seconds he'd talked her into making it appear as if she held the tipsy tower on its side. Not only that way, but also two more using only her index finger and a third where she pretended to do a kickbox pose. Later that afternoon, while sifting through the photos with him, she'd laughed so hard her stomach hurt. The moment was well worth lowering her guard.

She continued to flip through the photos, stopping at a selfie taken at the organic farm on the outskirts of Lucca. Fresh air, fabulous food, fields of grapes, and views the masters painted. Thinking about their simple meal of Tuscan bread soup, a bowl of olives, and a platter of cheese and meats made her stomach juices gurgle. Sitting side-by-side at a picnic table, with the vineyard a perfect backdrop, she'd snapped away. They could be any couple in Tuscany, laughing while making a toast with their wine glasses raised and trying to snap the photo at the same time. Happiness had rippled inside of her all day in Lucca.

"That's a cute picture." Sandra leaned over Mamie's arm.

Mamie quickly lowered the camera. "Thanks."

"You were with Julian, huh? I thought you met that other guy. The one who took you on the scooter."

"Um, no. I'm not sure I'll see him again." Mamie glanced to the front of the bus, where Julian busied himself with some paperwork. She dropped her voice. "Julian offered to show me things a little off the tour track."

"Then you two had fun?" The innuendo in Sandra's tone couldn't be missed.

Mamie smiled, even though she should downplay the outing. "We did. But, please don't say anything. I don't think he's supposed to hang out with passengers socially."

"I won't say a word. But I'm pretty sure he's single and so are you."

"Yes." Mamie should've been more discreet. "He's just a nice guy, trying to show me the sights. Nothing more."

Sandra rested a gentle hand on Mamie's arm. "I understand, dear. Not a word to anyone."

Julian took that moment to turn and look around the bus. His gaze stopped at Mamie and his eyes softened before he turned back to his paperwork.

His attention felt nice. Maybe he'd enjoyed their time together yesterday, too. Mamie remembered Sandra at her side and dared to peek her way.

Sandra smiled then looked out the window.

* * * *

Mamie and the others walked in a single file on the narrow sidewalk. On either side, old buildings made of thick grey brick and gold stucco exteriors held modern storefronts, tempting passersby with leather, ceramics, and other tourist delights.

Julian talked loudly over the traffic and pedestrians. "Florence was known as the capital city of Tuscany, the birthplace of the Renaissance, and was once ruled by the powerful Medici family."

Mamie hung on every word, but some in their group kept stopping to peer into the store windows.

Julian sounded impatient. "Folks, there'll be time to shop later. Right now, we're headed for the Piazza del Duomo, in English, Cathedral

Square." He pointed ahead. "Please note the *campanile*—also known as the bell tower. After we see inside the cathedral, I'm going to climb to the top. Those interested can join me." Julian raised his chin and cocked an eyebrow. "Bob? I assume you're up for the challenge?"

"Dude, you just keep bringing those towers on."

Carol, who rarely spoke and allowed Bob center stage, patted her husband's arm. "Don't push it, honey. You know what the doctor said."

Bob put his arm around her. "You worry too much, hon."

Julian smiled as he watched the couple. Mamie enjoyed how he'd find a reason to joke with or at least talk to all the passengers.

She'd worried she wouldn't like the bigger city, at least compared to the small, walled-towns of Tuscany. Yet Florence spoke the same voice as the other medieval towns, only louder.

A few minutes later, they entered the piazza. "Okay. We've arrived." Julian opened his arms. "Take a moment and soak in the grandeur."

Mamie swept her gaze over the magnificent cathedral. Towering above the public square, the structure stood like a gothic giant, the rusted copper-colored dome so enormous it filled the sky.

"Pretty awesome." Julian appeared at her side, speaking softly. Their arms brushed as they stood close, staring up at the cathedral. "You can never get lost in Florence. Search for the dome to find your way around."

"It's massive."

"The Florentines' philosophy was 'go big or go home.' Their dreams for this dome were so big, it almost didn't happen."

"Why not?"

"The original church design included a wood dome. But something this large was impossible to construct using traditional methods and material. Yet the Florentine people didn't give up. The story goes they had faith God would send someone who could figure out a way. Many years later, Brunelleschi showed up and made the largest masonry dome ever built."

A few others gathered around to listen. Julian's tone shifted back to tour director mode and he continued.

Mamie stopped listening, awestruck by the church standing before her. So many years to reach these incredible heights, yet the Florentines' faith made them hang onto a dream. The notion punctuated her lost belief in God. This building reached up to the heavens, like a beacon to guide people to a familiar place if they ever got lost. Her parents, being true believers, would've loved all this symbolism.

Mamie appreciated the beauty, but didn't believe God got this job done. If God was so powerful, why would he have taken from her people she loved and—stop! Not now. She refocused, as Julian's voice rose above the noise in the square.

"Folks, stay together and let's head inside."

Thankful for the interruption, Mamie followed them into the entrance. Lost in the eclectic beauty surrounding her, she forgot the negative thoughts about God and enjoyed the tour. Everywhere she turned were artistic expressions of strong faith, done so creatively some of her apprehensions about the church and God lifted. Afterward, they climbed the cathedral's tall tower, blessed when they reached the top and could observe the city with a bird's-eye view.

When they left the church, Julian guided them to a street lined with outdoor cafes and bars, explaining how bars in Italy also served food like sandwiches. Mamie hoped to get him alone, but he disappeared while she admired leather jackets in a shop window. Instead, she ate at a trattoria on a quiet side street with a few people from the tour.

An hour later, they met up with Julian and headed to the Galleria dell'Accademia. He walked ahead of them with Joel at his side, talking excitedly and pointing at different buildings. Mamie battled with her disappointment. Maybe she'd read too much into yesterday's outing. She sighed. Best to stop sulking and enjoy the day.

They stopped in front of a smooth, white stone building, with pillars cut right into the front facade. A burgundy banner above the door carried the museum's name and a long line of people ran down the street leading to a ticket window.

"Wanderers?" Julian held his hand up and smiled. "Stop wandering and gather around." He laughed at his joke and got a few chuckles from the others.

The group circled around him. Mamie stayed in the back feeling sulky.

"We can bypass this line because we booked ahead. Your tickets include an audio guide. Everyone, try to follow the guide so we all end up in the same place in the end." He glanced at his watch. "In two hours, we will meet in the lobby where we will enter. I'm going to give you your tickets and then head inside to the audio guide table." He glanced around, avoiding her eyes. "Questions?"

When nobody replied, he went about his task handing out the tickets. He slipped her one without making eye contact. Ouch. As they filed inside, further disappointment owned Mamie. The care she'd taken to put on a pretty sundress and delicate sandals, and to straighten her full hair now seemed ridiculous.

She entered the museum and veered toward a display with maps. She wanted to be alone right now. Solitude, a close friend these recent years, always made her feel less needy of others. Part of her needed something from Julian, reinforcing vulnerability she'd spent years trying to avoid.

"Coming, Mamie?" Sandra stopped and waited.

Mamie squashed down the sadness waiting to erupt. "Go on without me. I'll catch up at the end."

Sandra frowned and didn't move. Bernie took her by the elbow and, as he drew his wife away, he said, "Give the girl space, honey."

Mamie watched them leave, took a map, and studied the layout. The museum housed many treasures. Besides several of Michelangelo's famous statues, including David, she wanted to visit the display of musical instruments and catch a few Italian painters. She planned to soak in all the culture she could before this trip ended.

Someone grabbed her hand before she took a step.

She twirled around.

"Hello." Julian stood there, a grin on his face. "Want to come with me?"

"Where—"

"No questions. It's a surprise."

"Another one?"

He shook his head. "You underestimate me, don't you? Didn't I promise to deliver on our agreement?"

Her sullen mood lifted and as much as she hated to give into her needs, she did. "Okay. I'm game."

He led her around a corner, his warm hand in hers. After guiding her to the wall so people could pass by, he dropped her hand. "In a minute, we'll go through the entryway behind me."

She looked over his shoulder to an arched opening leading to another hall.

He glanced both ways, then moved closer to her, dropping his voice. "But you have to do something first."

Her heart stuttered, flustered by his nearness. "Now you've got me worried."

"Oh ye of little faith. All I want you to do is close your eyes and let me guide you through into that hallway."

"Close my eyes?" She laughed. "You do know this sounds weird, right?"

"It's all about trust, Mamie." His gaze skipped around her face. "Simple trust."

"This surprise of yours, it's *really* list-worthy?"

"Then you're curious?"

"Only about your mental health." She cocked a playful brow.

He laughed. "Mamie Weber, you're a tough customer." His eyes didn't leave hers as he reached out and brushed a piece of fallen hair from her face. "Guess what? For the second time, I'm going to accept your apology when we're through."

"Wait." She placed her hand on her hip. "There's something so great in that hallway, you think I'll apologize? Confidence in a man is a very attractive quality, but whatever is in there would have to be epic for me to apologize."

He took a step back and extended his hand. "There's only one way to find out."

She didn't hesitate and placed her hand in his.

He drew her near and his voice grew husky. "Now close your eyes."

Her body tingled, both from his tone and the suggestion. She did as he asked, any foolishness at standing in the museum like this overpowered by the game he played.

His warm breath fell close to her ear and he gave her hand a quick squeeze. "I won't let you trip."

She let herself fall into the safety net of his handholding gesture.

He started to move and stopped. "Hold on a sec. I'm letting some people pass us."

Voices echoed against the museum walls. Julian's hand held hers tightly. Anticipation mounted. Her heart fluttered fast.

"Okay." The warmth of his breath brushed her ear. "Let's go."

She took slow, careful steps. Did others watch them right now? Wonder what they were doing? She must look ridiculous.

"Almost there." After three more steps, they stopped. "We're in the hallway but don't open your eyes yet. I'll tell you when."

She nodded, her mouth suddenly dry, her heart racing.

He squeezed her hand, then let go, but immediately she felt the heat of his body behind her. "Okay. Open them."

She did as he asked. Straight ahead, a long hallway with high vaulted ceilings stretched out before her. Mamie blinked to adjust to lights after having her eyes closed. A series of unfinished sculptures lined the walls, but her gaze drifted to something beyond the hall, to a magnificent form at the end.

Michelangelo's David.

Pictures barely did justice to the statue before her. Standing here, in the atmosphere produced by centuries of Renaissance creations, Mamie drew in a breath, awed by the sight at the hall's end. A wide opening led to a separate room, framing the large sculpture in a space of its own. Positioned on the ceiling over David, a domed skylight cast a beam of natural light onto the carved marble, brightening it as if the heavens themselves demanded visitors pay heed to this magnificent work of art. Mamie's eyes pricked with tears, the reaction catching her by surprise.

Julian whispered, "It's beautiful, *si*?"

She nodded, her throat too thick with emotion to speak.

"Seeing this never gets old."

She glanced over her shoulder. Julian's eyes glistened as he stared straight ahead, his raw emotion mirroring hers.

He looked at her. "Ready for a close-up view?"

"Yes."

Hand in hand, the moved toward the statue. Each step brought a new view. As they entered the room, Mamie's spirits elevated with awe as she feasted on the artistry. Thick veins ran down David's arms to his hands. In one he clutched stones, the other his slingshot. Skillfully crafted cuts made the curls of his hair seem soft and his expression filled with both concentration and cunning.

She turned to Julian. "Want your apology now or later?"

His gaze skipped over her face then he smiled. "Nah. Forget about it. Your reaction is all I need. Want to hear about David?"

"Tell me everything."

"He's nearly seventeen feet high and was made from a single piece of marble. This pose shows him before facing the behemoth Goliath. At the time this was made, Michelangelo was the first artist to sculpt David *before* the fight. Do you know the story of David and Goliath?"

"I'm familiar with it."

He pointed. "See the tension in David's arm? This is the moment right before he strikes Goliath. Michelangelo catches him at the apex of his concentration. He stands relaxed, but alert."

Julian put his hand on her lower back and guided her to another angle. "Check out the eyes. They're watchful. Michelangelo creates tension other ways, like by the pulsing veins on the back of the hands." Julian paused for a moment, his gaze trailing the statue from top to bottom. "But all in all, David's bravery shines through. It's a masterpiece."

Mamie studied the statue's face and the details Julian noted. Bravery. She'd faced a giant the day she lost her family. Sure, she got up each morning and started a new day, but those days started with dread and sadness. Not bravery. "If I faced a threatening giant, I'm pretty sure my face would show fear."

Julian studied her for a long moment. "Yes, I suppose one would." His gaze drifted to the sculpture and for a long moment he didn't speak. "I guess David's fears were backed by the best insurance anyone can buy."

"What's that?"

"His faith in God." A flash of pain crossed Julian's face as his Adam's apple rolled along his throat.

She couldn't be certain what caused him to react that way; faith, fear, or something else. Yet something deep drove Julian.

His cell phone rang and he let go of her hand to pull his phone from his pocket. When he glanced at the display, his jaw tightened. He pushed a button and it stopped ringing.

"Everything okay?" Mamie asked.

"It's fine." He stuffed the phone away, but the tense expression remained on his face. "Let's walk around to the other side and take a look."

Mamie followed him through the crowd. Julian was avoiding something.

She didn't understand the distant sadness in his eyes at times, but one thing was certain: they'd both carried some extra baggage on this trip.

Chapter 10

"I love Siena, but not during Palio week." Ricardo stared out into Siena's busy main square.

A frown marred his rugged face. Julian liked the Spanish tour director, a twenty-year veteran in the travel business and Julian's trainer when he joined Wanderlust. But he could be a bit of a complainer at times.

Ricardo lifted his drink. "When I got stuck with this tour again, I was one step from quitting."

Ricardo seemed edgier than usual. Or it could be Julian's own bad mood. Gary's call in the middle of his museum tour with Mamie had ruined a perfectly good day. He drank down the last of his wine but the angry edge caused by his persistent ex-boss still lingered.

Josef chuckled. "My friend, you said the same last time I saw you in Rome during Holy Week." Behind his German accent, his mocking tone couldn't be missed. "I think Claudia is testing your patience."

Julian nodded his agreement.

Owen piped in, the British company employee always the voice of logic. "One of my mates who lives in London, he quit his tour company and opened up one of his own." He leaned back in his chair and stretched his long legs out into the open space near their table. "A small operation, but enough to keep him afloat."

Ricardo leaned forward, placing his bulky weight-lifter arms on the table. "Sounds like too much work."

Julian picked up the wine bottle and topped off their glasses, finishing what remained. "Then just have another drink and relax." Ricardo was starting to annoy him. Julian held up the empty bottle of wine as the waiter rushed by. "Another, *per favore.*"

He watched the town staff set up barriers to form an inner circle in the ancient square for the famous horse race. The setup would effectively trap the tourists in the center during the race, where stepping out could be dangerous. The way Julian felt trapped in his own skin these days, unable to make any movement toward a return to his old self.

"I don't know, Ricardo. I love the Palio's excitement," Julian said, wanting to veer the conversation from his friend's pessimism. Anything to boost his own mood.

"*Ja*. Me, too." Josef's rich blue eyes trained on two pretty brunettes in tight dresses and pointy heels as they walked by. He picked up a pack of cigarettes from the table and removed one, eyes on them until they disappeared into a shop. He turned to Julian and motioned to the pack. "Want one?"

Julian shook his head. "Since medieval times, this city has gone through a tremendous amount of work in preparation for the Palio. That's a long time. All for a one minute and fifteen second bareback horserace. Pretty remarkable if you ask me."

"I'd say I have to agree." Owen reached for a cigarette when Josef tipped the pack his way. "Ricardo, I think you're plain old knackered. You've been with Claudia's outfit longer than any of us."

A distant drumbeat grew and silenced the conversation. Seconds later a line-up of men wearing white and blue silk medieval costumes marched into the Campo. A drummer led the entourage, the full arms of his costume billowing as he pounded on the drum. Behind him followed men with flags emblazoned with the mascot for their Siena neighborhood.

Julian marveled at the strong sense of community, so prevalent in many Italian towns, like the place he'd lived when his parents weren't filming. He missed that feeling, maybe why a part of him enjoyed this job with Wanderlust. The waiter dropped off a new and uncorked bottle of wine, pulling Julian away from his memories.

The men quietly watched the parade pass by while Julian topped off their glasses.

Wine. An elixir to the agony tearing him apart. Michelangelo's David always cut deep. The artistry. The message. Today, though, when Mamie mentioned fears, her words reached inside his chest and ripped open a wound. One waiting to burst since...

Damn it! All he wanted was one day where he didn't think about watching Carlos die or the part he played in convincing him to make the jump. The statue of David mocked him with a reminder that some men face their Goliath. Julian had run from his.

The timing of Gary's call today was uncanny. While the massive statue's message almost swallowed Julian whole, Gary left another message asking to speak to him, this time his voice more emphatic, almost pleading. Julian had wanted to pick up the phone and scream, "Go away," only the tone in Gary's voice left Julian feeling bad. He hadn't always hated Gary and they'd had some damn good times on the road.

No, it wasn't Gary he hid from. Julian simply couldn't face the man he once was, ever again. The only thing making him better lately was Mamie. He loved the way she'd played along with his game at the museum. Closed her eyes. Let him guide her inside. While doing so, he couldn't stop staring at her, breathing in her wholesome beauty, her perfectly shaped lips, and those cute faded freckles. The ones she told him she hated while they'd pedaled along the Lucca wall during the bike ride. What was it about her that made him feel...? Damn, he couldn't pinpoint the emotion, but every single time she popped into his mind, a force inside his chest squeezed. A feeling he couldn't recall having before—

"And you, Julian?"

He turned to Owen. "I'm sorry?"

"Your group, will they see the race?"

"Only the trials. We leave before the race begins."

His phone buzzed in his shirt pocket. He removed it, seeing the same name and number that sent him reeling into a dark hole this afternoon. He almost picked up, but stopped when all his reasons for avoiding Gary cast a shadow on the nice moments they'd shared. He hit the button, sending Gary into the pile of his other messages.

Another parade group entered the square. Ricardo stood. "A good time to visit the men's room."

Julian and Josef watched the passing parade, following the spectacle until it disappeared down a side street further up the plaza. Owen had leaned over to talk to some British tourists at the table behind them.

Josef glanced at Julian. "Just call him, would you?"

"What?"

"The producer. Call him back."

"How'd you know who called me?"

Josef took a drag off the cigarette then exhaled a stream of smoke. "Your poker face sucks."

Josef had an apartment in Rome, not far from Julian's home base in the city. When tour duty didn't call, they'd sometimes hang out. One night they'd gone out to a bar, had a little too much to drink, and he'd confided to Josef about the death on the show and the truth about Eddie. Josef vowed to keep it silent, but he'd been the one person Julian could talk to about his problems this past year.

Josef flicked some ashes into a glass tray. "Look, if you're not interested, tell him and the calls will stop. You'll get rid of your problem."

"Who said I have a problem?" Julian knew he sounded defensive, but didn't care and tipped back his wine.

Josef stared back, his silver-blue eyes softening with compassion. "Jules, if anybody understands denial, it's me. Listen, what is the worst that can happen if you return his call?"

"What have you been in denial about?"

Josef stared at his cigarette, but his jaw tightened as he knocked some ashes off into an empty glass. His gaze slowly lifted and he smiled. "A story for another day, my friend. Let's just say I understand your pain and didn't want to accept the reasons why. Now why aren't you talking to your old boss?"

"He *might* want me to come back to the show. I'm not ready."

"Okay. So you tell him the truth. Phone stops ringing. *Ja*?"

"You don't understand how stubborn Gary is." Julian remembered Gary's persistence the day Carlos died. "His demands helped push Carlos to his—"

He stopped, unable to say the words aloud. Growing disgust for himself threatened to drown him, only this time, he considered Josef's words. Each call from Gary revived the sights and sounds of a day he wanted to come to terms with. For the rest of his life, that day would stay with him. Julian's unresolved issues with Gary made the accident memories ten times worse; however, Josef's idea had some merit. If these calls from Gary stopped, Julian's healing could begin.

"You know what, Josef? You're right. Excuse me for a minute."

Julian left the restaurant's outdoor seating area and headed down a quiet narrow street. He dialed, the noise from the campo fading the further he walked.

The phone rang four times, his heart pounding wildly as he waited for an answer.

"Well, it's about time." Gary's usual cheery tone sounded annoyed. "I've been busy. What's so important you keep calling?"

"I'm about ready to tell you forget it."

"No you're not. What do you want?"

"We want you back. We'll double your old salary."

"And if I say no?"

"Then you're a bigger fool than many people around here already think you are."

Julian tensed, every muscle in his body one step from exploding.

* * * *

"I'm telling you, Bernie," Joel stopped walking with his arm around Tina's shoulder, but glanced to his side to talk to Bernie, who waited while his wife window-shopped for a moment. "We can blame the Republicans."

Mamie walked behind the two couples on the way back to the hotel, devouring her hazelnut gelato, far more interesting than a discussion about the U.S. budget deficit. Both parties owned responsibility for what was wrong, as far as she was concerned.

"Enough about politics, Joel." Tina tossed him an annoyed glance.

Mamie appreciated how the two couples included her on their dinner outing, but on this beautiful night in Tuscany, Julian remained in the forefront of her thoughts. Being the fifth wheel only highlighted the loneliness of being single.

They neared an intersection where a side street led to the campo and Mamie stopped. "I'm not ready to head to the hotel. I think I'll walk around and burn a few more calories."

Joel and Tina said good night and kept walking, but Sandra hesitated with a slightly concerned frown.

Bernie took his wife's hand and winked at Mamie. "We'll see you tomorrow then." And he dragged his wife off to catch up with the other couple.

Mamie leaned against a brick wall to finish her gelato. Loud drumbeats neared the area and people stood back to clear a path. Seconds later, a parade of men in colorful medieval costumes emerged.

On their bus ride home from Florence, Julian talked about the Palio and the events surrounding the historic race. "The Palio is more than a horse race," he'd said. "It's about the politics of each contrada, the history of Siena."

This must be a parade from one of the *contrade*, what he'd defined as neighborhood. Excitement pumped through Mamie's blood as she took in everything. From the other tourists' awed expressions as they snapped photos to the band of stoic men marching by, playing their parts with the seriousness such a role deserved. As exciting as Julian promised.

The parade passed and she kept on walking. Whenever Julian spoke about the history of Italy, passion burned bright in his expression and emotion filled his voice. Every historical story carried a personal feel, like it mattered to him. Or the way he talked about Michelangelo's *David*, with passion making her appreciate details she'd have otherwise missed. Their time in the museum ended too fast. Mainly because the phone call he'd ignored seemed to dampen his enthusiasm.

On their way to dinner earlier, she'd spotted him with a group of men at a restaurant in the campo. If he were still there, maybe she'd try to get him alone and ask about the call.

Mamie scraped up the last of her gelato. She'd have sworn the waistband of her new skirt tightened with the last bite. The deep red skirt, laced on the bottom with a Venetian pattern of pencil-like sketched gondolas, had fit perfectly in the shop. But that was after a light breakfast. Did it really matter? These wardrobe updates of gorgeous Italian styles lifted her morale to a new place, where feeling plain didn't exist and she walked tall, almost forgetting about the ache in her hip. The only touches of old Mamie were the ballet flats, not the serious heels the store clerk suggested. Heck, she was nothing if not sensible.

After wiping her mouth with a napkin, she went to the nearest side street leading to the piazza.

As she turned down the tight alleyway between two brick buildings, a loud voice made her pause.

"Screw you, Gary."

Julian stood straight ahead in the alley, his back to her.

"You want to know what I think of your offer? I think you can shove it up your ass."

She froze. On the tour, he'd always been so pleasant sounding and confident. Never upset or angry. Before she could turn around and walk away, his voice rose.

"Why? Because of you, I'm responsible for a man's death. Now don't call me again."

A man's death? Julian hung up the phone and stormed from the alley, forcing Mamie to stop so he wouldn't see her. She didn't move a muscle. When he vanished around the corner, she breathed a sigh of relief and went the opposite way, heading for the hotel.

As she pushed through the crowd, Julian's words rang in her ears.

I'm responsible for a man's death.

Had she heard that correctly? What could he have done? Murdered a man? An accidental death he somehow caused?

Her mind raced as she hurried away, but deep in her heart she didn't believe he'd purposely done something to harm another human being. She reached the quiet, dark street leading to the hotel. As she came within sight of the entrance, a sad thought walloped her...loss of life haunted both her and Julian.

But what was his story? The other morning at breakfast, one passenger suggested Julian looked like someone on TV. The personality's name escaped her, but she remembered the tension on Julian's face over the comparison. In fact, she'd meant to do a search on the Internet the other day, but got sidetracked by Paolo's call.

After what she'd heard tonight, the time had come to finish the search. Doing so seemed kind of nosey. Even a violation of his trust. But she sensed Julian barricaded himself behind a brick wall, something she understood all too well. As his friend—yes, she was a friend—it simply seemed like the right thing to do. Like he'd been helping her enjoy the sights of Tuscany.

Chapter 11

Mamie wrapped her wet hair in a towel and tossed on the thick, terrycloth robe. The little extra sleep she stole as part of today's free time had been well needed and it was still only seven o'clock. A whole day stretched ahead of her.

She grabbed her laptop and plunked onto the bed. On her way through the lobby last night, she'd run into Bob Leon. After striking up a conversation about the upcoming Palio race, she casually asked if he remembered the talk show host a couple of passengers thought Julian looked like. He gave her a name and she'd rushed upstairs, but a Skype call from Allison delayed her hunt until this morning.

She typed in the name Eddie Morrison, hoped Bob was right, and hit search. A Wikipedia page for *Exploring the World with Eddie* popped up.

Glancing through the text, she learned Eddie Morrison hosted an adventure show cancelled a year ago. The producers didn't say why. Another website speculated it had to do with an episode where someone was killed during a wing suit jump. Mamie had never heard of wing suits and there were no added details about the sport.

A photo halfway down the page showed the host. Right away, she understood why Frank had seen a resemblance. She compared Julian with Eddie, each with the same rugged jawline and boyishly handsome face, but Eddie's short hair and cleanly shaven face did make him look like another person. Dressed in khaki-colored safari clothes, he beamed at the camera, his face tan and confident.

Yes, this man might be Julian. Except for one big difference: Eddie's green eyes carried a vibrant and excited shine, his demeanor that of a man who reached out, grabbed life by the collar, and never looked back.

She couldn't say the same about Julian. There were moments he'd share his knowledge of Italy with the group and she'd see a spark of life. He engaged with others politely, often joking around. But Eddie popped off the computer screen while Julian seemed to blend in.

So if Julian was Eddie, then why guide a bunch of seniors—and one desperate thirty-nine-year-old woman—on the tamer sights of Tuscany?

Her Internet search continued, going to other websites that talked about the show. Nowhere did Julian's name appear. Yet based on Julian's white-faced reaction when Frank Bruno shouted out his revelation, she had to be missing something.

On page five of her search, she hit an article in *The New York Times Magazine*, "Does the quest for ratings go too far?"

She rose from the bed, made a cup of coffee from the Nespresso machine and returned to the computer. The discussion centered on zany reality shows, doing the absurd to get viewers. The topic shifted to adventure programs, like those where survivalist techniques come into play or extreme sports are performed. Several paragraphs talked about *Exploring the World with Eddie*, including the sport of winged suit flying.

Mamie learned participants glide through the air with the help of wings that are part of a suit they wear—almost like flying squirrels. The wings add surface area to the human body to enable a significant increase in lift.

Sometimes flyers exit an aircraft to fly. Other times, they base jump from a site, such as a cliff, or from a helicopter. The second was deemed far more dangerous because the initial airspeed upon exit would be absent.

In Eddie's case, his show had been filming an episode with a well-known base jumper. Though vague on specifics, the article stated how the conditions that day were questionable. Yet the activity launched as planned, with a camera crew waiting to film. A chill crept through Mamie's body as she read how the jumper slammed into a bridge, severed a leg, and died. Eddie had participated, too, but made a safe landing.

A picture showed Eddie Morrison photographed at the accident's scene. Deep anguish, the kind of unimaginable pain Mamie understood, resided fresh on his face. Her heart writhed in agony for those involved in the accident.

A paragraph beneath the photo read, "Show host Eddie Morrison is no stranger to tragedy. His parents, Allie and Alfred Morrison—who hosted *The Wild Adventures of Allie and Alfred*—died in a hot air balloon accident when Eddie was only fourteen."

Fourteen. Sadness of another kind ambushed Mamie. She imagined losing her parents at such a young age, at a time when children still needed them for so much even though they were getting older. How did this play into the man she knew as Julian?

This entry on the Internet alone didn't tie Julian to Eddie, but her gut told her to keep going. She finished her coffee, continuing her search while the sun outside her window rose. A solid hour passed while her stomach growled and she tried to ignore it.

The silence in her room broke when she yelled, "Eureka!"

A nugget of gold appeared in the archives of Michigan library. A very old article about a couple named Peter and Gabriella Gregory. As a student at Michigan State, Peter attended a college semester in Florence. There he met Gabriella, a native of Tuscany and the woman who later became his wife. After college, they began to organize small adventure tours around the world. They married and their family grew. One day, they got an offer to do a show about their travels. The program billed them under the new names of Allie and Alfred Morrison. Their children joined the show and worked under stage names, too.

She flipped back to the *New York Times* article, this time zooming in on the sadness on Eddie's face. Then she saw it. The same expression Julian wore while they were at the statue of David yesterday.

While the resemblance proved nothing, with the non-stage name of Gregory combined with his appearance she believed they were the same man. And if Julian and Eddie were the same man, it meant he and Mamie had something in common...they'd both witnessed death.

A hard lump settled in her throat. Had he handled it well or did he bear scars like her? Did it still haunt him all these years later?

Voices from other guests in the hallway echoed loudly and startled her. She got up and stretched, her thoughts drifting to last night's call she'd overheard. Who had he spoken to on the phone? And what kind of offer had he passionately refused?

From the look on his face in the *New York Times* article, Julian might blame himself for the death, but any man who partook in diving in a wing suit pretty much knew the risk involved. But if he felt responsible, Julian might have run from the show for tamer pursuits...like a tour of Tuscany. This tour job might be a place for him to hide, the way she'd closeted inside her house.

Julian's reaction to her bucket list suddenly took on a new light. His choice of tamer sights might be because it was all *he* could do right now.

Her own bravery in taking this trip suddenly became more real. Nobody would've ever called her bold, yet on this trip, she'd become exactly that. Better than she'd felt in some time. It also left her sad for him.

She wanted to help Julian. Everything he'd been doing with her made her transition back into the real world easier. So what could she do for him?

Directness might work, simply toss out how she'd figured out his identity. She threw away the idea as quickly as it arrived. If he'd wanted people to know he played the role of Eddie, he'd have admitted it that morning when Frank Bruno drew the parallel.

The activities they were doing were a perfect way to become better friends. If they continued down the same path, maybe she could do for him what he'd been doing for her: point out alternative ways of looking at the world. Over time, they might test the waters of some real risk-taking adventures, even face their fears together.

She stepped inside the shower, her mind whirling with ideas about how to help him face why he hid. Become the man he once was.

Sometimes all people needed was a friend willing to listen and let them be themselves. Julian, without knowing it, had done that for her and he deserved the same.

* * * *

Julian opened his eyes. The phone's second sharp ring zapped his already throbbing temples like a bolt of lightning. Who the hell...?

After a few slaps on the nightstand, he grabbed the hotel phone. "Hello."

"Julian? It's Rick."

Julian processed the name, his head spinning lightly and his mouth dry. "I'm downstairs." After a pause, Rick added, "You okay?"

Julian glanced at the clock. Eight-forty. Right, Rick. The local guide, an American ex-pat and spectacular photographer, had been hired to take some of his passengers on a photo expedition today.

Julian coughed and wished for water. "Yeah, I'll be fine. Rough night with the guys."

"Sounds it. Figured I'd let you know I'm here to meet your group. We should be back around five. Does that work?"

"Perfect. They should be in the lobby soon." He thought about Mamie, who hadn't signed up, so he wondered what she was doing. "There are fifteen in total. I'm laying low in town today. Call if you need me."

He hung up, ambled out of bed, and hung the Do Not Disturb sign on the outside of his door. After a trip to the bathroom and drinking a full glass of water, he flopped back into bed and closed his eyes.

The pounding inside his skull got worse. What was he thinking, drinking that much? Yesterday started out with his mood riding high, and then abruptly turned sour. Taking Mamie to see David worked out exactly as planned. The awe in her eyes as she feasted on the remarkable statue carried an intensity shooting right to the core of his chest. Maybe because the statue affected him so deeply, too. All the joy he'd had in showing off Michelangelo's masterpiece slowly diminished with her question about fear. He could've lied to her, but the question cast a spotlight on his cowardly behavior these days.

He'd recovered enough to hide his raw emotions until returning to the hotel. Meeting his buddies last night helped drown the shitty feeling with alcohol. Then Gary's call. Josef's encouragement coupled with Mamie's remarks about fear almost shamed him into finding the bravado to call the producer. Sure, he'd told Gary off. But it didn't make him feel one bit better. Instead, the call to Gary drove him straight back to the table, where more booze almost helped Julian forget.

Money. It was—and had always been—the only thing his damn producer cared about. Finances drove the show's every decision, always putting them on an aggressive schedule. The bottom line came up in every conversation. The holy grail of their business model.

Julian would argue how expeditions like his couldn't be managed from only a financial perspective. Outside circumstances could change their day, a fact to which Gary always turned a deaf ear.

Including *that* day.

Gary had argued with him from the cliff's edge, minutes from jumping, that they couldn't wait. If there was ever a moment for Julian to push back, it was that one. But he hadn't. Instead, he'd convinced a man to jump to his death.

Julian's gut clenched and he flew from the bed. Running straight into the bathroom, he held his hand over his mouth and reached the toilet just in time before he got sick. Once. Twice. He sat on the floor, back against the wall, and waited until the nausea seemed over. Stepping inside a steaming shower, he prayed for the hot water to wash away his sins.

Forgiveness. It never came easy to Julian.

In recent months, while he blamed himself for the jumping accident, it occurred to Julian the matter of forgiveness wasn't a new issue he struggled with. The day he'd watched his parents being burned alive, flames of quiet rage burned inside Julian. They'd betrayed him with their recklessness on the show, by not settling down somewhere and allowing their family to lead a normal life. Morsels of anger toward them dissipated fast as they surfaced, though, because his fury felt wrong considering he'd lost them forever.

He shut off the water and stepped from the shower. While toweling dry, he glanced up at the large mirror over the vanity. The tattoo on his pectoral muscle mocked him, reminded him the man he used to be was a fake. Inked with a three-dimensional effect, the bold tattoo showed a circular tribal ornament, the masked face of a warrior in the center. The crew insisted he get it done after a shoot in southern Ethiopia, where the tribe leader told Julian he possessed a warrior's heart.

All it took was a few drinks for Julian to agree. Now he wanted to rip it off his skin.

As he blinked at himself in the mirror, the pain in his head disappeared only to be replaced by a truth ringing loud as a bell: unruly behavior came easy after losing his parents because he had nothing left to lose— including his own life.

He dried himself, wishing for a way to relieve the anger always pulling him down. Once, while touring a church in Orvieto, he overheard a priest talking to someone about forgiveness. Would granting himself mercy make the heaviness in his chest lighter? Or did he just need a shrink?

Once back in the room, he turned on the television. Watching a morning show, he dried his hair with the towel then wrapped it around his waist. An empty day ahead of him doing paperwork while his tour did other things added to his lousy mood.

Yesterday, he'd planned on asking Mamie to spend the day with him. Another tame adventure, meant to keep her focused and out of trouble. Only what happened at the museum left him emotionally spent, forcing enthusiasm the rest of the gallery visit. Mentally, he'd run away from her.

Running.

A path Julian followed since the age of fourteen. When would he stop?

Chapter 12

"Thanks, Sandra." Mamie left the lobby and took the stairs to the second floor to the room Sandra told her belonged to Julian.

Armed with Julian's real story and the desire to help him through a crisis she didn't fully understand, she continued until she stood outside room 207. Mamie lifted her hand and, only after she banged three times loudly, did she spot the Do Not Disturb sign on the knob.

Before she could turn and make a fast escape the handle jiggled and the door swung open.

Julian stared back, naked except for a white towel wrapped at his waist. Her gaze drifted to a tattoo of a symbol just above his left breast, peeking out behind a few sandy brown hairs. She followed the narrow trail of hair in the center of his broad chest, stopping as it hit his naval.

He cleared his throat.

She quickly looked up, her gaze landing on bags beneath his eyes. "Sorry. Good morning."

His jaw tightened as he dropped his gaze to the door handle.

"Yeah, sorry about that. I didn't see the sign until it was too late." Voices in the room caught her attention. The reason he didn't want to be disturbed took on another meaning. "Oh, never mind. I'll catch you later."

"It's the TV. I'm alone."

"It's nothing important. I can tell you're—"

"What's up, Mamie?"

In spite of his obvious bad mood, her mission today was Julian's happiness. "I was wondering if you wanted to hang out today? That is, if you're free."

He drew in a deep breath and his broad chest lifted, forcing her to ogle again like a desperate woman. An awful way to feel, and yet she fit the bill.

She looked him square in the face. "I asked because you've shown me some wonderful things and, well, I enjoy your company."

His face softened a little.

Feeling bolder, she added, "In fact, I can't think of anybody I'd rather spend my day with." Then she smiled, the most hopeful, upbeat smile she'd probably put on her face in the past five years.

He studied her with an impassive stare for a long few seconds. "Have you eaten breakfast?"

"Not yet. I'm on my way down."

"Let me get dressed. I'll meet you downstairs. Grab us a table. We can talk then."

"Great."

He nodded, shot her a half-smile, and then shut the door.

Mamie let out a breath, letting go of tension in her tight shoulders. Once in the dining room, she got a plate of food then found a table in the corner, away from the other patrons. Getting the man who she suspected was Eddie to open up a little wouldn't be easy.

The waiter delivered her coffee while she sat picking at a bowl of fruit. A penance after days of ignoring anything too healthy. Only if she finished the fruit would she let herself dive into the nearby plate of salami, cheese, and Nutella.

A few minutes later, Julian entered the room. He said something to the waiter and, after taking only a roll from the buffet spread, approached her table.

Julian pulled out a chair and sat, his knees bumping hers.

She glanced at his plate. "All those yummy things to choose from and you got one roll?"

His gaze drifted to her heaping plate and she swore he turned white. "You feeling okay?"

"I'll be fine." He sipped his water.

She chewed on a piece of melon, debating whether to mention she'd seen him in town last night.

"How'd you like Florence?" he asked.

"Nothing short of remarkable."

"Favorite part?" He tore a corner from his roll and slowly chewed it.

"There were two things. I loved the view of Florence from the Boboli Gardens. Simply breathtaking." He nodded, watching her with a deepness that made her almost forget to breathe.

"I'd love to show you Fiesole," he said. "Different city views, but equally beautiful. Maybe while we're at the farmhouse we can take a ride."

"I'd like that."

"And the second thing?"

"The statue of David." She reached out and touched his hand for a second. "Really, Julian. Thank you. I'll always remember how you introduced me to it."

He offered a close-lipped smile. "My pleasure."

She smoothed the hazelnut spread onto half a crusty roll wishing she could just ask about the call of his she'd overheard, but it wasn't the right approach. After taking a bite and swallowing, she said, "Last night, I was Googling things about Italy and stumbled on a quote from Mark Twain. Something like Michelangelo's designs—no wait... Ah, yes. 'The Creator made Italy from designs by Michelangelo.'"

Julian laughed. "Great quote." He watched her for a moment then reached out and touched a spot beneath her lower lip, his touch gentle and surprising. "You wear your Nutella well."

She dabbed with her napkin, hoping her cheeks weren't as red as they felt. "I can't resist this stuff. Is it gone?"

He picked up his napkin and wiped beneath her chin. "Now it is."

She couldn't remember the last time a man touched her with such care, in a way so...so...familiar and almost intimate.

"Twain's comment carries some truth." Julian put down his napkin. "This country is so beautiful. Easy to see what inspired the Renaissance artists, you know? I've traveled to many beautiful places during my life, but Italy is special." He stared into his coffee cup for a fraction of a second, then met her gaze and spoke more softly. "I like watching you see everything for the first time."

Her cheeks warmed knowing he'd been watching her so closely, his awareness a surprise and the kind of attention she once loved receiving.

To want it was also scary. This new and fun thing with Julian could vanish in the time it took the second hand to tick. What did she really know about him? She didn't want to like being around him so much. Yet the mystery surrounding him intrigued her.

"Tell me about your tattoo?"

His shoulders stiffened, but he replied calmly, "It's an Aztec warrior."

"Cool. Why did you decide on that and not, oh, let's say, Tweety Bird?" When she smiled, his shoulders relaxed and he grinned.

The smile faded. "A few of my buddies talked me into this after a little too much to drink." He glanced down at the tabletop for a second, then looked up. "That's it. Just a crazy impulsive decision."

She nodded, certain there was more to the story. "What kind of adventure can we take today?"

"There's tons of treasure right here in Siena."

"Sounds good." She sipped her coffee, watching him over the rim as he ate small bites of his bread. "Guess we won't be using my list at all."

He chewed then swallowed. "Have I disappointed you yet?"

"No. But my list is still on the table, right?"

"Maybe for another day." He wiped his hands with his napkin. "Finish eating. We've only got until five, when the others come back and we've got a lot of ground to cover." He paused and studied her for several seconds. "How do you manage to get me to do things I shouldn't be doing?"

"It's a gift." She waggled her brows and loved the way his face softened in response.

She ate while Julian shared a story about a trip that went awry from one of his other tours. In the back of her thoughts, the fact she wasn't completely honest with Julian about her life made her feel awful. The topic of work bringing her to Tuscany was legally off limits, but she did have a personal story to share. Not the made-up story about a divorce.

Julian laughed. "And then Beppe spent five minutes trying to get the goats to cross the road..."

His joy and improved mood made her happy. It made her want to be truthful and reveal to him the true Mamie.

So what was she waiting for?

* * * *

"Some say this church is the soul of Siena, while the main square is the heart."

Julian glanced at Mamie from where they stood in the back of Siena's Duomo, looking out to the nave. She stared straight ahead, her dark eyes wide and her full lower lip slightly open, giving him a minute to study the gentle slope of her nose and creamy skin.

She seemed interested in the tour he'd given her. He never tired of looking at this place. Lined by columns made of white/black marble and layered in a striped motif, the cathedral displayed sculptures of Siena's past religious leaders, while the floor displayed storytelling done in mosaics.

Her intense gaze canvassed the interior of this medieval gothic masterpiece, then she turned to him. "And when did you say it was built again?"

"They started construction in—I think—the early twelve hundreds." Instead of staring at the artwork, he couldn't take his eyes off Mamie. She seemed... What was it? More confident? He usually didn't notice women's fashions, but lately her clothing was less plain, more like what he saw on local women. Like the long halter dress she wore today.

"Just remarkable." She reached inside her purse and removed her sunglasses, glancing his way as she looked around one more time but her mood had shifted abruptly. "Thank you for being such a thorough guide. I'm ready to leave whenever you are."

Thorough guide? That's exactly the part he'd played for her, though. Not that of a man who'd taken notice of her, loved to talk to her, was interested as all hell about her. Damned if he didn't do the showman thing with everyone. When he was Eddie, he was always on and entertaining. Never giving those around him a glimpse into his personal side. Now as a guide, he rarely took off this same hat. Much easier than being himself.

They headed out the doors and into the large piazza in front of the church. A warm breeze blew by, making her lightweight dress flutter around her slender legs and giving him a peek of her shapely calf where the dress slit on the side. Where was she putting all the food she'd been eating? Certainly not on those lean curves.

"Are you getting hungry yet?" She glanced around, definitely avoiding Julian's gaze. Yup, her good spirits during the cathedral visit had disappeared.

"Sure. I can eat now. There's a nice place in that direction." He pointed to his right.

As she slipped on the dark glasses, he swore he caught glistening in her eyes.

She started to walk away, but he reached out and took her hand.

Pulling her closer, he asked, "What's wrong?"

"Nothing." She shook her head.

He lifted her sunglasses and placed them on top of her head to find the tears he suspected in her eyes. "Mamie. What is it?"

She dropped her chin to her chest. "I'm sorry. Being inside there..." She looked up at the cathedral. "It made me think about someone I lost who'd have truly enjoyed this place. Hell, he'd have loved everything about Tuscany."

He? "How about we sit and talk?"

She hesitated then finally nodded. He led her by the hand to the cathedral's side, where the front steps wrapped around the building. They found some shade and fewer people. He motioned for her to sit and, when he joined her, their legs touched. He held tightly onto her hand and waited for her to say something.

Her shoulders stooped as stared at her lap. "The story I told you about my life isn't completely true. I'm not divorced. My husband...he died and also—" She stopped and shut her eyes, her face contorting right before tears streamed down her cheek.

"What is it, Mamie?" he asked quietly.

She shook her head then drew in a deep breath. "Nothing."

His heart ached for every tear she shed, but he wouldn't push her right now. "I'm sorry. How long ago?"

"Five years."

All the sadness displayed on her expression when she first arrived became clear. No wonder he'd related to her. The agony of such a loss always painted the same picture. Torment he fully understood. "I'll bet it's been a tough five years."

"Yes." Her lip trembled and she let go of his hand and wrapped her arm around her stomach. "It was a car accident." She drew a deep breath. "It's the reason I limp."

He nodded, remembering what she'd told Joel after the scooter accident.

"EMS said I was lucky to have survived." She bowed her head and whispered like a passing breeze, "I never felt lucky."

Julian put his arms around her shoulders and drew her trembling body close to his chest. Words escaped him. All he could feel were the pieces of his broken heart stirring inside his chest, reminding him how it felt to lose a loved one. Tightness made his throat thick, and an unexpected tear ran down his cheek.

He hugged Mamie even tighter, though it didn't stop the control he'd mastered for many years from slipping away. Mamie's pain became his own, causing his throat to swell and his eyes to water. For once, he didn't fight his pain. Not only for Mamie, but for his own losses, too.

They stayed on the steps, Mamie settled against his chest and Julian supporting her—or maybe she was supporting him. No matter. Being with her at this moment felt so right. But why? He hardly knew her. Yet something had drawn them together. Perhaps their suffering.

She looked up at him. Tears stained her cheeks. He reached into his pocket, found a napkin, and wiped her wet face.

"I'm sorry." She said, watching him through watery, vulnerable eyes filled with pain so raw he couldn't let go. "You're crying?"

"I-I..." Words escaped him. The story of his parents' death had been neatly brushed under the carpet for a long time, so he didn't know what to say. Besides, this was about her. "Yes. I'm sad for your loss."

She frowned and her eyes skipped around his face, her scrutiny making him uncomfortable. He didn't want to talk about his problems.

"I'm sorry to dump this on you."

"Don't be. I'm not sorry you did."

"No?" She watched him, her brows furrowed and a desperate gleam in her eyes. "It's been a relief to be someplace where nobody knows about it."

He nodded. It was why he changed his appearance and made sure nobody knew he was once Eddie. A fact he could share with her right now, so she understood she wasn't alone with the emotion.

Instead, he used his finger to wipe off some wilted mascara beneath her eyes. "Thank you for telling me."

She took his hand. "You're welcome."

They sat together for several minutes, their shoulders touching while they quietly watched the crowds.

She shifted and faced him. "I think I'm still hungry." She smiled, so slight and quick he almost missed it. "Pitiful, huh?"

"Not one bit." Right away, he felt better, surprised how much her happiness suddenly mattered so much to him. "My plan was to grab some food from a deli in the old part of town, find a place to eat and people watch, then head to a park called All'Orto de' Pecci. They have medieval gardens you might like. We can even take a short afternoon siesta."

She grinned. "You need a rest?"

"I'm running on very little sleep after a rough night."

"Don't let the rest of the tour hear you say that. You'll never hear the end of it."

He laughed. "Can't I count on you to keep a secret?"

"For now. But if the time ever comes, I may use it against you."

"Oh so this is how it's gonna roll, huh?" He stood and held out his hand to help her up.

"You bet." She took his hand and rose just as her stomach growled loudly. She laughed and pressed her hand to it. "Jeesh, down Rover! I've never eaten so much in my life and still find room for more. Can you explain that to me?"

Taking in her eyes, now lively and energetic, he couldn't ignore how good her joy made him feel. "It's part of Italy's magic."

Chapter 13

"Peter, *sbrigati. Siamo in ritardo.*"

Mamie opened her eyes and lifted her head. Right near the blanket where she and Julian had lain down to relax then fallen asleep, a woman holding a child's hand hurried by.

Staying on her side, Mamie nestled her cheek into the soft blanket. The owner of the deli where they'd purchased a bag of olives, bread, and sliced meats for their lunch turned out to be a friend of Julian's. The two men had spoken in lively Italian and next she knew, the gray-haired owner handed Julian the blanket they now used, winked at them, and sent them along with a bottle of wine.

From this angle, her gaze trailed the line of connected gold and tan stucco buildings with terra-cotta tiled roofs separating the park from the busy city. Beyond the buildings, the sky opened and the tall tower she and Julian planned to climb this afternoon jutted into the sky.

Julian. An awareness of his arm draped at her waist and his slow breaths close to the back of her head swept over her. How had they ended up in this position? They'd been on their backs, side by side, staring up into the blue sky and puffy clouds. Then she shut her eyes for just a second and rolled to her side... That's the last thing she could recall.

His nearness offered comfort. Same as when he'd take her hand out of the blue. Maybe he was just a guy who touched people easily, but part of her wanted it to mean more.

The cathedral tour should've been wonderful. Well, it was at the start. But while Julian discussed works done by Michelangelo, Donatello, and Bernini, she couldn't stop thinking about Ted and how he'd have loved this tour, loved this country.

At least she'd told Julian the truth about her marital status and why she was single. She couldn't quite mention Zoe. Her daughter's wide, dark eyes and freckled nose flashed in her mind's eye, causing Mamie's gut to quiver. Talking about Zoe brought her back to life, leaving Mamie clinging to precious memories where she'd later drown in her grief. No, she couldn't share that loss with him. Not yet.

"Ready to climb the *campanile*?" Julian's tired voice rumbled near her ear.

"The what?" She rolled over to face him, burying the angst over losing her daughter and forcing a smile.

He watched her through sleepy eyes. "It's another name for the tower."

"How many steps did you say?"

"Five hundred."

"It doesn't look so bad, so I'm game. The real question is, are you?"

He narrowed his eyes. "Did you just throw down the gauntlet?"

"Did you forget about our bet? Ten euros are at stake, although I think the incentive should be greater."

"Oh? What do you want?" His voice shifted, huskier than before.

His smile faded and his serious gaze made her still. She wanted to reach over and touch the soft grain of his beard, run her fingers through the waves of his hair. Kiss him and let the thin mustache above his upper lip tease her skin. Yes. That's what she wanted to do. What she wanted to feel.

Julian studied her face, the intensity in his eyes making the space between her thighs ache for his touch. Old Mamie would've waited, but new Mamie's desires were strong. She leaned in, pushing aside any concern about right from wrong—

Julian swung an arm up and blocked his head just as a soccer ball landed between them.

"*Scusi!*" A young boy approached.

"*Non c'è problema.*" Julian handed off the ball with a smile.

"*Grazie.*" The young boy ran off to his friend.

Julian sat up and Mamie did the same.

He turned to her. "I guess we should get going."

"Sounds good."

Only he didn't move. He stared at her face, searching and assessing, then slowly his gaze drifted to her mouth. His lips parted, such perfect lips partially hidden beneath the outline of his beard and mustache. *Kiss me. Kiss me. Kiss me.*

He glanced away and cleared his throat. "The Wanderers have a talent show planned while we're at the villas."

"Yeah. Bernie mentioned it." She worked hard to sound normal, despite disappointment over the swift change in the atmosphere.

"I was thinking, do you want to do a number with me? The others would love it. I mean, since we're the group's youngsters."

"At thirty-nine I'm not exactly a youngster."

His gaze trickled over her, pulling her back to the near miss of a kiss. "You're younger than me."

"Not by much."

"Two years, and I'd gladly take those back. So? Are you up for it?"

"I don't have any talent." She straightened out her legs and wiggled her toes, freed from her sandals. "What are you going to do?"

"I play the guitar. Beppe said I could borrow his brother's. He lives close to the villas where we'll be staying." He smiled, a grin sly as a fox. "Want to know a secret?"

"Sure."

"My dad attended Woodstock, like the others in the group."

"Why haven't you told them? They'd eat that right up."

He shrugged. "This is their trip. Not about me."

"Bet your dad will love hearing about this tour." As the words fell out of her mouth, Mamie remembered the article about him losing his parents in a hot air balloon accident.

"My dad passed away." He showed no outer reaction. "Many years ago."

"Oh. I'm sorry."

He waved a hand. "It was a long time ago. Anyway, Dad taught me how to play the guitar. And trust me, he made sure I could play the music of his generation. I figured I'd surprise them with a number from the concert."

"Great idea. I can tell they really like you."

"You think? Well, I like them." He rose off the blanket and extended his hand to her. As she took it and stood, tenderness visible in his eyes said far more than his words. "Let me know if you want to join me on stage, but for now it's time to hike the *campanile*. We've got to be back in a while."

They packed their things and headed back toward town. Julian returned to acting like a tour director, describing all the sights along the way. Good thing that soccer ball rolled onto the blanket. She must be misreading his cues and was rustier about the dating scene than she thought. Even though he'd asked her to join him at tomorrow's Palio trial race, it wasn't like a date.

He stopped in front of a brick building. "This is the Sienese Government building. Our entrance to the tower." He pointed up.

Tipping her head back, she took in the edifice, its height more daunting close up than from a distance. "Gosh, it *is* tall."

"Don't back out on me."

"Did I say I was backing out?"

"*Vamos, Señorita* Mamie. Our race starts here."

He placed his hand on the small of her back and guided her inside. After paying a fee, they started the ascent.

At first, Mamie sprinted, glancing back at him and laughing about her possible win. The tight chamber narrowed the higher they went and soon she couldn't see Julian. A dank scent closed in on her and natural light disappeared. She stopped near a small window set into the thick brick. Mamie bent over a half-wall edging the stairs like a railing, from this view able to stare down the levels within the squared staircase. "Julian?"

His head popped into the stairwell opening, about ten or fifteen steps below. "You might want to pace yourself. Remember the turtle and the hare?"

"Which one are you?"

He laughed and then pulled in his head so she could no longer see him, like a turtle hiding in its shell.

"I think you're the turtle," she yelled and his laughter echoed inside the closed chamber.

She continued up slowly, getting winded and hoping he'd reach her soon. Other voices carried from above and a moment later, Mamie pressed her back against the cool brick walls while a family passed on their way down.

Julian finally appeared around a tight corner and grinned. "Thanks for waiting, Bugs Bunny."

"So you admit you are a turtle?"

He shook his head and smiled then motioned with his hand. "After you."

She started up, slower now. The stone stairs were steep and her legs ached. She stopped to catch her breath and he waited at her side.

"We're almost there." He sounded winded himself. "It'll be worth it."

She could only nod and they kept climbing.

Less than a minute later, the sky beckoned beyond a doorway. She stepped out and the fresh air rushed her skin, a welcome break after the musty stone structure.

"Come on." Julian took her hand and headed toward brick wall maybe four or five feet high surrounding the observation platform. "Let's call this race a tie."

When they reached the wall, their shoulders brushed as they stood close, his hand in hers. The hot sun warmed her skin. She inhaled, fully aware of her racing heart. Be it from the climb, Julian's hand in hers, or the view, she couldn't be certain.

Nothing could've prepared her for the panoramic view of Siena's orange roofs dotting the cityscape, blending the hand of nature and man. Architecture so rustic and perfect that the buildings appeared to have sprouted from the soil. Directly below the tower, tourists the size of ants milled in the Campo. The large fountain in the square's center looked small enough to be a toddler pool. Beyond the city walls, the rolling hills of Tuscany wrapped its arms around the walled fortress. Safe. Peaceful. That's how the Sienese of centuries past must have felt here. It's how Mamie felt.

"What do you think?"

"It's..." Mamie searched for the right words. "Magnificent."

"Look to your left."

Mamie turned, further awestruck when she caught sight of a massive cathedral in the distance. She hurried over to the corner, waving to Julian to follow.

"Is that where we went earlier?" she yelled before he could reach her.

"Yup."

Close up, the church had seemed enormous, and somehow even from this distance it majestically enveloped the city.

He caught up and stood beside her.

She lifted her sunglasses into her hair as the sun disappeared behind a billowy cloud. "I think this tower is as tall as the church. I hadn't realized how high up the church sat, like it's built on a hill."

"You're very observant. The Sienese were making a statement by doing that, giving both government and God an equal importance in their lives, although the tower is taller, so you be the judge of their message."

"How do you know all this?" She faced him and found him watching her, not the view. "I really love all these little details you share."

"Do you now?" He spoke softly and his lips lifted in a slight smile.

"I do." She leaned against the stone wall as the sun reappeared and cast its heat over her. Or did she feel this way because Julian stood close, his gaze brimming with a different type of heat. "Why are you smiling?"

"Because I love your excitement." He reached up and brushed a few strands of her hair from her face, his smile fading. He took a step closer and stretched out his arms, resting his palms on the wall and trapping her between them. Close enough to kiss.

He lowered his voice and watched her. "The views up here are nice, but I have the most beautiful view of all."

Julian kissed her. A tender and careful kiss. His soft lips treated her with a kind of patient handling she needed, yet still conveyed his desire. She lifted her arms around his neck and pressed close as he slipped his hand to the curve of her back, holding her there while he deepened his kiss.

He leaned back, watching her with a satisfied smile on his lips. "What do you think? Was this worth the climb?"

"Oh yes." She stretched up on tiptoes and this time she kissed him, the way she'd wanted to earlier.

Little did he know that her real climb had been the one taking her to the airport and sending her on this journey. An ascent returning a few pieces of herself she'd previously lost along the way.

* * * *

"If I could have everyone's attention."

Mamie looked away from the bus window to where Julian stood at the front of the bus. Their eyes met and he gave her a quick smile then turned his attention back to the tour.

His simple glance revived their last kiss, hiding out in a quiet alley not far from their hotel after they left the tower. Passionate. Forbidden. The secret nature of their Siena tryst made it all the more tantalizing.

"This is our last night in Siena—"

Groans filled the bus, cutting him off.

He laughed. "Now come on. We're headed to a beautiful villa. It'll be a Tuscan communal living experience. I thought hippies liked communal living?"

"That's a stereotype," Tina piped up from her seat across the aisle from Mamie. "I'll miss Siena. Strolling around town after dinner has been a joy. Plus, I like not cooking my meals."

"I'm glad you mentioned that, Tina. My boss made arrangements for a chef while we're there. Listen, this place is beautiful. You can still take day excursions, photograph nearby, or simply relax to enjoy the pool or visit the hot springs."

"It'll be a chance for you to rest up, Julian." Bob grinned.

"Well played, Bob."

The others laughed and started to talk again, but Julian's silence and raised brow quieted them.

"For dinner tonight, we're headed for a small town called Staggia. It's just past Monteriggioni, where we had dinner your first night here. There's a castle nearby, located on an old pilgrimage route between Poggibonsi and Monteriggioni."

Their first night seemed like a lifetime ago. Mamie sure wasn't the same person who'd gotten on that plane back at JFK.

"This dinner, it's a very special one for me. My mother was from Italy. So while I was born in America, Italy has always been a second home. The chef here is a close family friend. Like an uncle to me. It's been way too long since I've seen him, so..." Julian looked at the ground for a few seconds and his Adam's apple rolled along his throat. He lifted his head and, voice filled with emotion, he continued, "While I don't usually join you at dinner, tonight I will. For me, it's about old friends and new ones."

Everyone applauded. Julian smiled gently and took his seat. The small drop about his past confirmed what was written in the Michigan library article about his mother being Italian and meeting her husband during his study abroad. Armed with this new fact, she vowed to be patient and let Julian tell her about himself, not divulge what her Internet search revealed. Him telling her would mean he wanted to open up to her, rather than her backing him into a corner with her suspicions.

The bus slowed and entered a narrow street. They passed a row of blemished white stucco connected buildings, all with aging evergreen shutters.

Beppe pulled into a spot and had barely stopped before half the passengers stood, anxious to exit. Mamie waited more patiently and was one of the last few to step off. Julian waited outside the door and offered her a hand down.

His eyes searched hers. "Careful. Did you enjoy your day free from my grueling tour?"

"Oh yes." She tossed him a coy smile. "I explored Siena. Seems I have a deep passion for the city."

His eyes hooded, making her want to drag *him* to a quiet alley and make out again. Who was this stranger she'd become?

He quickly turned to Tina, right behind Mamie. "And how about you, Tina?"

Mamie walked over to the others, but had a hard time taking her eyes off Julian.

Bob Leon stepped off last, a grin already set on his face as he raised his voice loud enough for the group to hear. "A few of us are hoping for a late night of partying. Right, Bern?" He tipped his head to Bernie, who waited near Mamie.

Bernie laughed. "Now don't scare the kid, Bob. Didn't we say we'd ease him into it?"

"Take it easy on me, you guys." Julian patted Bob on the shoulder. "Last night I had a rough one with some friends."

Bob shook his head. "I'm not sure you'd have survived Woodstock, kiddo."

"Sometimes I wonder that myself, Bob."

Mamie wondered what Bob would think if he knew he was talking to a man who, at one point in his life, challenged himself with more dramatic feats than most mortals.

Julian waved his hand and they followed toward a row of stucco buildings, slowing at a door marked "Ristorante del Castello."

"This place is small and ours for the night. Head on in and take a seat." He motioned to a doorway where gold fabric cords hung from the top frame and danced with a breeze.

As she reached the door's threshold, the aromatic scent of garlic and good cooking bombarded her senses, making her mouth water and hungry stomach beg for satisfaction.

An older man, wiping his hands on a food-stained white apron, exited the kitchen. He had a long, thick nose and stark white hair. His dark eyes sparkled as he smiled and lifted his long chin to inspect the group.

When Julian walked in after the last passenger, the man's face brightened. "Julian! *Benvenuto.*"

They hugged. Julian shut his eyes and the two men stayed that way for a long moment, the depth of their affection so deep Mamie could feel it.

They spoke in Italian while the others got seated then Julian turned to the group. "I'd like everyone to meet Ernesto."

The group responded with waves, choruses of hellos.

Ernesto smiled wide, making the cracks of age lines more prominent and showcasing his yellowed teeth. "Howdy. Welcome."

Julian placed a hand on his shoulder. "Ernesto's asked me to translate for you, because he only knows a little English. Ernesto grew up in Staggia and left here as a young man to work at a popular Milan restaurant. In his sixties, he retired and opened this place. He specializes in cooking traditional Tuscan food. Tonight, Ernesto promises to serve us some of his regional recipes. As an added treat, he will also perform some of his music."

A minute later, small tumbler glasses were passed out by two helpers, who then filled them from large bottles of Chianti.

Mamie watched Julian as he talked to Ernesto, their closeness clear. Ernesto spoke with authority. Julian listened more than spoke, appearing to hang on Ernesto's every word in what Mamie recognized as a sign of deep respect for the man. Their conversation ended and Julian turned around, heading for a table across from Mamie where he took the only remaining seat.

She didn't miss the glow in his expression. Happy. Relaxed. The kind of comfort and ease that comes with being with people who know you better than anybody else.

People you call family.

Seeing Julian happy lifted something inside Mamie's heart. He deserved happiness. After all, he'd brought some to her. He'd made it easy for her to flirt again, and showed her she was still desirable to the opposite sex.

She'd just found him and now the clock ticked on their time together. A reminder she'd better make the most of what was left.

* * * *

"I'm excited to try this food." Martha turned to Julian.

"You won't be disappointed." Across the room, Julian watched Ernesto give instructions to the wait staff. He looked back to Martha. "I have fond memories of being at my family's Tuscany home when Ernesto would come to visit to escape the busyness of Milan on his days off." Julian laughed. "My mom would always walk him into the kitchen and say 'Put on an apron. I need help.'"

Martha laughed. Jesus, he'd been babbling like a fool about himself without a second thought. What had brought that on? Joel started talking and Martha's attention drifted to him.

Julian looked to the kitchen, where he could see Ernesto bustling around back, shouting out orders to his two helpers. When Julian began to work for the tour company and moved back to in Italy as his home base, the first thing he did was look up the old family friend. For too many years they hadn't talked, mostly due to the show's schedule. After being fired from the show, Julian's need to secure a tie to the past seemed as critical as air.

Opening up about his background to Martha just now came out of nowhere. Another unplanned moment today, like kissing Mamie.

He glanced to the next table where she sat listening to Sandra speak. Seconds later, Mamie's gaze drifted to him. She stared, bolder than the way they'd made eye contact in the past. All pulling him back to every time he kissed her. First in the tower, then again as she made a purchase in a Campo gift shop, and later inside a store filled with ceramics.

Was it a mistake? He'd been a wreck this past year and no woman had gotten close to him. Shit, he'd never let *any* woman he'd dated within arm's distance, at least emotionally. Damned if Mamie didn't feel so right in his arms, though. So perfect he didn't care about breaking the company's rules.

"Have you been there, Julian?"

"I'm sorry." He focused on Joel, who sat in a seat across from him. "Where?"

"An Etruscan burial site, not far from here."

"I have. There's also one close to the farmhouse we can visit."

Ernesto stepped from the kitchen opening, announcing his first course: assorted crostini, followed by cold cuts, and in the center a nice chunk of Pecorino Toscano drizzled with *aceto balsamico*. Julian ate and drank in a way that reminded him of family gatherings while growing up. Laughing and talking with this group filled his chest with familial joy, the kind he craved after losing his parents.

After they devoured wild boar stew served on pappardelle noodles, Ernesto exited the kitchen holding his guitar.

"*Questo si chiama, il mio cuore.*" He paused and added in heavily accented English, "A song called 'My Heart.'"

Ernesto sang, his Italian rich and pure, each word settling on Julian's ears and touching him with a loving hand. He glanced around the room. All eyes were on Ernesto, passion in their faces, despite none of them understanding what he sang. The Italian language was like that, carrying a melody of its own.

Mamie's eyes glistened as she watched, deeply moved like the others. Julian couldn't stop watching her while Ernesto sang about Tuscany. History. Golden fields. A strong culture. And pride. God, these people were proud. The same pride Julian had once found in Tuscany, both in the company of blood relatives and friends, new and old. This place nourished him. It was home.

At that moment, Mamie's eyes drifted from Ernesto to Julian. Beautiful Mamie, with eyes dark as chocolate, and lips he wanted to feel on his again. Right here, right now. This week had been special, in a large part due to her. And just like the things written in Ernesto's song, she filled a space in Julian's heart.

Was he falling for someone, during the lowest point in his life?

Loud applause and shouts of "*Brava*" drew Julian back to the room. Ernesto stood, took a bow, and moved to Julian's side.

"You read the words of my song to them? *Sì?*"

"Of course." Julian stood to address the group and translated the words on the paper. But he didn't dare look into Mamie's eyes while reading this, afraid the turmoil and vulnerability inside of him would come spilling out.

He finished reading and excused himself to get some fresh air outside.

On his way out, a hard, cold reality hit. He wanted Mamie to understand him, but what would she think of a man who'd coaxed another man to his death? Probably not much.

* * * *

"Next time I see Ernesto, I'll pass along your message." Julian turned away from his hotel room window, where he'd been staring out into the darkness. "Great talking to you, Jen. Love you."

He hung up the phone, got undressed, and slipped on some boxer shorts. Before crawling into bed, he detoured to the bathroom to brush his teeth. Since leaving Ernesto's restaurant, Julian had a strong urge to talk to his sister. In part because tonight reminded him of their family, but he had another motive, too.

As he'd walked into his room, he calculated the time as five o'clock in the States and found her exactly where he thought he might: fixing dinner while the kids did their homework.

The call had been made with a personal agenda in mind. On the bus ride home, his strong feelings for Mamie got all twisted up with fear she'd reject him once she knew what he'd done the day Carlos died. By the time they reached the hotel, he'd figured out a way to test the reaction of another woman he was close to…his sister. After he'd been fired from the show, his email to his sister simply stated he was pursuing other interests. She only wrote back to say she was glad he no longer led that life, not asking for specifics.

If Jenny didn't blame him for what happened during the winged suit accident, maybe he could feel more confident speaking to Mamie about it.

Only when Jenny answered the phone and he talked about the dinner, her excitement at hearing about their childhood family friend had squashed the topic at hand. Or maybe he'd grabbed it as a handy excuse to avoid talking about the real reason he'd called.

So how could he ever raise this with Mamie?

He lifted the toothbrush, but instead of using it, he stared in the mirror, ashamed of his image watching back. The tattoo mocked him. If he could, he'd rip it off his skin. After quickly brushing his teeth, he went to bed.

Lying in the dark, a new kind of fear took hold, found in his real feelings for Mamie. A rejection from her might push him off the edge. In all decency, though, he couldn't have her in his life, even briefly, without telling her the truth, which represented the worst of him.

The road ahead. A game of risk.

He couldn't have her if he couldn't be honest, but that honesty could make her want nothing to do with him.

There was one other way out. As it stood right now, they'd only shared a few kisses and close moments. Ending it now would surely mean they could stay friends. As friends, he didn't feel an obligation to tell her about his shameful act on the show.

Guilt pounded him hard and fast. This was a shitty thing to do, but in her, he sensed strength. More strength than he possessed lately. Further proof she deserved better than him.

The real question was, if he went ahead and suggested they cool it a bit, could he handle it?

Chapter 14

Knock, knock, knock.

Mamie put down her toothbrush, rinsed her mouth with water, and grabbed a towel as she went to the door. Peeking through the peephole, she caught Julian glancing both ways down the hallway.

She opened the door while wiping the side of her mouth dry. "Am I late?"

He jerked his head her way. "No."

"Good. I thought we were leaving for the trials at eight sharp."

"I wanted..." He pointed inside. "Can we talk inside?"

"Oh sure." She moved aside and tossed the towel on the dresser. He sounded nervous. "Something wrong?"

He stepped into the room. In the entryway, the overhead light showed his tired eyes. "Let's talk."

"Okay."

He took her hand, led her to the bed and motioned for her to sit at his side. He inhaled. "You know I like you."

"Oh, shit. You're ending things?" Said half-joking, she worried when a pained expression flashed across his face.

"I'm sorry. I started thinking about us last night while I tried to sleep. My job. I can't lose it right now."

"You worry too much."

"Come on, Mamie. I've broken so many rules, letting you on the bus—"

"You could've said no."

"But I didn't."

"And you offered to take me on those *not-a-date* things we've done."

"So I could keep an eye on you."

The words struck like a sucker punch to the gut. Julian babysat her so she didn't do anything drastic while on his tour. "Oh. I see. Well, last I checked, *you* kissed *me*."

He hung his head. "I'm sorry, but I shouldn't have. I wasn't thinking."

An ache pulsed in her chest. She stood and walked to the window.

Starting over again sucked. Married life had been filled with certainty. Learning to date again wasn't. Her recently discovered desire was now battered and bruised by his abrupt shift.

He came up behind her, putting his hands on her shoulders. "Mamie. Look at me."

She couldn't. Rejection brought a return of all the vulnerability that came with loss. Alone. Again. In a way, so much easier than needing others.

He turned her around. "Please, Mamie."

She lifted her gaze to his sad eyes. "What?"

"This past year, I've had some problems. You deserve better than a broken man like me."

"Isn't that my choice?"

He shrugged. "I think you can do better."

"You could talk to me about your problems. I told you about my husband and the accident." She swallowed, aware she hadn't told him everything, including the reason she landed on this tour.

"Yes, you did." He thought for a moment then shook his head. "I'm sorry. I can't talk about me right now. You'll have to believe me when I say you can do better. I'm not a good man."

"I hate hearing you say that." She wanted to blurt out the story about him she'd read on the internet, tell him she figured out he was Eddie from the adventure show. Only she found the information by snooping behind his back, and so she'd have to wait until he was ready to tell her. Instead, she took his hand. "That's not true. Everyone likes you." More quietly, she said, "I like you."

He shut his eyes while shaking his head. "But you don't know me or what I've done."

"Only because you won't talk to me."

He opened his eyes and frowned. "It's not you. I don't want to talk about my problems with anybody."

"I didn't think—" Hard as she wanted to believe she'd become special to him, that she wasn't just anybody, it counted as her first mistake. Reasonably, what they'd done together just barely scratched the surface of dating. No matter how intense their moments together had seemed.

She stepped to the end of the bed and sat down. "You know what? This is fine." She tried to sound chipper. "Just go. Easier to end whatever we started after eighteen hours. Let's pretend this thing between us never happened for what's left of the tour."

His voice cracked. "It's for the best."

She wanted to scream how it wasn't best, but instead she dropped her chin to her chest and bottlenecked all the upset swirling inside her, waiting to sprout.

"I can still take you to the trials."

Her throat grew thick. "No, but thank you."

He got down on one knee in front of her, reached out and tilted her chin up so he could see her face. "I'm sorry. You don't deserve to step into my mess. I'm trying to protect you."

Her head pounded. Maybe this was personal. Maybe it wasn't. But she couldn't handle getting attached to a man and having him leave. Or maybe she could, but this first time hurt.

He watched her intently, the despair in his eyes obvious. She pulled herself together. "My life has been a mess since the car accident. I didn't appreciate all the wonderful things I had"—she swallowed the hard lump in her throat—"until the Goddamn forces ruling the universe decided I wasn't worthy of them anymore."

She inhaled deeply while trying to gain perspective on her reaction to what Julian had done this morning. "I don't need you telling me what I do and don't deserve. This was a vacation fling, Julian. Nothing more. But if it's over for you, then so be it." She stood, went to the door, and opened it. *Stay strong.* She turned to him. "I'd like to be alone, if you don't mind."

Julian stood. Approaching the door, he watched her then opened his mouth to say something. Instead, he crossed the threshold into the hallway. She shut the door and let her tears flow.

* * * *

"Are you okay, sir?"

The hotel maître d' paused on his run past Julian, who sat on a barstool hidden behind a tall plant.

Julian forced a smile. "Yes. I just wanted a quiet spot to have breakfast."

The short, dark-haired man nodded. "Certainly."

Julian stayed away from the rooftop with his food, worried about running into Mamie. Right from wrong tugged. Anticipating her judgment over what happened on his show had sat like a dead weight in his gut while he'd tried to sleep last night. The reason he woke determined to save himself the pain. Now, though, he felt sick in a whole other way.

Voices in the lobby made him glance out between the ficus tree branches.

Mamie walked by with Bernie and Sandra. Probably on their way to the trials. Mamie looked less upset than when he'd left, but certainly not herself.

He downed the rest of his coffee, took one more bite of the roll. The logic to end things suddenly seemed thin. Without further thought, he got up from the stool and followed them out the door.

He stayed behind the three of them, lurking far enough back while trying to think about what he should do. Ending things with her hadn't fixed his problem. In fact, since their talk, an avalanche of doubt bombarded him. He needed to face one undeniable fact: the moment Mamie stepped onto that bus, he'd felt alive for the first time all year. It's why he hadn't been able to share what had happened to him on that jump. It would be like dragging out a dark cloud on a sunny day and ruin the one good thing he had going for him…. Her.

By ending things, he'd hopped right back to square one. Ending things was dumb. An impulse decision. So, how the hell could he fix this?

Following them on the cobblestone street toward the center of town, he remained back trying to come up with a solution. As they neared the square, loud booms from cannons mixed with excited voices from the crowds.

He moved closer, worried they'd get separated in the midst of Palio fever. These crowds were rowdy, one of the reasons he'd invited her to go with him in the first place. Ever since he first laid eyes on her, he wanted to be there for her...even if it was obvious she didn't really need him.

They stopped at the back, behind a pack of people not far from the starting gates. The bleachers were about half full, the center of town the same. By this afternoon, every inch of space would be filled with people. Mamie kept rising on tiptoes, scanning the area. She said something to her friends, then started to weave through the crowd, moving closer and closer to the main event.

He almost laughed. Leave it to her to thrust herself right into the action. Throwing herself into everything seemed all she wanted on this trip, and he'd diverted her efforts every step of the way. All in the name of keeping her presence low key from his boss, but now he wished he'd given her more leeway.

The horses entered the arena, causing the crowd to roar, elevating energy in the town square. Several of the large animals whinnied and fussed, making it difficult for their riders to keep them in line. In past Palio trial runs, Julian had seen jittery horses ruled out for the real race.

Unable to see Mamie, he hoisted himself up on the edge of nearby bleachers to look. Finally, he spotted her right against the barrier gate, maybe fifty or one hundred yards from the starting gate.

In the stands, across from the gate, a lively group representing a local contrada broke out in song. They finished and people clapped. An announcer said the trial was about to start. Seconds later, a loud boom exploded in the square.

They burst from the gate. Before Julian could blink, two nervous horses stuck in the pack's middle slammed into each other. Loud cries from the animals carried above the crowd noise, sending a chill up Julian's spine. A dark brown horse nearby reared on its hind legs, tossing the rider into the air and sending him crashing to the ground. Behind them, a white horse reared and as his front legs returned to the pavement, Julian cringed. The fallen rider had landed in the same area. The horse dropped, crumbling to the ground.

The crowd gasped. A woman screamed.

Julian searched the crowd for Mamie, finding her staring at the scene on the ground, her mouth opened wide and terror in her eyes. He headed in her direction.

* * * *

Blood. Rich, red blood spilled from the jockey's temple and dripped down his face.

Mamie numbed. Her head got light, her knees soft. The car accident. Images she couldn't erase, always rising at the sight of blood. The rider and horse blurred as her temples began to throb. She couldn't move, her body shocked by the impact of being hit by another car. The bang of impact echoed in her ears. Ted. Zoe. Pain shot through every muscle, but she forced her head to turn as her gaze landed on Ted in the driver's seat, his eyes closed and shards of glass all over his bloody body. Numb, her head pounding, she tried to turn to her daughter but her body didn't work right. "It's okay, baby." Silence. *Zoe. My Zoe.* Pushing past her pain, Mamie turned around. Zoe's limp body, pinned in the car seat. Mamie slowly stretched her arms, ignoring the ache. The short distance seemed like a mile, but with effort she reached the strap and fumbled until she undid the belt. Her hands circled Zoe's torso and wet warmth coated her skin. Mamie withdrew them, her head spinning as she stared down at her blood dripping off her fingers...

The thundering sound of a loud neigh jarred her back to the commotion, to the jockey and the blood trickling down his neck and onto his shirt. Her heart throbbed. Head spun. Faster and faster. She turned to escape, but the crowd formed a human blockade. Using all her strength, she pushed people away. Panic stole each breath. A nightmare. A bad dream. It would end soon and her family would be alive. Safe.

"Let me through," she screamed.

The crowd pushed against her like a strong current. She fought, a salmon going upstream, her instinct to run the only way to free herself from the images still exploding in her mind.

Somehow she reached the crowd's edge and gasped for air as she ran into an open space. When she spotted a quiet alley not far away, she ran toward it. A place to hide. *Run. Run!*

Halfway down the alley, she slowed and caught her breath. What was happening to her? Running. Hiding. Five years later, the memories still haunted her. Five years later, she still tried to hide from them.

She sat on stone steps leading up to a weathered wooden door. Several deep breaths slowly stopped her tears.

The uproar in the square carried into the alley, the crowds still buzzing over what she'd witnessed. Another front row seat to a horrible accident. Even now, on the sidelines, the ache inside her body throbbed. The same ache consuming her while she'd watched from the ambulance as the paramedics removed her family from the car, while onlookers who'd stopped witnessed the moment changing her world.

She rubbed her sore temples, trying to forget about the terror seizing her a moment ago. Instead, her stomach turned and bile choked her throat. Tears streamed down her cheeks. She wrapped her arms around her body, closing her eyes and wishing she were back in her room.

Footsteps echoed in the alley. Bernie and Sandra. They hadn't wanted her to move up front. She glanced up. Julian headed her way.

"My God, Mamie. Were you hurt?" He squatted down in front of her, watching her through worried eyes.

"No. No." She wished he'd leave, hating that he'd found her like this. "I'm not hurt."

He studied her, his own face contorted with the agony she felt inside. "Something is wrong. Was it because of what I did this—"

"No!" she said sharply and buried her face in her palms. "It has nothing to do with you." But, in a way, it did. His visit this morning shattered a little piece of her that had finally started to feel good, leaving her to face that accident with her heart's wound exposed.

Her throat grew thick as anger toward him festered. For ending their fling so quickly. For everything else she'd lost. For indulging in joy around Julian, the mere act of doing so reminding her of happiness and love she used to shower on Zoe and Ted. A fact she couldn't hold against Julian for reviving, yet she could steer clear of him to save herself further grief again.

She wanted to find a place to hide, but Julian's breathing clued her to his closeness.

"Just leave me alone." She brushed wetness from her cheek. "Leave me...please..." The energy behind her anger dissolved, leaving only her sadness.

He sat next to her.

"Please. Go away."

Instead he put an arm around her, held her head to his chest, and stroked her hair.

She wanted to claw her way out of his hold, scream that she could take care of herself. Only the gentle way his touch soothed her made her stay put. Support, not being alone, was something she missed.

His warm breath fell near her ear. "Mamie, please talk to me."

A quiet desperation resonated in his voice, and her anger softened. "The rider, he was bleeding. It brought back some memories."

He didn't say anything at first, then he asked, "From the accident?"

"Yes."

She hadn't told Julian about Zoe. Nor had she told him any details about that day. The only person she ever discussed the accident details with was the officer who interviewed her for the accident report. Every word split the wound in her chest open wider, so painful she never wanted to discuss it again.

Julian's presence reassured her, though. Even with this morning's reservations about a romance, that he'd helped her turn a corner in healing couldn't be denied.

She lifted her head. "We were on our way to go shopping..."

Though difficult to speak at first, slowly she got out most of the story. When she reached the part about finding Zoe, the words lodged in her throat and came out as tears.

Mamie reached for her purse, still hanging from her shoulder. After taking out her wallet, she flipped it open to a photograph of her with Ted and Zoe during a trip to the Rhode Island beaches. The day was clear as yesterday, and yet a moment she could never get back.

Julian blurred behind her watery eyes as she passed him her wallet. Her voice cracked as she said, "I lost Zoe, too."

Julian took the wallet and studied the photo, his eyes glistening.

"Mothers should protect their offspring," she whispered, each word twisting the dagger already plunged in her heart. "I didn't. It's goes against the natural order of things, me here but she isn't."

"My God," he said quietly. "I'm so sorry."

She shut her eyes and embraced images of her precious girl, who sometimes seemed so close Mamie could still feel her tiny hand in hers or smell crisp apple juice on her breath. The girl she'd never see mature into a teenager or a grown woman, never know her dreams and desires. The ache inside her chest swelled until it exploded into an avalanche of pain, but this time instead of running, she stayed at Julian's side.

They sat together like that for some time, neither saying a word. Every so often someone would walk past them, but she didn't look up.

Julian leaned back, but kept her in his hold. "Is this why your uncle sent you on this trip?"

She opened her eyes and looked at him. "Sort of."

Work. She wanted to be honest. Only her head hurt and she just couldn't decide how angry the powers at the publishing house would be if she was. But she could share more about herself.

"Recently, at the fifth anniversary of losing them, I started to think about how I was wasting my life. So the trip came at the right time."

He nodded. "I see. Listen, sorry about this morning. I panicked."

"It's fine, Julian. I'm sure you had your reasons."

"No. It's not fine. I made a mistake and want us to enjoy the rest of our time together. But I think you should know something about me. It's the reason I did what I did this morning."

A shift, and his expression carried the same distraught weight as in the photograph on the Internet, the one taken immediately following the accidental death.

Mamie took his hand. "What is it?"

"I'm not the man you think I am."

She squeezed his hand gently. "I can't imagine that's true."

He frowned and drew in a deep breath. "I used to be host of a show on a cable network. A travel show."

"You mean the one Frank Bruno mentioned at breakfast one morning?"

He raised his brows. "Yes. You remembered. Do you know the show?"

Telling him she'd looked it up might only change the topic, and making this confession appeared to be a big thing for him. "I've heard of it."

He nodded. "Our last show, we were filming in Colorado with a couple of guys who were considered amongst the best wing suit jumpers in the world..."

Julian looked at the ground while continuing his story, often filling in the blanks from what she'd already read, including his efforts to stop the jump and the pushback from his superiors to make it happen. Several times he stopped talking and swallowed. Finally, he looked up, his eyes filled with tears. "So now you know. The real me is someone who coaxed a man to his death. I'll understand if you want to back off from being…I don't know, whatever we were starting to become."

"Why would I do that? It was an accident."

His voice dropped, a breath of a whisper. "Not really. Carlos died because of me. I should've stood up to my boss."

She placed a hand on his shoulder. "You can't blame yourself."

"Why not?" Julian closed his eyes and dropped his head. "I'd rather it had been me that died that day."

The words underscored his pain. "I understand, probably better than most. I'll tell you something I've never shared before. I've thought that, too. After the car accident, I'd have given anything to give my family back their lives. Even my own life."

He lifted his head. "Really?"

She blinked away fresh tears and nodded. Listening to Julian offered Mamie a clearer view into everything she'd been doing wrong. "Sounds like we both carry around the baggage, but I just realized how we have no real control over the hand dealt to us."

"Yet that doesn't change what makes us hurt."

"No, but it gives it some perspective."

He considered her words then shook his head. "I'm a fool. So caught up in my own problems, I'm not even thinking about anybody else." He reached out and swept her lips with his thumb. "I'm glad we talked. Will you forgive me for what I did this morning?"

"Of course."

He leaned in and tenderly kissed her, so sweet it cushioned the blow of what had just happened.

"Well, would you look at that?"

They pulled away and turned to the sound of a familiar man's voice.

Tina and Joel watched them from the middle of the alley, their brows raised and grins plastered on their faces.

Tina elbowed Joel. "I told you they like each other."

"Yes," he chuckled, "you did, dear. Mamie, are you okay?" Joel tilted his head.

"I am."

She still worried about Julian's job and let her hand go limp so he could let go.

But he held it tight and brought it to his lips, leaving a little peck on the top. "There was a horse accident and she was close to it. It's more upsetting than people think."

They nodded.

"I've got a favor to ask of you both," Julian said. "Can you two keep what you just saw a secret?"

"Of course," they said in unison.

As they walked away, Mamie looked at Julian. "Are you worried about what they saw?"

He drew her close. "I've spent a lot of time worrying this trip. It's time I stopped and let it run whatever course it intends to take."

Chapter 15

Mamie leaned against the window as the tour bus turned onto a wide dirt road somewhere in Tuscany, close to the Umbrian boarder. Fields stretched to the horizon, the tracts of land dotted with cypress trees standing tall as soldiers, guarding the endless fields of emerald and gold.

A mile down the road, they passed a field filled with trees. Mamie recognized the familiar olive branches on them. She reached up and touched one of the dangling earrings Julian had surprised her with an hour ago, delicate gold earrings in the shape of olive branches. His gift to apologize for what he'd done to her this morning, given to her privately in her room before leaving the hotel.

They'd joked about the symbolism. The sincerity in his eyes while he stood behind her at the mirror and watched her put them on sent a much stronger message.

Julian's gift restored any lost faith in their slowly building relationship.

She turned away from the view and looked up front, to where Julian sat lost in his own thoughts. An intense expression. Was he thinking about her? Their losses? Their kiss? Or was he thinking about how they'd both made confessions this morning that weren't easy to share?

"Hey!" Joel's voice rose from the bus's back. "Our first field of sunflowers!"

Julian turned around, his face full of interest, like he always did when he slipped on his tour director mask. "Thanks, Joel. Beppe, let's stop for pictures."

The bus pulled over and everyone got out their cameras, leaning to one side to get the perfect picture. Mamie snapped one, but much as she loved this beautiful setting, she felt strangely sad leaving Siena. The city had begun to feel like home. Even with what had happened at the race earlier today, she still loved the city, its people, the food, and the atmosphere.

But the melancholy inside her went deeper. The drive to the villa started their second and last leg of their trip. Endings weren't her thing.

Her gaze drifted again to Julian, who now leaned forward in his seat, talking quietly to Beppe while they waited. She could still feel the strength of his arms, supporting her after the accident with the horses and his lips on hers. Tender, soothing, and just so right.

He turned away from Beppe and stood with a ready smile for the passengers. "Okay, a little bit about sunflowers. They're a symbol of Tuscany, but were brought here by European explorers who visited the Americas. They became a crop over time when someone patented a way to squeeze oil from the seeds."

"Very rich in vitamin A and E, too," Joel said, then turned back out the window with his camera aimed at the field.

"Thank you, Joel. Sunflowers are called *Girasole* in Italian. It means 'sunturner.' It's a characteristic called heliotropism where over the course of a day, they follow the sun from east to west."

The passengers were busy snapping pictures and barely listened. He glanced at Mamie and winked.

"We go now?" Beppe interrupted the moment.

Julian startled and nodded. "Sure. Everyone, take your seats. We're almost there."

The bus took off and a mile or two down the round, they rounded the corner, turning onto a cypress-lined road.

Julian faced the passengers. "Straight ahead is our home for the rest of your stay." He pointed. "Up on the hill."

The entire bus full of people let out a gasp.

Verdant hills served as a backdrop to an enormous stone villa, elevated by its placement on a low hillside. Cypress trees dotted the grounds surrounding the majestic house, a place that appeared large enough to house a small village.

"Very funny," Bob yelled from his seat in the back row.

"Not a joke this time, Bob."

Mamie's pulsed raced at the thought of staying in such a place. Siena had tons of Tuscan charm, but this villa offered a total different element to her journey.

"This hamlet was originally built in the fifteenth century, but renovated ten years ago by the current owners." Julian's gaze scanned the passengers and a gentle smile crossed his face. "È bellissimo, vero?"

"Dude." Bob raised his voice. "It's really *bellissimo*." He sounded truly awed for the first time on the trip.

"We'll be there in a minute. When you get off the bus, I'll give you your villa assignments while Beppe unloads the luggage."

A few minutes later, the bus pulled up in front of a paved courtyard. The compound had several buildings, all with stone walls covered in creeping vines. Down a few steps from the courtyard, a flat area housed an in-ground swimming pool and further away, a tennis court.

"We have five different housing units here. Couples will be together. Singles, you'll have your own room. The apartments have several bathrooms and kitchen facilities to share if you prefer to eat on your own. If not, a cocktail hour begins at six each night, then our meal about an hour and a half later in a building designated for common use near the swimming pool. Chef Andre might ask you to help by setting the table, little things. Oh, there's tennis and swimming, some bikes to use for rides around town, and free Wi-Fi."

They exited the bus and Julian started calling villa assignments. Mamie stepped away from the group, enjoying the warm breeze, stunned by the gorgeous views of both hills and valley.

"Okay. I've got a three-bedroom bungalow. Room one goes to Joel and Tina, room two goes to Bob and Carol, and"—Julian glanced up—"third room goes to Mamie."

She waited to walk over until the others had taken their keys. She approached him, their gazes meeting as he reached into a bag and pulled out a key. Lowering her voice, she said, "Do you do private tours of this place?"

"I've been planning on it, for some of my special passengers." His suggestive little smile made her toes curl. He quickly returned to the key disbursement.

She followed the two couples to a relatively small stone cottage with clay-tiled roof, not far from two bigger houses. Stepping inside, she instantly fell in love. Terra-cotta floors held richly colored patterned rugs. Overhead, aged wood ceilings beams contrasted with contemporary, comfortable furniture surrounding a fireplace, yet together, they worked. Behind her, a kitchen opened into the main area, separated by a trestle table big enough to seat eight.

Tina set down her Gucci luggage. "I have a bottle of wine from our vineyard visit. Everyone want a glass?"

"Sure." Mamie's key tag was marked bedroom three. "I'm going to unpack first."

"Good idea," said Tina. "Then we'll all meet."

"Perfecto." Bob winked at his wife. "See, honey? My Italian is getting better."

Carol just laughed, always her husband's biggest fan.

Mamie found her bedroom in the back of the house and opened the door. The tile floor and rustic-beamed ceiling carried into this room. A large bed covered by a white and creamy yellow bedspread was set against the far wall. She tossed her suitcase on the bed and began to unpack her clothing into an antique armoire stationed near sliding doors covered by light, white drapes. When she finished, she went to the sliding doors and parted the curtains.

The sun rushed inside. Mamie opened a glass door and stepped out to a small balcony with a wrought iron railing. From here, she had a clear view to the empty fields edging gently sloped hills. Footsteps below on the stone walkway made her look down. Julian walked along, carrying a piece of luggage.

"Hey, where you going?"

He stopped and used his hand as a visor to block the sun. "Hello. We're neighbors."

"Oh?"

He pointed downhill to a small bungalow. "That's where I'm staying."

"Coincidence or careful planning?"

"You have to ask?" He moved closer, into the shade beneath her balcony. Dropping his voice, he added, "I like to keep an extra close eye on my adventure-seeking passengers."

"Is that so?" His suggestive tone and hooded eyes made her wish they were here alone, not under such watchful eyes. Mamie leaned on the balcony railing. "How much trouble can I get into around here?"

"Guess that's something I'll find out." He smiled slyly and turned, walking toward the cottage down a small hill, away from the complex's other buildings.

She watched him all the way, hoping he might turn around.

When he reached his door, he did. "See you at dinner," he yelled.

She waved and ducked back inside the room. Dinner. For the next week, her life would be living in this rustic, charming setting with a man who'd revived her in both body and spirit.

Maybe the adventure she craved wasn't about the thrill of hang gliding or wandering inside caves. It could simply be found giving herself to a man who, by the hands of fate, had entered her life.

Opening up to him offered a gentler danger. Sure, things could go wrong, like this morning. But if she didn't do it now, she might never take the final steps needed to restore her life to normal.

* * * *

From Julian's seat at the long patio dinner table, surrounded by the uplifting conversation of his passengers, he leaned back and feasted on the view. Dusk had arrived, changing the orange-streaked sky to a palate of dark blues, leaving only shadows of the surrounding hillside.

When Claudia assigned him this tour, and he saw the villa as the second stop, he was glad. He loved this place, especially at this moment. White candles arranged in a row in the teak table's center brightened the satisfied faces of his passengers. Or maybe it was the meal's second course served by Chef Rao, a simple dish of fusilli with a raw tomato sauce served with generous glasses filled with Chianti.

He tuned into the group's laughter.

"Okay, I've got one more joke. You're gonna love this one..." Bob glanced around the table, looking pretty pleased with his attentive audience. "Sophie just got married and, being a traditional Italian, was still a virgin. On her wedding night, staying at her mother's house, she was nervous. But mother reassured her. 'Don't worry, Sophie. Luca's a good man. Go upstairs, and he'll take care of you.' So up she went. When she got upstairs, Luca took off his shirt and exposed his hairy chest. Sophie ran downstairs to her mother and said, 'Mama, Mama, Luca's got a big hairy chest.' 'Don't worry, Sophie,' said the mother, 'All good men have hairy chests. Go upstairs. He'll take good care of you.'"

Julian looked around the table, smiling to himself at the anticipation on everyone's face.

"So, up she went again," Bob continued. "When she got up in the bedroom, Luca took off his pants exposing his hairy legs. Again Sophie ran downstairs to her mother. 'Mama, Mama, Luca took off his pants, and he's got hairy legs!' 'Don't worry. All good men have hairy legs. Luca's a good man. Go upstairs, and he'll take good care of you.' So, up she went again. When she got up there, Luca took off his socks, and on his left foot he was missing three toes. When Sophie saw this, she ran downstairs. 'Mama, Mama, Luca's got a foot and a half!' 'Stay here and stir the pasta,' says the mother. 'This is a job for Mama!'"

Everyone laughed, but Bob's wide grin said it all. Julian couldn't remember a group he'd enjoyed more than the Wanderers. They'd convinced him to let Mamie on the tour, too.

His gaze drifted to her as she reached for her wine glass, her face still bright and glowing, her full smile a delight. Warmth for her flooded his heart. Yes, happy Mamie brought him joy. This was what he wanted for her. Every single time he thought about the agony of her expression when telling him about her daughter, a pain shot straight to the center of his heart.

She'd handed him something precious by unveiling herself to him. More than any other woman had ever given him. All because worrying about her happiness, thinking about her even when she wasn't around, gave his brain something to do besides dwelling on his problems. And when he'd handed her the truth about his job and why he lost it, she didn't judge him.

He watched her laughing. Since her arrival, she'd bloomed. Like the sunflowers of Tuscany followed the sun, Mamie responded to the magic of the region. He tried not to stare, but couldn't drag his gaze away from the way her eyes shined like topaz in the flickering candlelight. For once, he felt inner peace.

Could his honesty with her have been the key?

Julian's own losses had taunted him for most of his life. Starting with his parents, and over time, lost girlfriends—even though he'd ended things before he grew too attached. And now Carlos. But today, he'd opened the drawer on pain stuffed away long ago. A beautiful stranger who fell into his orbit proved loss didn't have to leave one disabled.

Chef Rao stepped outside onto the patio carrying a tray, his assistant behind him with one, too. "Lamb spiked with rosemary and garlic along with zucchini with potatoes and thyme."

Julian eased his self-reflection as the cooks placed platters at each end of the table.

The portly chef smiled. *"Buon appetito."*

Food passed from person to person. Lively talk filled the air. Wine flowed like a fountain of happiness. The familial sounds of this gathering reminded Julian of growing up in Italy when they weren't taping the show. For four months every year, they'd have a normal life. Tutors home schooled him and his sister while his parents researched future shows. A regular nine to five endeavor. For two additional months, they'd return to the States and visit his dad's family. Then the cycle of taping would repeat.

What would his life have been if they had normal jobs? Lived in Michigan where his parents were married and Julian born. What if they hadn't died? Questions with no answers that only made his heart ache.

"Hey, Julian." Joel leaned across the table. "Want to show me where the wine cellar is and help me grab a few more bottles?"

Julian snapped out of his stupor. "Sure."

Standing, he glanced to Mamie's seat, now empty. He followed Joel through the sliding glass doors and toward the kitchen.

Joel turned to him. "Do you ever get tired of your job?"

"No. Not yet, anyway." For a second, he considered sharing about his childhood on the road, but to discuss it might lead to more and more about himself. Pieces he feared revealing, because he never easily opened up about himself.

On their way through the large living room, the downstairs bathroom door opened. Mamie exited and smiled at them.

"I was just telling our chef this might be the best meal I've had in my life."

Chef Rao's voice carried from the kitchen, "And I told her, wait until tomorrow's surprise."

"The anticipation is killing me." She laughed, the sound light and carefree. "God, I love everything about this place."

Julian wanted to pull her close, feel those soft lips against his. Instead he smiled and motioned for Joel to follow him through a doorway leading to the cellar.

At the bottom, Joel approached a wall made of stone with built-in wine racks. He took out a bottle, read the label, then put it back. Removing another, he said, "So? What's going on with you two?"

"Who? Me and Mamie?"

Joel chuckled. "No. You and Chef Rao." He removed another bottle. "Yes, you and Mamie."

"Nothing. Look, when you saw us at the horse race...she was upset about the accident during the trials. The jockey was bloody, and—well, I hated to see her upset."

Joel read a third label and placed the bottle of Chianti on a small mahogany table before moving to the next section of bottles marked Pinot Grigio. "So those were kisses of comfort?"

"Yeah, that's all."

Joel removed two bottles of white wine and turned to Julian. "You sure about that?"

"Positive. It's against my boss's rules for me to get involved with any passengers."

Joel lifted the bottle of red and tucked it in the crook of his arm. "I won't tell." He started toward the stairs, but stopped and his expression grew more serious. "Take it from a man who hasn't always lived life to its fullest...carpe diem, buddy. Best decision I ever made was to admit to myself how I felt about Tina."

"And I'm glad for you. But I've got my job to worry about."

Joel continued to the stairs. "Wanna grab two more bottles of Chianti?" He took the first step and stopped. "Like I said, seize the day, Julian. The things that matter in life don't always make themselves so obvious."

He walked up the stairs, but the weight of his words hung in the cool basement air. Yes, Mamie did something to him. So why the hell did he tiptoe around it and use work as an excuse?

He reached for the same bottle he'd seen Joel take upstairs, grabbing two. Footsteps on the concrete stairs made him turn around. Mamie appeared at the landing and approached him.

"Joel sent me down here for some sparkling water. Do you know where I can find it?"

Seize the day...

"Over there." He motioned behind her and placed the bottles on a nearby shelf.

Seize the damn day!

Julian took one long step toward Mamie, slipped his hand around her back, and then drew her close. She inhaled a sharp breath, but he waited no longer and lowered his lips to hers. They were soft and warm. Carefully, he moved her against the cellar stone wall, closed her in with his arms on either side of her shoulders.

She parted her lips, her chest heaving with each breath.

Julian cupped the curve of her cheek, swept her beautiful full lower lip with his thumb.

"All night..." he whispered. "All night I've wanted to kiss you."

She searched his face then stretched on tiptoes until their lips met with a hard kiss, jolting him with a message strong as espresso and casting aside any doubt. He touched the soft dip in her waist, the curve of her hip. Slipping his hands to her back, he drew her body near as she softly moaned, making his desire for her soar. Not only for the same physical needs that pushed him to one-night stands, or with the passion found in his never-ending risky adventures.

No. This thing with Mamie came from a different place deep inside the gaps of his heart, left unfulfilled for too long. This desire offered another kind of risk. A sweeter kind that, if achieved, yielded greater life rewards.

Chapter 16

Mamie sank into the warm tub water, her head fuzzy from the wine and her heart glowing like the glimmering candle's flame now dancing on the golden bathroom walls. What an unbelievable day. She tipped back her head and stared at the rustic ceiling beams overhead, a contrast to the modern plumbing. This villa was perfection.

She lifted her hand from the water and touched her lips with damp fingers, still imagining Julian's generous kisses during the night. Their cellar kiss had kicked off a flurry of passion for the meal's duration, Chef Rao's creations taking a back seat to the sweetness of Julian's lips. Subtle glances they shared at the table held enormous power. By night's end, when Julian found her alone in the kitchen rinsing out a glass, he'd leaned her against the sink, placed his hands on her hips, and whispered, "You're so beautiful." The space between her thighs had burned for more of him. Much more.

No man had ever spoken those words to her. Ted often called her pretty or adorable, always said in a way that showed his love for her. But now another man had claimed a stake in her heart. Guilt edged toward her, a challenge of loyalty she hadn't prepared for.

If common sense were to dictate, she shouldn't have any guilt. Ted wasn't the first or only man she'd slept with. He was, however, the only man she loved so deeply she wanted to share a lifetime together.

Intimacy with Ted had carried an intense spark since their first kiss in the back of a movie theater, a blind date that made her believe in love at first sight. In the months after losing him, she'd lie in their bed wishing to wake just one more time with his body curled close to hers, his hands caressing, slowly rousing her to wake. Like he had the last time they'd made love. A lazy Saturday morning, where Zoe had slept in for once. Ted had unexpectedly nuzzled alongside Mamie and she rolled over into his arms. She reached out and ran a hand through his messy hair.

Desire had burned in his sleepy blue eyes. "Morning, doll. I think we've just been given the gift of time."

The gift of time. Handed to them so casually and jerked away later that afternoon thanks to a drunk driver.

Goosebumps zipped along Mamie's arms. She glanced up and spotted the thin white curtain near the bathroom window flapping from the open window. She stood, grabbed a towel off the rack, and quickly shut the window, although the chill remained. Mamie dried off, but Ted's words haunted her.

The gift of time.

A rarely acknowledged handout. With this trip, it had been handed to her again. It started with the spellbinding Tuscan countryside, like CPR for her soul. Then another present arrived, slowly revealed in the connection to a man who made her less lonely. Made her forget her problems.

She'd hoped Julian would invite her back to his place after dinner ended. She'd have gone. But he didn't, and she wasn't the type to push. Having him say no might steal all her recently found bravado.

She hung the towel, tossed on a thick terrycloth robe, and removed the band holding her loose bun, shaking her head to relax her hair. Leaving the bathroom, she went to the balcony doors and stepped outside. The cool air raised goose bumps on her skin. She ignored the chill and watched Julian's villa. A light burned in a back room. Was that his bedroom? She imagined herself walking over, knocking on the door. Opening her robe...

She sighed and tilted her head back to a canopy of glittering stars leading up to the heavens, if they did exist. *Please, Ted. You know how hard this is for me. A sign. Any sign that I'm supposed to move on.*

She shut her eyes, wishing as hard as she could something, anything, would happen. When she opened them, her gaze drifted back to Julian's place. A broad-shouldered silhouette stood in the back window and waved. Julian. They stared at each other for a few seconds. He opened the window and his face brightened from the light of a nearly full moon.

He motioned with his hand for her to come over.

Beneath her robe, she wore nothing. All her bathtub fantasies got very real. As far as signs went, this qualified.

She nodded, came inside, and hurried down the dark steps, quietly to make sure she didn't wake her housemates. Swiping her key off the table near the front door, she slipped outside into the moonlit walkway.

On her way, she glanced to Julian's window but he wasn't there. She hurried along the stone pavement, smooth against the pads of her bare feet. Cool air drifted to the naked skin beneath her robe, heightening this deliciously forbidden venture.

She reached the door, her heart pounding fast as she lifted a fist to knock. The door swung open.

Julian stood on the other side, still in the jeans he'd worn at dinner, his button-down shirt now open with nothing underneath. Taking her by the arm, he guided her inside the room, closed the door, and pressed her against it. Anticipation of his touch made her heart pulse fast. The glow of a full moon brought in a pale stream of light, enough for her to see the need burning in his eyes.

He dipped his head, brushing her lips with a quick sweep while he dropped his hands to her waist and silently undid her belt. His gaze didn't leave her face.

She rested her palms on his bare chest, the firm muscles rising with each breath he took. Slowly, he slipped his hand beneath her robe, resting his palm on her shoulder. Moving aside the robe's shoulder, he leaned over and placed a gentle kiss. His lips traveled to her mouth where he kissed the corner, to her throat where he left a warm trail, to the soft spot right above her breast where the bristles from his facial hair teased her skin and sent heat spreading through her core. She gasped and clung to him, her knees going soft.

He drew back. "Are you sure about this?"

She moved her hands along his shoulders, pushing his shirt until it dropped to the floor. "That answer your question?"

Julian placed his hand beneath her robe and pushed it off. He took her in from head to toe with a bold gleam in his eyes, the way a conqueror might admire his prize. And she let him look. Tonight she was bold, no longer owned by vulnerability.

He stepped closer, cupped her cheeks in his hand, and covered her mouth with his. Demanding. Possessive. She responded in kind so he'd know she felt it too. When the kiss ended, he led her by the hand through the dark room to the bedroom door.

At the threshold, he gathered her close and kissed her again. He drew back and studied her with a hint of humor on his face. "Okay, gorgeous. Now the real adventure begins."

* * * *

In the dim dawn light, Julian watched Mamie sleep, each breath even and slow. A strand of her shiny chocolate hair stretched across the pale mound of her breast. He reached out to brush it away, but stopped and retreated to avoid disrupting the peaceful expression on her face.

He glanced at the time. She'd need to return to her villa before anybody realized she was missing, but he wasn't ready to give her up. He studied her perfect lips, swollen from their intimacy, to her long ivory neck, to one exposed, hardened nipple. He shifted, desire for her so easily stoked. A change in her breathing made him look up to her face.

Mamie smiled through sleepy eyes. "Have you been watching me for long?"

He kissed her and slipped his hand beneath the sheet. "A bit." Running a hand along her slender thigh, he inched closer. "What do you think, Cinderella? Do we have time for one more round before the clock strikes and everyone wakes up?"

Her arms looped his neck. "Cinderella? She didn't sneak out for a booty call."

"Is that all I am to you? A booty call?"

She laughed and arched a brow. "It's possible."

"What?" Her sleepy eyes still sparkled with the residue of her laughter and he raised himself over her. "If it's a booty call you want, that's what you'll get."

Julian kissed her with all the tenderness swelling inside his chest.

She moaned softly into his mouth. "Jeesh, Prince Charming, is that a sword in your pocket or are you just happy to see me?"

He laughed and wrapped her in his arms. Rolling onto his back, he brought her along with him so she straddled his hips. "I don't remember Cinderella being this sarcastic."

She slowly moved her body against him, the motion driving him wild. "In the new millennium, she is."

Dipping her head, she kissed him, sweeping him into the undercurrent of her passion. Every passing minute, he needed her more and more. As he wandered in the tenderness of this moment, he cast aside his usual caution and allowed his heart to soar.

When they finished making love, she lay quietly in his arms, her head on his chest. Julian tried to clear his head, wishing he didn't feel the need to figure out why *this* woman was so different. Every touch, every conversation, every single kiss filled a vacant space inside his heart.

The rising sun brightened the room. He looked at the nightstand clock. "It's almost six-forty."

She lifted her head off his chest and propped herself up on an elbow. "Guess I need to leave soon. I've got a question. How bad is it that you're doing this with me while on the job?"

"Goes against company policy. Something you have a habit of making me do."

"Me? Hey, you have free will." She grinned while tracing a path along his chest with her fingertips. Her smile drifted away, replaced by a serious expression.

"What's wrong?"

"Do you think your boss might actually fire you?"

"Based on the stories I hear, I do. We need to be careful around the others. If Claudia catches wind of it—" His cell phone vibrated on the nightstand. He leaned back to read the display and saw his producer's name. "Jesus Christ." He pushed the button to go into voice mail and returned to facing Mamie, who was smiling at him. "What?"

"Everything okay?"

Hell, he'd told her the worst of his story—getting fired and why. Might as well dump the latest problem. "The call was from my old boss. From the show."

"Is that who called you the day we were in Florence. At the statue?"

He nodded. "You remember that?"

"Well, the call seemed to bother you. Why would he call so early this morning? Is he in another time zone?"

"I don't know where Gary is right now." Julian knew he could be anywhere. "He's been bugging me to come back to my old job."

"I imagine that would be hard after what happened."

"Yes."

"I have a confession to make." She frowned. "I read about you on the internet. And I also found an article about your parents, their show..." She quieted. "And how they passed away."

His chest tightened. "So you know all about me, huh? My sad little story."

"All things considered, you are a remarkable man." Mamie reached for his hand. "That was a lot for a kid to go through."

He shrugged it off, like it was no big deal. But it really was.

She looked him in the eyes. "I was just feeling so desperate to know about you. It started with the show, but somehow I ended up on things more personal. I hope you'll forgive me."

"Of course I do." He drew her into a hug, unsure if it was meant to help her or himself. It didn't even matter. The truth was being with Mamie felt exactly like where he was supposed to be at this moment of his life.

Chapter 17

Julian entered the common room, not surprised to hear opera music playing. Gigi loved the opera and, as the person in charge of setting out breakfast for guests during their stay at the villa, her personality added to the atmosphere. The tour had been lucky to find the local grandmother of ten who lived in town and was happy to make extra money.

He posted the day's activity offerings on a corkboard near the entrance and went to get breakfast.

"Okay, here's another one." Bob turned from the buffet spread and nearly bumped into Julian. "Oh good. Just in time, Julian."

Bob approached the long wooden table where ten or so other guests already sat eating. In a loud voice, he asked, "How do you know the concert you're attending is *not* Woodstock?"

In unison, the diners yelled out, "How, Bob?"

Bob, dressed in a black T-shirt that read "Peace on Earth," grinned and puffed out his chest. "Because Santana turns out to be a jolly bearded guy with a sackful of presents."

A few people laughed, but Carol sat shaking her head. "Honey, you told some people that yesterday."

The group quieted with the rare rebuke from Bob's wife, who always seemed to go with *his* flow.

"Did I?" Bob shrugged and pulled the lid off the yogurt, grinning the whole time. "Mamie, you weren't there, were you?"

"Nope. It was cute." She smiled at Bob and cracked her hard-boiled egg on her plate. "I hadn't heard it before."

Julian grabbed some yogurt and headed toward the table where Mamie sat near Tina and Sandra.

"Good morning," Julian put his yogurt in front of a seat then went to a nearby table holding coffee and condiments. Glancing back over his shoulder as he grabbed a ceramic mug, he asked, "Everyone happy with their quarters?"

"Ours were great," Tina said. She elbowed Joel, nose buried in a book. "Right, sweetheart?"

He glanced up. "Hey, Julian." He slowly turned to his side. "What, Tina?"

"Nothing."

"So were ours." Bernie glanced over the top of reading glasses while he spread butter on a chunk of Italian bread with surgical precision. "Gorgeous view out into the courtyard. Damn it, I forgot jelly."

He stood and approached the table where Julian filled his mug with coffee. Bernie stopped close to Julian and picked through a basket filled with jelly packets. "Yup, beautiful courtyard views."

"Good. Glad you liked them."

Bernie gave Julian a slight tap with his elbow. Julian glanced sideways.

Bernie's full white brows lifted. "I hope Mamie liked hers." He waggled his brows, either a hint he'd seen something last night or he was doing a bad Groucho Marx impersonation.

Julian shrugged. "You'd have to ask her."

Bernie grinned, waving his brows again in a manner as subtle as a symphony gong. He lowered his voice. "Nah, I don't want to embarrass her."

Luciano Pavarotti's voice rose as he sang a popular number from Rigoletto, the same moment Bernie added, "I was up early taking a walk. I saw her leaving another villa this morning." Bernie winked as he lifted a strawberry preserve packet. "Ah, here's what I want."

Julian's stomach flipped, but he hoped to God the background music prevented anybody from hearing. "Out with it, Bernie," he whispered. "What exactly did you see?"

The older man grinned. "Ah, don't worry about it. I knew something was up with you two. Your secret is safe with me." He started to leave, but then turned back around. "But you could tell the others. Heck, all us Wanderers are pushovers for a good romance."

"Right now, I'd appreciate it if you kept it quiet."

"Consider it done." Bernie gave Julian's shoulder a paternal pat and returned to his table.

First Joel and Tina had caught them kissing in Siena. Now Bernie, who would surely tell Sandra what he'd witnessed this morning. Somehow, it seemed only a matter of time before others found out. He'd been careless.

In fact, since the second Mamie stepped on his bus, he'd taken risks. Like he wanted to get caught or something...which he didn't.

"What's on the agenda today, Julian?" Joel looked up from his seat as Julian sat down.

"Glad you asked." He raised his voice. "If I could make a quick announcement. I just posted the daily activities offerings on the board. After lunch, you can either hop on a van from a local vineyard to visit there, or see an Etruscan site not too far from here on the bus with me and Beppe."

All eyes rested on him. Julian struggled to keep his head in the game as he wondered if every person in this room knew what he and Mamie had done last night. Would any of them report him to Claudia? Travelers expected a lot from their guides on these tours, and some could frown upon anything personal between passenger and guest. The reason Claudia had the rules she'd put in place.

Everyone started talking, so he cleared his throat. "Please sign up if interested. If you want to relax around here, feel free. There are bikes, swimming, hiking. Tonight after dinner, I've planned a Woodstock trivia contest with the help of Sandra. Seems there's been a little debate going on amongst the group about who knows the most about the three-day concert?"

Joel puffed out his chest. "No debate. I'll be glad we can finally put this question to rest."

Tina rolled her eyes, but Julian couldn't help but notice the head shaking and laugher from several men. The door into the common room opened behind him. He waited a moment while whoever it was came inside before finishing the morning announcement.

"Well, well. I've finally found you."

That voice. The last person Julian expected to hear right now. Julian turned around, anger and disgust churning inside of him.

Gary Simon stood in the doorway. He could've looked like any other tourist in his khakis and creamy yellow polo shirt, not the way the locals dressed.

Gary glanced around the room while running a hand through his short, light brown hair. When he stopped, the spikes of his bangs remained pushed up. His gaze landed on Julian. "You're a hard man to track down."

"Didn't I ask you to leave me alone?"

"On the one call you answered, yes. But you didn't even let me talk. If you'd answered my call this morning, me showing up wouldn't be such a shock." Gary took in the group and a smirk crossed his face.

"Hello, everyone. I'm Gary Simon, producer of *Exploring the World with Eddie*. Did any of you realize you're traveling with a real-life celebrity in your midst?"

"Well I'll be damned!" Frank Bruno belted out in his thick Bronx accent. He slapped his hand on the table. "I knew it!"

Low murmurings filled the room. Panic swallowed Julian whole. Did they know about the wing suit accident and Julian's role in it? Or what had happened the day he got fired? He'd avoided all media after he got fired, so he wasn't sure how much was disclosed to the public. Far as he was concerned, Eddie had died jumping off that cliff, too.

Gary's arrival resurrected Eddie from the dead.

Anger pooled in his fists. He stomped toward Gary. *One, two, three...* Counting didn't soothe his rage. Gary's smug expression mirrored the one he'd worn the day they'd filmed in Hawaii, three weeks after Carlos's death and the day Gary had fired Julian.

Julian barreled forward until he stood a few feet from the man he'd loathed upon waking every single day for the past year.

"You're not welcome here, Gary. I'm leaving. Call yourself a cab." He stepped away but stopped and turned. "And learn to take no for an answer."

He walked out the door.

* * * *

Mamie debated. She wanted to go after Julian, but her bottom stayed rooted in her seat. Never had a man looked more like he wanted to be left alone.

Frank Bruno brought Gary a cup of coffee, offered him a seat on a sofa near a stone fireplace. Several others went over, too, excitedly asking the producer questions about the show. Gary answered like a pro. Easy. Confident. Crest bright smile. On the surface, his clean-cut appearance seemed about as threatening as Mr. Rogers at the start of his show.

"Poor Julian," Tina said.

Sandra nodded. "He looked very upset."

Bernie leaned in, lowering his voice. "Remember the day Frank first mentioned how he looked like the show's host? Julian didn't look thrilled. I wonder what happened to make him leave the show?"

"And take a job with this tour company." Sandra shook her head. "It can't be that exciting after everything he's done."

Mamie wanted to tell them about the death on the show, Gary's role in it, and how Julian blamed himself. For her to tell others would be wrong, especially since he'd gone to great lengths to keep that story hidden. She understood. The past five years, she'd lived in the shell of another persona.

Seemed they both found a way to hide in plain sight from their pasts.

But Gary's arrival proved one thing: the past never really disappeared.

Joel reached across the table for a packet of sugar. "I can't imagine why he'd hide all this from us."

Joel's comment drew Mamie back to their conversation. "I'll tell you why."

They all looked her way and Tina placed a hand over Mamie's. "Oh, honey. Did you know? I mean, you two are...close."

"Yes, we're friends, but..." She stopped. Tina had seen them kissing after the horse race. "Yes. I knew."

"Mamie?" Bernie placed a hand over hers. "It's okay. I saw you saying goodbye to Julian this morning."

Sandra winked at Mamie. "He's a sweet boy. I'm happy for you both."

Lowering her voice, she said, "Then you all know about us?"

"Yup." Bernie reached for his coffee. "None of us are going to tell. We're happy for you. I mean, we were the generation of love."

"It's fine, honey." Sandra patted Mamie's forearm. "Did you know he was on the show?"

"I just learned about it recently." Mamie turned to Joel. "You wondered why he'd hide it, Joel?" She glanced around the table. "Maybe all of you do. It's not my place to tell you why, but sometimes people need a break from their lives. That's all Julian has been trying to do."

She swallowed and readied herself for what she was about to tell them. Just like she and Julian had confessed to each other, it was time the people of this tour met the real Mamie—at least her real personal side. She still couldn't share her work mission.

She drew in a deep breath. "I haven't been honest with all of you, either. The story I told you about getting divorced isn't the real me."

They watched her, brows furrowed and faces marked with concern.

Mamie lifted her chin, about to cross a line she'd avoided for five years. "I was once married. But I lost my family in a car accident...."

She shared details that often got stuck in her throat. Eyes watered. Tears fell. But there were hugs. Loving hugs from new friends, who made her see how the support of others wasn't something to run from, but embrace.

Why it had been so difficult to accept the same kind support from people she'd known much longer remained a question she couldn't answer. One thing was certain, though. She'd crossed a line into a new part of her life where she let others in for a change.

* * * *

Julian sat on the grass staring out at a hillside, a perfect Tuscan view of an olive grove to his left and a field of bright red poppies to his right. The strong morning sun hung amongst puffy clouds in the blue sky. Another gorgeous summer day. One he'd looked forward to until Gary showed up.

Julian imagined his passengers gossiping over everything they learned this morning. The same way any group of people would if they'd been lied to.

Frank Bruno had called it, a fact Julian had no doubt he'd remind the others. Mamie knew more about his past than anybody, though he trusted she wouldn't tell more than was already out there. Gary could have a field day about his life and Julian didn't trust him at all.

The tall grasses behind him rustled and he braced himself. If it was Gary, he couldn't be responsible for—

"Julian?"

Mamie. Relief rushed through him. He didn't want to kick Gary's ass, but left alone with him, he just might. He glanced back over his shoulder.

She frowned. "You okay? I've been looking all over for you."

He turned back to the view, crisscrossing his legs to get more comfortable. "I needed to be alone."

She lowered herself to the grass, slipped her flip-flops off her feet, and adjusted the straps of a pair of denim bib overalls so they sat properly on her shoulders.

On any other woman, he wouldn't have looked twice at such an outfit. But on Mamie, her hair twirled into bun and her long legs stretched out before her, the word cute popped into his mind.

"How'd you find me?"

"Beppe suggested I look here. He said it was your favorite place."

"My friend, the traitor."

"You're lucky to have such a good friend."

He turned to her. She'd been watching him. "I know."

She put a hand on his knee. "You okay?"

"Not really." He rubbed his cheeks with his palms. "What kind of scene did I create back there?"

"Not so bad. Mostly they're worried about you and"—she drew in a breath—"curious. They're wondering how they could've been in the presence of a TV celebrity and not known it. Although several times Frank Bruno reminded them he'd called it."

Julian laughed. "I figured."

Mamie took his hand and drew it to her lap. "Bernie said he saw me leaving your place this morning."

"He told me while I was getting my coffee." Her soft hand in his gave him the comfort he'd been looking for on this hillside, but hadn't yet found. "Guess the ol' cat's out of the bag."

She shrugged. "It's a matter of time before the others figure it out. Plus, I'm not sure those who know will do a good job of keeping it a secret. Not to hurt us or anything. They just seem to not mind us being together, even if it's not allowed by your boss."

"I don't care if they all know about us."

"No? What about your boss?"

"If Claudia finds out, I'll deal with it." He squeezed her hand. "I can only imagine what they think knowing about Eddie, the show, Carlos dying on my watch." Self-hatred tore at his inside. "Even about me getting fired."

She frowned. "First, I'm not sure they know all those details. Second, why do you blame yourself? Through my eyes, Gary is to blame."

He turned back to the view. Blame. It came easily to him. Logically, he understood the ease of owning blame came from a deep-rooted place. He contemplated the risk of saying it aloud, struggling for a long moment but when Mamie squeezed his hand, he took the leap. "For years, I wished I could've saved my parents the day they died. I just stood there. Helpless. The moment Carlos slammed into that damn bridge, the old feeling I had watching that hot air balloon go up in flames returned. I couldn't do a damn thing and he was up there because of me."

She drew her legs to her side and faced him. "I know how that feels. There are days I still replay the car accident, if only I'd seen the car veer into our lane, if only I'd suggested a different route, left the house earlier or later..." Her eyes watered then she sighed. "Problem is when fate drops a bomb in our path, we're powerless to stop it." She lifted a hand and touched his cheek gently. "All we can do is move forward. You're helping me move forward, you know?"

"Me?"

"Yes, you," she said softly. Her eyes glistened, but they seemed like happy tears. "I'll always be thankful to you for that."

He kissed her. She'd handed him a gift, in believing he was capable of good. He leaned back, happy to see her tears gone. "Now maybe you can help me figure out how to deal with Gary."

"What happened that you're no longer on the show? I mean, did you quit after the accident?"

"Didn't you read it on the internet?"

"It didn't say."

He drew in a deep breath and stared out at the hills. "We were in Lanai, the Hawaiian Island. The Kaunolu cliff jump. An eighty-two-foot drop into the ocean."

"Sounds terrifying."

"Normally, I wouldn't have blinked. But this was three weeks after Carlos died. Gary wanted to film at a popular local site for cliff diving. I didn't think anything of it. At least until I stood on the edge, staring down in the choppy water. Hell, it wasn't even a bad day to dive. The old me would've talked to a few locals, listened to their advice, and gone for it."

"But not that day?"

He shook his head and his throat grew thick with the pain owning him that day. "I was something I've never let myself be."

"What's that?"

He turned to her. "Scared." His stomach trembled, the confession never before uttered aloud. "The fourteen-year-old boy in me who missed his parents terribly never allowed himself to be afraid. I grew up to be a man who had to prove to the world nothing scared me. But that day in Hawaii, all I could hear while waiting to make that jump was the sound of Carlos hitting that bridge. The cliff edge seemed as daunting as stepping off the edge of the world." He sighed and looked up at her. "Gary threatened to fire me if I didn't do it, so I walked off and told him to do it."

She watched him carefully and nodded. "So why does he want you back now?"

"The show's executive producer wants me back. Is offering to double my salary."

"Did you like doing the show?"

"I loved certain things about it."

"Like what?"

"Seeing new places, meeting new people. I've always loved that and it's been an important part of my life."

"And what didn't you like?"

"Sometimes those dramatic stunts didn't sit right." Speaking so truthfully carried a great sense of relief. "Gary thought they were a ratings grabber. After Carlos died, I realized I only did them to prove I could."

"Prove to who?"

He met her serious gaze. "Myself I guess." Then the real answer hit him. "No...ever since losing my parents, I almost wonder if I've been trying to prove to the world I'm like them. Someone who isn't afraid to try new things, explore places others wouldn't dare visit." The reality of his current fears took a swing. "I'm not, though."

"Julian, you've risked your life, multiple times. God, you're about the bravest person I know." She gathered his hands in hers. "You let me on the bus without authorization." She grinned. "And took me on some dates, and into your villa. A rule breaker if there ever was one."

He drew in the warmth of her pretty smile, but it disappeared as fast. "That wasn't bravery." He put his arm around her shoulders and they sat quietly for a moment.

Mamie broke the silence, quietly asking, "So feeling brave really matters to you?"

"Sure. I may not want the same level of risk going forward, but being adventurous is part of who I am."

After a few minutes, she looked up. "I have this great idea for you, a new kind of adventure."

"What?"

"I want it to be a surprise."

"Haven't I had enough of those this trip?"

"Please? I trusted you..." She raised her full dark brows.

"True, you did." Her persistence left him curious. "Then run with it."

"You won't be sorry."

He couldn't imagine anything she could do would make him sorry.

She stood and wiped some dried grass off her thighs. "How about we go see if Gary has left yet?"

"Sounds like a good idea."

She extended a hand to him. He took it, and as he stood, pulled her close and kissed her deeply.

Julian tried pinpointing the exact moment this smart, pretty woman came out of nowhere and swept him off his feet. She'd worked her way into both his heart and his head, despite many problems of her own.

Hell, yeah. He trusted her.

Chapter 18

Mamie pulled herself across the pool's length with long strokes, but her mind rested on the activity outside of the water.

Earlier, while she and Julian enjoyed a swim, Frank Bruno came poolside and told them he'd invited Gary to stay at the villa for a couple of days, using the spare bed in his room. Julian had started to say something about his tour instructor's strict rules, then stopped talking, dove deep, and swam like an angry shark chasing prey.

So Gary was here to stay. Like it or not.

Julian now stretched out in a lounge chair on the opposite side from his former boss, a clear message if Mamie had ever seen one.

She kicked off the pool wall for a new lap. Gary staying might not be such a bad thing. His arrival served as a catalyst to what ailed Julian. Which was why before dinner last night, she'd brainstormed with Beppe on ways to help Julian get through his personal crisis. Together, they'd hatched a plan and today Beppe talked to his cousin, who said he could help them with it toward the end of their villa stay.

Mamie popped her head from beneath the water, surprised to hear singing. On the far side of the pool, beneath the shade of a curtained cabana, several tour members and Gary rocked out about the summer of '69. A version that would've made Bryan Adams cringe.

Mamie climbed up the pool ladder and settled quietly into the lounge chair near Julian. Water glistened on his tanned arms and chest. With his sunglasses on, she couldn't see his eyes, but he appeared to be sleeping. Her gaze drifted to the Aztec Warrior tattoo near his shoulder. He deserved to wear the emblem, even though he didn't see himself as a warrior. Warriors came in all forms. Especially when facing the battle of their lives. Exactly what he'd been doing the past year.

Just as she tipped her head back and shut her eyes, Julian mumbled, "Look at him. He waltzes in and takes over. Hell, he didn't even go to Woodstock."

She turned her head sideways and found him wide-awake, his sunglasses pushed up into his damp curls. "Neither did you, and you sing along with them."

"Are you always so reasonable?" His gaze softened and slid along her body. "And sexy?"

She laughed. "Oh yes, my one-piece Speedo is the stuff men's dreams are made of."

His voice grew husky. "Then maybe it's you?" He ran his index finger along her shoulder and her skin tingled. "Oh, while you were in the pool three more from our group came up and told me know they knew about us." He reached for her hand and gave it a squeeze. "So how about we call it safe to openly enjoy ourselves?"

"I vote yes."

"Yo, Julian," yelled Bob over the chorus. "Come join us!"

He waved. "Thanks. Maybe in a bit."

Beppe's van appeared at the crest of the winding stone driveway.

"Good. Lunch is here." Mamie let go of his hand and reached for her tunic cover-up. She stood and slipped it over her head. "Let's help Beppe get food set up in the common room. I'm starving."

"Sure." He stood, slipped an arm around her waist, and drew her close. In the space of a heartbeat, he dipped his head and swept his lips against hers. He leaned back and grinned. "Let's give 'em something to talk about. And while we're on the topic, why don't you move your bags into my place? Let's make the most of this time together."

She forced a smile. This would end soon, but she'd enjoy every minute while she could. "I'd like that."

He winked and turned, heading toward the patio, where Beppe had just dropped off a box. Julian turned to her, holding out his hand. "*Andiamo, mia bellezza*. I thought you were hungry."

"I am." She hurried to catch up with him, knowing the others looked on. Glancing to her side, she found only smiling faces watching them. Any background worries she had about him being reported to his boss vanished.

* * * *

Laughter and conversation filled the patio air. Julian couldn't wait to sample this feast of Italian delights. Olives marinated in spices.

Thick sliced tomatoes nestled near mozzarella, both glazed with fresh, fruity olive oil. Tangy cheeses accompanied by sliced ham, salami, and prosciutto, waiting to be enjoyed on slices of fresh bread baked by Beppe's brother-in-law.

He glanced to his side and studied Mamie. She sipped her second glass of Chianti, not seeming to mind one bit the way he slowly massaged her thigh beneath the table.

Loud laughter from the far end of the long table rose above the other sounds.

"Is it true, Julian?" Bernie raised his voice above the noise. "Gary here is telling us about the time you visited a tribe and they wanted you to marry the chief's daughter?"

"Yup. One of our earlier shows. Let's just say I wasn't ready to commit." A voice inside his head reminded him he never had been.

Gary chuckled. "I never thought we'd get out of that one. Thank God she didn't like you."

"I'll admit it now. My ego was a little bruised. Hell, nobody likes to be turned down. But that was a blessing in disguise."

"I remember that show." Tim, a short man with dark glass frames who seemed to be opening up at the villa, looked toward Julian. "Wasn't there one where you went in a river filled with piranhas?"

"Yeah. In the Amazon. Funny, but those damn fish scared me more than a lot of things I've done for the show."

Memories of the good times he'd had doing the show ambushed him. Moments he'd erased like they'd never happened a year ago, but now brought back with some fondness.

Gary reached to a platter in the table's center and took a rolled piece of salami. "That guide told you they were more scared of you than you were them, but you didn't believe him."

"Hell no." Julian smiled. These types of encounters always bonded the show staff. "Remember when he started talking to his buddy in some Amazonian language our translator didn't understand? I was pretty sure he was making fun of me."

Mamie laughed, giving him a burst of unexpected joy. It felt nice to share this part of himself with her, too.

Bernie leaned forward. "What other crazy things happened on the show?"

Gary looked at Julian. "Enough that we talked about doing an episode devoted only to some of our craziest moments, right, Jules?"

"Yeah, we had some great stuff planned." Nostalgia for good times wrapped him like a snake, leaving old memories to choke him with regret for his actions. For years, the people on the show were friends, almost like a surrogate family. "Remember the tape you have of a rhino charging at me?"

Several people seated at the table gasped.

Gary scrunched his face, in deep thought. "Oh yeah. Nepal, right?"

Julian nodded, then panned the attentive audience and dove right in. "The rhino stood about fifty meters away. I was trying to back off slowly and this one"—he motioned with his thumb to Gary—"he's saying, 'Puff out your chest. Let him know you're not afraid.' The rhino decided to call my bluff and as he attacked, Gary was yelling 'Don't move until the last minute.'"

"Hey, we had a great shot." Gary shrugged, not looking one bit apologetic.

"Great shot of what? The host about to have a heart attack?" Julian shook his head.

He waved his hand. "You'd have been fine."

The vineyard bus pulled in, stopping the conversation.

Julian stood. "I hate to end the party. Those going to the vineyard have to catch this bus and I have to get ready for the excursion to the Etruscan site. For those who want to join me, Beppe will be ready to drive us in an hour." He picked up two empty platters. "Feel free stay at the villa. If you're joining me, let's take a minute to clear dirty dishes and load the dishwasher. Give our help a little hand."

The table emptied and everyone participated with clean up. When all was done, Julian took Mamie by the hand and led her outside the kitchen door.

He twirled her around and pressed her to the building's stone wall. Pushing aside the shoulder of her sleeve, he kissed her exposed skin. "How about we get your bags now? Are you going with me this afternoon?"

"I am." She pressed her lips to his, a soft sweep. "I loved those stories about your show."

"It was fun talking about it." Gary's arrival had pissed him off at first, but right now he had a taste of his former self and it felt damn good. Besides, the way Mamie looked at him at this moment, having Gary blow his cover this morning was worth it. "We have an hour before the bus leaves. I can think of one way to put this time to use."

"And they say men can't multi-task." Mamie grinned. "Let's go."

They returned to her villa to grab the luggage then headed toward his place. For once, his soul felt in harmony with the world. A kind of lightness Julian wanted to grab tight and hold on to forever. A tranquil sensation that had escaped him for a long time, perhaps his entire life.

She glanced his way. "You loved your old job, didn't you?"

"Yeah. After what happened, I forgot how much."

"Would you ever go back?"

"I don't know. The people I worked with were like family."

"Even Gary?"

"No," he said right away. "I had a work respect for him, but somehow I sensed he looked out for number one. It always put me off."

She nodded, and they silently walked to the house. He wondered what she thought about, but by the time they reached the house and got behind a closed door, he only cared about the time they had left together.

* * * *

Mamie burrowed her face in the pillow and inhaled Julian's scent, a faded mix of soap and spice. The Etruscan tour had been interesting, but being back here now, alone with Julian, was even better.

She shifted against the crisp sheets, listening to the shower running, but still able to feel the touch of his hands as they'd explored her skin. God, how she'd missed sex. Just the thought of being in his bed for the remainder of this trip made every nerve-ending tingle.

Gary's presence brought mixed results. Having him here tossed Julian's past on the table, which strangely enough seemed to relax him. A fact that also made her happier. Yet the smooth producer possessed a disingenuous air about him. She only hoped he didn't do anything more to upset the good karma of this magical villa.

The clock ticked on their villa stay. Tomorrow morning she'd get a chance to reciprocate the support Julian had given her with a special moment for him. Nerves tugged at her gut as she thought about her plan. Julian might hate the challenge she proposed, and all she could do was pray that he didn't.

Julian's happiness mattered and doing this for him brought a kind of purpose she hadn't felt in some time. The kind she'd felt, as a mother and wife, when giving support to her loved ones every day.

Her cell phone rang. She rolled over and grabbed it off the nightstand, happy to see Felix's name flash across the display.

"Hey, stranger." She sat up and pulled the sheet over her chest.

"It's the world traveler." Felix's deep voice and melodic British accent sounded more rested than usual. "Allison tells me you're holding your own out there."

"Surprisingly, I am. How's the new Mrs. Carrol?"

"Gilda is making me the happiest man in the world. If someone had told me love could feel like this, I'd have made myself find it years ago instead of traveling the world."

"That's how I feel about Tuscany."

"Most people do. Are you still in Siena?"

"No. We're at the villa, near the border of Tuscany and Umbria."

"Beautiful, yes?"

"*Sì. Bellissimo.*"

Felix laughed. "Mamie, dear, it does my heart good to hear you this happy."

"I am happy, but a little sad, too. I've made some nice friends on this tour. Hey, did you really go to Woodstock?"

"Believe it or not, I did. I was in college and traveling abroad in the U.S. that summer. And yes, I am a member of the Wanderers, too. They're nice people. Every couple of years I go on a trip with them. On my own time. When I don't have to take notes and write about a place. You know, when the publisher asked me to go on the tour with the group, I talked to her about my conflict of interest. But then meeting Gilda... Ah, well it all fell into place and seems I didn't belong on the Tuscany trip after all. How's the piece coming?"

"Pretty well. I'm following your format. In fact, hold on, though. I have a couple of questions if you've got time."

"Absolutely."

She put the phone on the bed, quickly tossed on her underpants and a T-shirt, and pulled her notebook from her canvas bag.

After settling on the bed, she flipped through the pages until she found her questions to ask Felix. It only took about two minutes to get answers and she scribbled fast in case Julian finished soon.

"My goodness, you are right on top of it." Felix sounded impressed. "Nobody will miss me."

"Now we both know that isn't true." The shower shut off and she quickly tossed the book back onto the top of her bag. "Hey, quick question. Did you ever tell anybody who you really were? Between us."

"Never. Part of the deal to keep the job. You know that."

"Yeah, it's just not easy sometimes."

He was silent for a moment, then said, "Yes, it was hard to not be truthful with the friends I've made, yet I felt like I had no choice. Now I've got a question for you." Felix's voice took on a serious tone. "I'm thinking of leaving my job as the Covert Critic. Are you interested in the spot?"

"Oh, I don't know. I—I just thought I'd be back home at the end of this."

Home. Less than two weeks ago, it had been the extent of her world. Now a door had been pried open. She could run free.

"Don't answer right now," Felix interrupted her thoughts. "We'll talk when you return. Sound good?"

The bathroom door opened and Julian stepped out with a towel around his waist. He started to say something, must've seen her phone, and walked over to his luggage.

"Yes. I think that sounds good."

They talked about the details of her return then hung up.

"Everything okay?" Julian asked.

She turned to him just as he buttoned the top of his jeans.

"I guess. It was my boss confirming my return date." She swallowed the pain of her lie, seeming a thousand times worse given what happened between them in the past twenty-four hours.

He seemed quiet as he tossed on a button-down shirt. She got out of bed and picked up the damp towel he'd left on the floor. "Guess I'll go shower."

As she turned toward the bathroom door, he grabbed the towel end and drew her close. "Don't run off." He put his arms around her. "You sure you're okay?"

She shrugged. "My boss offered me a new job."

"That's good. What is it? Like bank president or something?"

"No." The lie grew like Pinocchio's nose. "A regional job. It involves some travel."

"In the U.S.?"

"I'm not sure. He said we could talk about it when I get home."

"So you have time to think about it."

"Yeah." Home. Just the thought of it left her with a lump in her throat. "Hard to believe this trip is almost over."

Julian frowned. "Let's not think about it." The towel fell to the floor as he slipped his hand under her shirt, the heat of his palm resting on the curve of her back, and caressed her gently. Desire in his eyes made her heart swell. She undid his shirt and pressed her hands to his chest, loving how his body was becoming familiar.

He eased her onto the bed and removed the clothes he'd just put on.

They made love. Not the urgent passion owning them before, but a symphony of gentle and tender movements, punctuating a message that made the trip's ending even more bittersweet.

Chapter 19

The debate inside Julian's head came to a halt. Decision made.

He rose from the kitchen island stool, walked to the bathroom door, and knocked. The shower water stopped. "Mamie? I've decided to talk to Gary before dinner."

"Hold on." A second later, she stuck her head out the door, a towel wrapped around her torso. "I think that's a smart move." She gave him a quick kiss. "Good luck. I'll meet you at the cocktail hour."

He left the villa and walked across the courtyard, knocked on the door.

Frank opened it, dressed for dinner in a loud Hawaiian shirt and dress slacks. His gray hair was slicked back for a change and strong cologne hung in the air around him. "Hi, Julian. Or should I call you Eddie?" He elbowed Julian and winked. "Come on in."

"Julian, please." He held in his irritation at Frank, who reveled in this find more than the others. "You all set for trivia night?"

"Are you kidding? I practice all year for this."

"Is Gary around?"

Frank pointed across the living room toward a set of sliding doors. "He's out on the patio having a beer. Grab one from the fridge and join him." He glanced at his watch. "I'm heading over for the cocktail hour. Don't want to miss any of those appetizers."

"I'll be there soon." Julian pointed to his shirt. "You know this isn't a luau, right?"

Frank's laugh bounced off the room's high ceilings. "This was the biggest shirt I brought along. I saw tonight's menu and wanted plenty of room for eating."

"Now why didn't I think of that?" Julian smiled, then stopped by the kitchen to take a beer.

As he headed out through the sliding doors, Gary looked up from his seat at a glass-topped table, a Peroni in his hand. "Hey. I was just thinking I should retire here."

Julian shook his head. "You're only forty-five."

"This is peaceful." He turned back to the hills surrounding the valley. "Makes me wonder why I'm working like such a horse."

Julian kept to himself it was because Gary's greed always got the better of him.

Sitting, Julian tipped back his bottle while watching the man he'd loathed for the past twelve months.

Seconds passed before Gary made eye contact with him. "Dude, what the hell's been going on with you?"

Julian lowered the beer, the answer even more complicated with Mamie in the picture. "To be honest, I wish I knew. A year ago, it had everything to do with what happened to Carlos."

"I wish I could do that day over." Gary shook his head and finished off his beer.

Julian snorted. "Are you kidding me?"

"What? That man dying was horrible."

"Carlos. His name was Carlos." Julian leaned across the table. "I begged, BEGGED you to cancel the dive, but you pushed."

"The executive producers pushed, not me."

"The only person I heard was you."

"Show biz sucks. Money means everything."

"Even a life?"

Gary's jaw tightened and he looked away.

"The executive producers, did they tell you to fire me, too?"

Gary stared into the darkening sky. "No. I made the call because you were pissing me off."

"Pissing you off," Julian said quietly, careful not to set off his mounting anger. "I had just watched a man die." The words clogged his throat. "Fuck you, Gary."

Gary flinched, but lifted his bottle, frowning when he noticed it was empty. "The executive producers want you back. I'm here to find out what it will take."

"Now I'm starting to see what happened. You're in trouble because you let me go."

"Trouble is a strong word. They would've been happy with a replacement, but turns out there's something about you viewers like."

On some level, the news made Julian feel good. The one thing he'd loved about his job had been the viewers, who often sent fan mail or showed up on location. "For what it's worth, I don't know what I want. This past year, I've done some deep soul searching. I don't think I've done that a single day in my life. Just jumped into what life had to offer without a second thought. It's how I landed on the show."

"You were a natural."

"I was naive."

"How so?"

"Naive about life. What I really want from both a job and career."

"Well, it can't possibly be this one. A tour guide? Jesus, Jules. You went from a hundred miles per hour to ten."

"I'm a tour director. And it has plenty of rewards."

Gary gave sarcastic chuckle. "Like?"

Julian scrubbed at his beard and realized Gary hadn't even mentioned his latest anti-Eddie look. "It's more relaxing than the show, for starters. I meet some damn nice people." Then there was Mamie. "I spend time in beautiful places. Oh, and the best one…the death rate is pretty low."

"Touché," Gary said, his tone filled with contempt. "Look, all I ask is that you think about what it'll take to get you back. We're open to anything. Even a new show format." Gary leaned back in the chair and crossed his ankle over his knee. "I miss working with you. And that isn't bullshit. It's how I really feel. I'll respect your decision not to return, but I'd like you to sleep on it." He stretched out his hand. "Friends?"

Julian wanted to hate him. This was Gary in full-blown salesman, backing Julian into a corner while he smiled, making it hard to distrust. Julian reached out and shook, feeling like he had no choice but to keep things amiable now that Gary was here as a guest. "How about we join the cocktail hour?"

They stood and walked around the villa, going uphill toward the patio. As they rounded the corner, laughter and voices suggested the party was in full swing.

"Who's your new girlfriend?" Gary asked.

The word dropped like a bomb. Sure, he'd had women who he saw regularly. They offered companionship and sex. Never had he called them girlfriends, but for some reason he struggled to deny Gary's use of the word. "Her name's Mamie Weber. She came with the tour."

"With all those old people?"

Julian smiled. How she fit right in with them was part of her charm. "Yeah. Her uncle gave her the ticket. It was his."

"It's looking cozy."

"We just met." He glanced at Gary and gave him a *no-biggie* shrug, but the words carried a flat ring.

"Speak of the devil."

Julian looked straight ahead, where Mamie had appeared at the end of the walkway and stopped near a row of torches leading to the patio.

The long, strapless dress she wore clung to her body, sliding down to her ankles, where a gentle breeze opened the flap and revealed delicate sandals. She'd twirled her chocolate hair on top of her head, leaving soft tendrils to frame her face. His heart swelled with emotion, and the words he'd just said to Gary became a bigger lie.

She smiled and Julian did the same. All the choices before him right now, and the most unexpected one was that Mamie had made it to the list.

* * * *

Beppe whistled to the music coming from his car radio as he sped along the dark, empty highway. His smaller car made the speeds seem even more perilous to Mamie than the bus and she struggled to refrain from backseat driving. She had bigger worries ahead, like how Julian would react when they reached their destination.

Julian yawned loudly from the front passenger's seat and glanced at Beppe. "I don't know what you're so happy about at this early hour. Someone"—he turned around and raised a brow at Mamie—"better have a very good reason for dragging me out of bed so early."

She sat straighter in her seat. "Trust me. If I wake you while we're in bed, you should never ask why."

Beppe laughed and looked at her in the rearview mirror. "She's got you there, my friend. You do what your woman asks."

She stuck out her tongue at Julian, then smiled. Deep down, though, butterflies danced in her belly and she wished they'd stop. What she was about to ask Julian to do pulled him out onto a limb he'd been avoiding.

His face softened. "Just you wait'll this car stops," he said quietly. "You'll pay for that."

"Oh? I hope so."

Julian grinned then turned around just as Beppe drove uphill.

Mamie searched for anything to talk about to take her mind off what was about to happen. "I'm surprised Bob's wife, Carol, won the trivia contest last night. So quiet this whole tour, then she went and clobbered all those men who boasted the entire trip about knowing the most."

Julian laughed. "Did you see Joel's mouth drop when she got that last question right? He was sure he had the win." Before Mamie could respond, Julian added, "Really, you guys. What's this about? I feel like I'm being kidnapped."

Mamie leaned forward, sticking her head between the two men. "It's something like that."

"You're impossible." He grinned and shot her a glance, before turning to stare outside the dark car window.

She sat back in her seat, but somehow knew he wouldn't be smiling when he learned the truth. A minute later, they rounded a bend, where a car with a trailer attached sat parked.

Outside the trailer, on the ground, a rainbow-colored hot air balloon lay on its side. Next to it, the operator stoked a fire that would fill the inside and take them on their flight.

"What's going on here?" Julian's playful tone disappeared.

Beppe parked near the other car and glanced back to Mamie as he opened his door. "I'll leave you two to talk."

Mamie scooted to the middle of the back seat as Beppe's door shut. Julian turned around.

Even in the dim light, his glare shone bright. "Why are we here?"

"Good question." Mamie couldn't remember a word of her prepared speech. "I started thinking how we both seemed in search of something—"

"*This* isn't what I'm searching for."

"Maybe not. But I thought it might help us both. You see, after what you shared with me about being afraid, I understood. I've been scared for a long time, too. Coming to Tuscany had me scared. But when I finally got on the plane, I knew I needed to challenge myself. Like my husband used to do for me."

Flame from the hot air balloon shot upward, brightening the car's dark interior and highlighting Julian's tight jaw. "Mamie, what's wrong with you? I watched my parents die in one of these things. Right now, I'm...I'm not myself. I'm..."

"It's okay if this makes you nervous. I'm nervous, too."

"This goes beyond that and you know it! Jesus, that contraption..."

She touched his shoulder, the muscles tense. "I'm sorry to dump this on you. But sometimes the thing we need has to come out of left field, leaving us no time to think about it."

"Maybe for you."

Mamie summoned up everything she'd figured out about herself in these two weeks. "For the past five years, I've lived with the daily and unbearable pain of losing my loved ones. Like you, I had to witness something nobody should have to see." She inhaled, hoping to squelch the ache squeezing her chest. If ever she needed to be strong, it was now. "I've wasted the life I'd been spared." She reached to the front seat and took his hand. "But this week, and being with you, has helped me come alive again." Julian's darkened face blurred through her tears. "But you... I can tell you haven't let go of the ghosts yet. Your reaction to Carlos's death, it's not only about him—"

"I know. I can see all this."

"Then let me help you. Like you've helped me see the wonders of Tuscany. You've shown me the most extraordinary pleasures from the most ordinary days. Now let's try the unexpected together."

He turned away from her and stared outside in the direction of the hot air balloon.

She whispered. "I'm willing to take a chance with you at my side."

A loud rush sounded and the fire burst higher inside the balloon, casting another bright glare inside the car. The flames danced high, making the balloon fill. Slowly it rounded out and reached to the sky, where the sun crested along the horizon creating a reddish-orange band.

Beppe knocked on the window. "My cousin, he's ready for you."

Julian's gaze met hers. She held her breath waiting for an answer.

Chapter 20

Risk. Julian had played the game for too many years. But never in a hot air balloon. Many years ago, Gary had suggested a show in one. Julian told him about his parents and asked him to never bring up the subject again. Gary obliged.

Now Mamie, a woman he'd shared the biggest part of himself with, had set him up. She stared at him from the backseat, brows furrowed, concern etched on her face. A woman he'd trusted. By making this decision, she might as well be shoving him off the edge of a cliff.

"Say something," she said quietly.

"I don't want to do it. How's that?"

She blinked. "I'm sorry. I don't understand how a man who faced such extreme danger for so long—far worse than this—can't face the one thing that's been owning him for most of his life."

"Maybe because you don't walk in my shoes."

"No. I don't. But I do understand why it's important to sometimes step onto the ledge, even if the view down is terrifying."

"Mamie, you picked the *one thing* I can't do."

Light from the balloon flames highlighted a glossy sheen in her eyes. "All the more reason to do it." She touched his cheek, leaned forward and kissed him gently. As she reached for her door handle, she said, "It's fine if you don't want to go, but I'm taking a chance. I may not get another."

She stepped out and walked toward Beppe, his cousin, and another woman Julian didn't know.

He quickly got out and yelled over the loud noise from the shooting flame. "It's not that I don't want to. I can't."

She turned around and stared at him for a few seconds. When he didn't budge, she frowned and continued to the balloon.

I can't. I can't. I can't.

His thoughts pummeled him as the logic he'd survived on for years refused to lift. Reasoning that made him spend a lifetime proving to people he *could* do the impossible. That nothing scared him, even though a part of him was terrified. Now, a woman who'd made him seek out the treasures found in the mundane things in life wanted to show *him* more? It made no sense.

What would happen if she got on that balloon alone? He'd regret it forever, that's what. Like he regretted what happened to Carlos.

He slowly moved toward the balloon. Mamie smiled as she talked to Dario, already inside the basket. Beppe had introduced his cousin to Julian once before. He had no idea the man flew balloons, though.

The balloon hovered above the basket, still staked to the ground by thick ropes. Every terrifying memory stealing his soul on the day his parents died gripped him tight.

This time, he fought back, guided by Mamie's brave gaze as she stared upward at the balloon then stepped into the basket. His heart filled with pride, knowing she had the courage to come to Italy. Even more proud to know she'd take this step with or without him.

She turned and looked at Julian, sadness in her eyes silently begging him to come. The sun inched higher up the horizon, casting more light on her.

All he wanted was to hold this beautiful, brave soul in his arms. A woman willing to take this risk because she knew it would help him.

His feet moved, almost on their own. When he reached the balloon, she extended her hand. He took it and got inside, drawing her close but unable to speak, the flames roaring like an angry dragon.

Dario yelled, "It is good to see you again. Are you ready?"

Julian glanced at Mamie, who nodded.

"Okay, we're ready."

"My wife." He motioned to a woman standing on the ground near Beppe. "She will follow us in the car and meet us when we land, *sì*?"

"Sounds good." Julian tried to sound confident, even though the raw edges of his nerves stung and his head tried to process the surreal act of facing his true goliath.

Beppe waved. "*Arrivederci*," he yelled over another loud blast, this one lifting the balloon off the ground. "I will be waiting, too."

Julian took Mamie's hand and squeezed it. She squeezed back as they drifted upward, the rising sun illuminating the sky from darkness into light. Dario watched out the other side, occasionally looking at a meter near the equipment containing fuel.

Higher and higher they lifted, the flame's intermittent thunder ringing in Julian's ears, terrifying as the roar of a tiger. Suddenly it got quiet. They floated in the sky, a sense of calm surrounding him. It silenced the noise in Julian's head, fighting inside of him not only today, but for decades.

Julian wrapped his arm around Mamie's waist and she glanced at him with a quick smile before returning to the view. Out on the horizon, the sun continued its climb, revealing a gentle morning mist lingering above the patchwork countryside, exposing rows of crops, roads, and rivers usually hidden when on the ground. As they passed over treetops and houses, Julian got lost in the beautiful countryside seen from this bird's-eye view. Tuscany as he'd never seen it before.

The fog below lifted, and so did the weight of his worries. He glanced at Mamie, who stared straight ahead. She'd done this. She got him up here. He leaned close and kissed her cheek. She startled and turned to him with a smile, but her eyes glistened with moisture.

"Are you okay?" he asked.

"I am. Just happy. I mean, my God… Look at this view!"

He nodded, trying like hell to hold back a power inside him about ready to burst, one filling his heart and soul. The balloon lifted higher and floated beyond the treetops to an open view. Fields stretching into more fields, all framed by the hills.

Mamie gasped. "Just when you thought the view couldn't get more beautiful," she whispered.

He studied her profile. Yes, she was beautiful. Inside and out. Passion for her brewed inside him. A deep and caring sensation toward another person he'd ignored for years, squashing those desires so much a part of his makeup since his parents died that he had forgotten how to use it.

She glanced up and tears rolled down her cheeks, making his own eyes water. He leaned over, gently kissed her salty lips.

"You're not mad at me, right? We're okay?" she asked sheepishly.

He lifted her chin with his finger, stared into her beautiful eyes, finally owning his hearts desires. "*Sì, amore mio*. We are better than okay."

* * * *

Mamie's eyes opened. She rolled over and found Julian's side of the bed empty. A second later, he stepped from the bathroom wearing cargo shorts and no shirt.

"Sleeping Beauty wakes." He grinned, but there was something so genuinely peaceful in his voice that she found herself speechless.

He removed a shirt from the dresser drawer and came over, sitting on the bed's edge. "We've had a busy morning. That nap did us both some good."

She inched closer, took his arm, and pulled him toward her. "Only the nap?" He lay at her side while she kissed her way along his neck.

He gave an appreciative moan. "Okay. *Everything* about today has done us both some good." He pinned her to the mattress and fenced her in with his arms. "Thank you again for the ride this morning."

"My pleasure." She cupped his face while tracing her fingers along his recently trimmed beard. "My husband always pushed me. I've never been the bravest soul."

He kissed her softly. As he leaned back, sincerity reigned in his eyes. "I think you possess more courage than you give yourself credit for."

She let the words sink in and embraced a sense of renewal that came with doing something more courageous than usual. "I worried you'd be angry at me. That I'd crossed a line."

He repositioned himself at her side, turned to face her. "It was bold, I'll give you that. Gary suggested shows with them, but I refused."

"So why this time?"

He gently smiled. "To be with you. To have no regrets. To let you know your bravery inspires me."

"And I have no regrets about asking."

Especially because since the moment she got up, one thought consumed her: this was her last day in Italy. Her last day with Julian. She'd leave, taking her lie about the real reason she came on the tour with her. This morning she'd taken a huge risk into the sky. What if she told Julian about her work here? Was it worth the risk of getting fired or sued if the legal department at the publisher found out?

"Tomorrow the tour ends." Julian frowned.

"I was just thinking about it."

"Now that I'm off the show, my schedule is a little more flexible. Maybe there's a way we can still see each other long distance."

Hope lifted in her heart. "You think so?"

He smiled. "Yeah."

"But Gary's offer was pretty impressive. You sure you don't want to return to the show?"

"Not if it means I can't see you."

The lie still sitting between them swelled. He'd forfeit a return to a successful career while she was afraid to take a chance and tell him the truth about her job. "You shouldn't only do it for that reason."

"It isn't the only reason."

She wasn't sure she believed him.

"Listen, I was getting up because I'm taking a group to Orvieto this morning. I figured you'd want to sleep, but since you're up, want to come?"

"No. I've got some things to do." She'd use the time to call Allison, ask her advice on the risk of telling Julian her identity. It wasn't as if she did the job all the time, and she'd decided to say no to Felix's offer to become the Covert Critic if he left. "Go on. I'll see you later."

"Okay. We'll talk more about us later. *Sì?*"

"*Sì.* Now how about a goodbye kiss?"

He gave her one and left.

She showered, tossing on a sundress with sandals for the warm day. On her way out, she grabbed her notebook and the copy of *The Covert Critic's Guide to London* she'd used as an outline. After stuffing the books in her backpack, she headed for the communal kitchen under clear blue skies. She entered the quiet stone building.

"Anybody around?"

No answers. At least half the gang had gone with Julian. The others must be on the property and had already eaten. She found some leftover breads and meats, wrapped them in a napkin, then stuffed it all into her backpack with a cold drink from the refrigerator.

As she headed for the dirt path she'd followed while looking for Julian the other day, she passed by the pool. Voices and splashing came from the area, probably those who stayed behind. After finishing work, she'd stop by and see them.

She turned at the path. Walking through walls of thick grass, she enjoyed the chirping birds and subtle sounds from farms in the distance, but she missed the sun, hiding for one of the first times on this trip. Instead, light grey skies stretched to the hills, still pretty but lacking their usual brightness.

At the clearing where she'd found Julian, she admired the hillside leading down to the valley, with lines of olive trees to one side, bold red poppies to the other. An old wooden bench waited beneath the shade of a large tree so she went and sat down. Gathering her hair behind her into a ponytail, she slipped the band from her wrist though it several times and looked around, wishing she'd found this place sooner. She unwrapped the soft roll, filling it with the meat and slowly taking bites.

Fields stretched as far as the eye could see, some farmed with produce, others with more olive trees. Twisting walls merged with winding roads and amidst the patchwork were square houses with red terra-cotta roofs. She tried to image this place centuries ago, when the Medici family ruled.

Who walked these fields? Women in long, peasant dresses and men in baggy pants and shirts who carried baskets of food from the fields, most likely. Not the fancier upper-crust Florentine families seen on PBS specials about the era, or the aristocracy in the paintings hung in the art galleries they'd visited.

After finishing her food, she took out her notebook and started to write. At one point, she pulled out the London guide Felix had written to make sure she covered all her bases for the piece. She scanned back and forth between the guidelines for the Covert Critic and her own notes.

A yawn slipped out. A few minutes later, her lids fluttered. Work suddenly seemed like more of a bother and a rest by the poolside had more merit. In fact, she should've gone with Julian. She closed the notebook. Today was all they had left. Reaching Allison to discuss telling Julian the truth about her job for the publisher seemed more important at the time. Unfortunately, Allison hadn't been there when Mamie made the call and her secretary promised to pass along the message.

Mamie lowered her work onto the bench and opened a bottle of cold sparkling water, letting it quench her dry throat. As she screwed back on the top, she studied the nearby olive trees and stood to walk over.

They'd been planted in straight lines, and she set out down one of them. The bark on many trunks had cracked and become twisted, knotting into strange shapes. An almost disorderly appearance compared to the formality of the rows in which they grew. She walked from row to row, noting all the trees looked like this. Around the fourth row, the trees took on a more youthful appearance. A straighter trunk, the bark a silvery color. Definitely younger plantings than the first few rows.

It reminded her of the people on the tour, whose appearances might have changed since the famous concert bringing them together, but inside, they had a spirit and zest for life that both she and Julian hadn't been embracing. At least not until this morning.

She reached up and ran a finger along a branch, its leaves long and strong, like fingers extended on a hand opened wide to the possibility of anything. The olive branch offered a message of peace. Peace she'd finally felt on this journey. A message the Wanderers brought with them to Woodstock so many years ago, their open hearts the reason Julian let her stay on the bus and fulfill her destiny on this tour.

She took a small sprig off the tree, tucked it in her dress pocket, and patted the spot near her hip for safekeeping.

She walked back to her belongings, satisfaction brewing inside of her.

As she came out into the open area where she'd started, Gary sat on the bench dressed in a pair of slightly big swim trunks and an open button-down shirt. He held her notebook in his hand. *The Covert Critic's Guide to London* sat on the bench opened flat with a water bottle next to it. "Hello."

He looked up. "Hi. I wondered who this belonged to." He held up her book. "Interesting stuff in here. It seems to mirror the same format as the other guide book."

She walked over and held out her hand with confidence, but the wild beat of her heart made her feel like a cornered animal. "Yes. It wasn't meant to be read."

He handed it over and stood. "Are you the Covert Critic?"

"No." She made herself to stare him square in the eyes. He *had* to believe her.

"But you've got a letter from the publisher with instructions on how to write the guides." He viewed her skeptically. "Why else would you have this?"

"You asked if I'm the Covert Critic. I'm not."

"Does Julian know you're writing about his tour?"

"No he doesn't but—"

"I expect he'd want to know, don't you?"

"I'm not the Covert Critic."

He raised critical brows.

Dread threatened to crush her bravado. Gary would surely tell Julian what he'd seen. If only she'd reached Allison to talk about her new relationship with Julian this morning, like she'd planned. This find by Gary would have less meaning.

She lifted her chin, because if she ever had to look self-assured, it was now. "I'd appreciate it if you kept what you saw to yourself."

"But Julian should know you're reviewing his tour."

"It's been a great one, with nothing bad to report. Does it matter?"

Gary shrugged. "It might to him. Are you sure you're not the Covert Critic?"

She turned away and stuffed the notebook in her pack. When she looked up, Gary watched her, his brows lifted as he waited for an answer.

Something. She had to say something or he'd tell Julian whatever he wanted. Julian would feel she'd betrayed him, although, in a way, she had. "It is for a travel publication. Not the one you think. Listen, you'd be doing me a big favor if you just kept this between us. I mean, this is my job on the line."

Gary studied her for a minute, then slowly nodded. "Sure. I get it."

"Thank you."

His expression shifted. "I heard you got Julian to go in a hot air balloon this morning."

"Yes."

"Good for you. He fought me like a wildcat when I asked. You know about his parents?"

"Yes. He told me."

"And you still tried to get him on one?"

"It helped us both, really." She immediately regretted telling him too much. Gary was the type to use information to his advantage.

"Maybe it's a sign he's coming to his senses."

"What do you mean?"

"We want him back on the show. The producers will do whatever it takes. Even change the show format. The audience loves Eddie and none of the guys we hired did well in focus group studies."

Everything Julian had told her. "I'm not sure how much that'll matter to him."

"He's still saying no." Gary glanced out into the distance. "But I'm not through with him yet."

She suddenly hated Gary and everything he represented. Selfish reasons really. A return to the show probably meant Julian would lead a busy life traveling all over the world with an aggressive filming schedule. She'd most likely never see him again. Even though he claimed to have no desire to return to his old life, that could change. Yet, given how Gary behaved, she believed Julian deserved better than what the producer or the show had to offer.

He leaned over and picked up his water bottle. "I'm heading back to the pool. Stop by when you're done."

"I will."

Gary nodded and walked back toward the path.

"Gary?"

He turned and raised a brow.

"Remember, please don't tell Julian about this. Let me tell him."

Gary smiled, but it seemed phony. "Not to worry. Your secret is safe with me, sweetheart."

Somehow, she wasn't sure she believed him. The only way to prevent him from turning this into something bigger was to get permission to tell Julian herself.

Chapter 21

The van pulled into the driveway and parked after the successful visit to Orvieto. While the passengers unloaded, Julian opened his door and glanced around the compound for Mamie. Voices carried from the direction of the pool, so he got out and walked over. A large group, including Gary, hung out, but no sign of Mamie. He turned and trudged uphill toward the path leading to their villa.

"Hey, Jules. Hold up," Gary yelled, a smile on his face as he pushed open the wrought iron gate leading from the pool area. He jogged up the short hill.

Julian had seen that strained smile a thousand times, usually before Gary was about to push him hard on what he wanted for the show. "Can you make it quick, Gar? I need to shower and don't want to be late for tonight's dinner."

Gary reached the driveway. "Sure, sure." He took a second to catch his breath. "Listen, are you giving my offer any more thought?"

"A little. But I haven't changed my mind."

"I heard about your hot air balloon ride this morning."

Julian nodded. Everybody knew, the gossip chain amongst the group more reliable than most news medias. It bothered him to have the private moment out there, but only Gary and Mamie understood about his past and the full importance.

"Big step. Now that you've done that, I figured...well, it was like a breakthrough. Right?

"Spare me the psychoanalysis, Gary." He moved closer. "I've found some peace of mind lately. I can now see I was doing the show for the wrong reasons and I'm not ready to jump in again. It's not a firm no, but I'm not ready to rush and make a decision."

Gary stepped back and shook his head. "You're crazy, man. They'll give you whatever you want. It's a deal of a lifetime."

"So? It's my life. What's in this for you if I return?"

"I won't lie. They're making it worth my time to talk to you. But I genuinely think I made a mistake firing you. You know how hot-headed I am sometimes."

Acting reasonable. Another Gary ploy, aimed at weakening Julian's stance. "Another reason to say no."

Gary shook his head. "You liked doing the show, didn't you?"

"I did. But my life has changed this past year and I'm not really sure what I want."

"Why? That girl you're sleeping with?"

Julian's shoulders tensed. Blunt Gary, they used to call him. "Mamie. And yes, she's part of it. But I like this job, too."

Gary looked away, his jaw drawn tight. When he snapped his gaze back to Julian, the tense lines of his face gave away frustration not visible until now. "I'm leaving tomorrow morning, when you and the others leave. Promise me you'll think about it? Can you at least do that for an old friend?"

With caution, he answered, "Sure. I'll sleep on it."

Gary rested a hand on his shoulder. "Thanks, buddy." He returned to the pool.

Julian felt helpless as a man about to be drawn and quartered. Two very different paths stretched out before him. Choosing one over the other could either be the biggest mistake of his life or the best thing he'd ever done.

* * * *

Ring. Ring. Ring...

Mamie sat on the bed's edge, her heart beating wildly while waiting for Allison to answer the phone. Of all days, this was the worst to play phone tag with someone. Now, with what Gary had seen, Mamie needed to talk to Allison even more urgently. What if she missed her again this time? Julian would be back soon and Allison needed to know how Gary had connected a thin thread tying her to the Covert Critic. Especially since she didn't trust the person who learned her secret.

Allison answered on the fifth ring. "Hey, I got your message but it's been hectic around here today."

"Thank God I got you. We've got a small problem."

She explained what just happened with Gary, including her lie that she wrote the piece for another publication. "My worry is he finds my name on our company website and draws his own conclusions."

"Shit. That's not good. Are you certain he's not trustworthy?"

"It's a gut read. He did say he'd keep it quiet, but he's got a good reason to tell someone else."

"Oh?"

"You know that fling we talked about?"

"Uh-huh…"

"Well, you should know, I've gotten close to the tour director, a man named Julian Gregory."

"Tour director? The very person whose tour you're writing about?"

"When you put it that way, it sounds so, well—"

"Inappropriate?"

"Kind of. What's going on with him isn't influencing my evaluation."

"The man who figured out your identity, does he know about you and the tour director?"

"Gary's his name and yes, he does. But I can't stress enough how the relationship isn't playing into my piece."

"Oh, Mamie." Disappointment in Allison's voice made Mamie wish she'd kept quiet. "I'm sure you think so, but how can you be certain? If Gary wanted to, once your guide is published, he could ruin the series reputation."

"I suppose, but I don't think that he has motive to do such a thing. However, I worry about something else."

"What else is there?"

Mamie talked about Gary's relationship to Julian on the show *Exploring the World with Eddie*. "Gary said the show's producers want him back."

"I've seen that show. Julian is Eddie? He's a celebrity?" She groaned. "That makes this worse. Is Gary the type to leak any of this to the media? I mean, it could bring people to our books. Everyone loves a good scandal."

"I don't think this qualifies as a scandal. Listen, I called, though, hoping you'd talk to legal, explain what's happened."

"Yes. I'll let them know you weren't to blame for his discovery."

"Do you think I can tell Julian my role with the publisher? In case he finds out from Gary, I don't want him blindsided."

"Absolutely not. At least until I talk to legal."

"Why not?"

"One, Gary just may stay quiet. So why risk telling another person? And two, did Felix call you about his latest plans to leave his job and who he wants to replace him?"

"He did. I'm honored he'd think of me and that the publisher is willing to take a chance on me. But—"

"You're the perfect candidate, and you'd get a significant raise in salary."

"It's very appealing." Mamie wanted to be as honest as possible with Allison. This week turned Mamie's worldview upside down. True, a new path work-wise could be exciting. But a life on the road? She wasn't certain that was right for her either. "I just need to make sure it's right for me."

"All the more reason to stay quiet about what you're doing on the tour. Nothing should point to you."

"But what if Gary tells him? He didn't like one bit that I was doing this behind Julian's back. A loyal friendship thing, I guess."

"Hopefully he won't say a word. Hold on." Some papers rustled in the background and Allison thanked her secretary, asking her to shut the door on the way out. "I'm back. We have to make sure your name doesn't go public as a fill-in. Even if someone knew you were a sub, speculation might run wild that you held the job permanently. You'd better hope that Gary keeps his mouth closed."

"Here's the thing, Allison. I like Julian and I don't like lying to him."

An audible sigh carried over the phone. "It's a chance you'll have to take. You know the success of this whole series, for all these years, has ridden on the fact that nobody knows who does these reviews. It's what gives the series five-star credibility. But sit tight while I get ahold of legal. But it may not be until tomorrow that they have an answer."

Disappointment slammed her chest. "Yes. I understand."

Just then, the villa door opened. The sound of footsteps coming toward the bedroom got louder.

"I'd better go."

Julian stood at the doorway, smiling at Mamie.

"Please, Mamie," Allison said. "Promise you won't say a word until I reach legal."

"I won't." She hung up and smiled at Julian. "How'd today go?"

He talked about the outing. His relaxed expression reminded her how much she wanted to enjoy this last night with him this way... Happy and without the added burden of her secret.

Or was that the excuse she needed to abide by Allison's request, knowing deep down Julian might be angry if he learned she'd misled him?

* * * *

"Thank you, Tina." Julian stood on the mock stage, a foot-high wooden platform at the patio. Above the stage hung a banner in bold letters reading Rock Out Talent Night. "Come on everyone, give her a hand."

The Wanderers clapped wildly over Tina's rendition of Melanie's "Brand New Key," a quirky number Julian had never heard before about a girl who likes a boy.

Tina blushed but took her bow. A band of flowers crowned her head and a colorful poncho covered her frame, making her look as if she'd time traveled to the new millennium from nineteen sixties Haight Ashbury.

The skills he'd seen here tonight were impressive. One couple dressed as Sonny and Cher. Besides singing "I've Got You, Babe," they did a few minutes of standup similar to the show from the early seventies, where Sonny played straight man to Cher's zingers.

Hopefully, he and Mamie could hold their own. She'd agreed to perform background vocals, complaining she wasn't a good singer.

Julian read the list to see who performed next. "After this next number, we'll have an intermission to enjoy the dessert table. I saw a preview in the kitchen. It'll be worth the wait. Without further adieu, let's give a big hand to a group calling themselves the Three Amigos, who'll be singing the Grand Funk Railroad hit "Some Kind of Wonderful.""

Bernie, Bob, and Joel swaggered to the stage, all wearing identical Hawaiian shirts. Joel's long-haired wig touched his shoulders and the other two men went from thinning gray hair to full heads of curls. Julian's parents had owned a Grand Funk Railroad album, and he found the seniors' attempts to mimic the band's appearance commendable.

He returned to his seat next to Mamie. Her seventies look came from a patterned gauze skirt she'd borrowed from Tina and a tight T-shirt worn with a lace choker necklace. An outfit she'd discussed in great detail with him while they got dressed, complaining that his jeans, sandals, and plain short-sleeved shirt didn't really represent the decade.

He draped an arm over the back of her chair and she moved closer to him. "You're a natural as MC. All that training as a TV host probably helped."

"I spent many years preparing for tonight's role. Not just anybody can host Rock Out Talent Night."

She chuckled. "Nope. It's certainly not a job for just anyone." She nestled against his side, and he tried not to think about her leaving tomorrow.

Glancing across the patio, Julian caught Gary watching them as he leaned against the building's stone wall. A cold stare. Julian shrugged it off. Yeah, Gary was pissed Julian wouldn't commit to returning to the show. So what?

What Gary didn't understand was how a return to his old routine didn't leave room for some new things he desired from his life. What that meant exactly, Julian wasn't sure. Not marriage. But to let himself get close to another person—an unthinkable idea in the past—felt right now.

Music poured from the two speakers attached to an iPod near the stage. Julian drew his attention away from Gary's demands to enjoy this act.

The upbeat opening had everyone clapping. Bernie stepped up first, singing about how he didn't need money or a fancy car because he had everything a man could want, even more than he could ask for.

He stepped back into the line and Joel took center stage. Looking directly at Tina, he crooned about how he didn't need to run around or stay out all night. Pointing at her, he winked before belting out his lyrics about his lovin' woman.

Tina let out a whoop then blew him a kiss. The audience devoured their antics, swaying and clapping to the rock beat.

As they got to the chorus, each directed their words to the women who they'd brought with them on this trip. Some married for decades, others finding love in their second marriage and dating. Yet all expressing affection for the women they cared about. An open display, regardless of their age or the passage of time.

The bonds of love. A need for such closeness unexpectedly flooded Julian's heart. A heart shut off because it hurt. Some Mr. Tough guy he turned out to be.

These men were happy, caring deeply for women who'd been in their lives for years. Togetherness appeared to make their lives richer. Like what he and Mamie had shared this entire trip, especially this morning during the hot air balloon ride. A moment of growth, for each of them.

He turned to her and she smiled. Leaning over, he kissed her with all the tenderness brewing inside his chest.

She leaned back. "What was that for?"

"For what you did this morning." He took her hand. "I'll have some time off touring soon. How would you feel if I came to visit you in the States?"

A flash of conflict crossed her face, but she smiled. "I'd like that."

"Anything wrong?"

"No. I just want to make sure I can take time off work."

"We'll work it out."

She nodded and returned to watching the show.

While the men sang, Julian listened with a weightlessness he couldn't ever recall feeling, finally aware of something those men on stage probably already knew. The fear of losing a person you cared about was a lousy reason to avoid love.

Chapter 22

Tables emptied when Julian announced intermission. He returned to his seat near Mamie. "We're up after dessert. Think we should practice once more?"

She frowned and stood. "I think what would help more is some tiramisù from the dessert table after a quick trip to the restroom."

"How about I get us both some dessert?"

"Now you're talking." She rubbed his shoulder and walked away.

He couldn't take his eyes off her. The gentle sway of her hips, the long curve of her neck. Everything he'd noticed the first time he saw her, but somehow different. Even her slight limp was less noticeable. Maybe because she carried herself with more confidence than the day she'd arrived.

He rose from his seat and headed for the long line at the dessert table. A car pulled into the compound entrance. The headlights shut off and someone got out. Julian bypassed the table and walked toward the car. Nobody else was expected here tonight.

A tall, slender woman approached him. As she walked closer to a lamppost at the walkway's end, Julian froze. Claudia? He'd never met his boss in person, but he'd Skyped with her enough times to know her face.

"Hello, Julian," she said, her German accent crisp and cool. A nearby lamppost cast its beam on her. In person, Claudia was prettier than he'd remembered, with a pert nose and wide eyes. Last time they'd Skyped, she had shoulder-length hair. Now the blond locks were short and layered.

"What are you doing here?"

"I got an anonymous call about this tour. Evidently, things aren't going as I expect."

Shock momentarily held Julian's tongue in check. The people he traveled with didn't seem to mind his rule violations. So who would've called?

Julian wasn't about to hand over the problems until he fully understood why she came. "What isn't going according to plan?"

"I knew something was going on," she snapped, her English crisp with emphasis on the vowels and all her "w" sounds spoken as a "v." "One of your passengers transferred a ticket to someone else, but they failed to call me until after the tour had started. But it seems you let them on anyway." She raised a brow. "Without my approval."

Shit. "Who called you?"

"A Mr. Carrol called several days into the tour. He gave the ticket to a passenger name Mamie Weber and, only after the tour began, he realized he needed to let me know. So he called to verbally confirm that he'd authorized the transfer. You should have contacted me then."

Julian had spoken to Claudia one night in Siena. "Why didn't you ask me about it when you called me to confirm the villa stay?"

"A moot point by then, but my call was your chance to tell me. You had clearly broken the rules; however, I needed you to finish out the tour. To be honest, I considered not firing you. But when I got an anonymous call you are dating a passenger, I decided to come out myself to find out what you were doing."

Everything he'd been afraid of this year suddenly didn't matter. The hot air balloon ride boosted him with new power. Even though he liked the job, the safety net it offered was no longer needed.

Claudia pinned him with her hard gaze. "Well? What do you have to say to defend yourself?"

"Nothing really. Mamie Weber is a guest on this tour. It just happened and she had a letter showing the package transfer."

Claudia raised a thin brow. "And the dating accusation? Is it true?"

"It is. I'm not ashamed or going to lie about it. Your rules are inflexible, Claudia. You need to look at circumstances, not jump to conclusions."

"Don't tell me how to run my company. I would feel justified in firing you now."

He took a breath, realizing she was right about that. "Listen, I like working for Wanderlust Excursions. But before you fire me, meet Mamie, talk to the passengers—"

She held up her hand. "*Nein*. After you get them to the airport tomorrow, you're relieved of your duties with my tour company."

Gary stepped out from the building's shadow. "Good. Maybe you'll reconsider my job offer?"

That exact second it hit Julian who might have reported his dating a passenger to Claudia. Of all the slimy things to do, although it shouldn't have surprised Julian one bit.

"Who's he?" Claudia motioned with her chin toward Gary.

"My old boss." Julian wanted to haul off and punch Gary, but he bit back his anger and waved a hand Claudia's way. "Gary, meet Claudia, owner and president of Wanderlust Excursions."

Gary tipped his head to her, but quickly turned his attention to Julian. "So? Come on. You don't need this two-bit operation. You can make more money if you come back to the show."

"What show?" Claudia stepped closer.

Julian ignored her. "Listen, Gary, I told you earlier. I like this job." He shot a glance at Claudia, hoping she'd reconsider. "Besides, now that I've met Mamie, I don't want the commitment of filming and the tight schedules."

"Filming what?" Claudia tipped her head, her expression confused.

Gary looked at Claudia. "Julian spent many years as host of a TV adventure show, *Exploring the World with Eddie*."

Her eyes widened. "You are Eddie?"

"I was." Julian turned back to Gary, rage for him flowing to the brim. The guy hated losing and Julian should've known he'd do anything to win their battle. "And I'm not interested in doing it again."

"Before you decide, you'd better make sure you know everything about Mamie. She's not being honest with you."

"What do you mean?" He stilled, not sure what kind of game Gary was playing now, but the smirk on his face suggested he had something good.

"You know those travel books, *The Covert Critic's Guides*?"

Julian had read an article about them in a trade journal. "I do."

"I think Mamie is the Covert Critic."

"That's ridiculous."

"Not really. She's been reviewing your tour this whole time and I caught her using one of the Covert Critic books as a guide."

Claudia mumbled something in German, then in English marked with clear sarcasm, she added, "Nice work, Julian. See what happens when you break the rules? I can't imagine what kind of review my company will get now."

"Claudia, could you just..." He turned to Gary. This had to be a lie. Mamie would've told him this if it were true. Wouldn't she? Julian wanted to believe in her, in them, so he pushed Gary for details. "How do you know all this?"

He told Julian about finding her notebook with an outline from the publisher and confronting her. "She wouldn't admit it. I'm not sure you want to make your choice about a career based on a relationship with a woman who isn't truthful with you."

"You promised you wouldn't tell."

Mamie's voice came from behind Julian and he turned around. *Promised you wouldn't tell?* All the warmth for her he'd built up over these past two weeks faded into a distant place, one he tried to reach for but couldn't grab.

She stared at Gary. "How could you do this?"

Gary shrugged. "Hey, he just got fired from the tour company." He pointed to Claudia. "I figured he needed a job and the only reason he's not taking the one I'm offering is because of you. He deserved the truth."

Her gaze drifted to Julian. "Is that true? You're fired?"

"Forget about that." Agony ripped him apart, but he needed the truth from her mouth, not Gary's. "You've been lying to me?"

"Not exactly lying." Her face contorted with pain. "I've signed a contract with my publisher that says I can't talk about it with anybody."

"But I bent every rule for you. Put my faith in you." The pain of her not trusting him stung. How stupid he'd been. "But on this one thing, you couldn't trust me?"

"It's not so black and white. I tried to get permission. I wanted to tell you, very badly."

"Hey! Julian, Mamie...." Bob stuck his head around the corner. "You're on."

"Perfect timing." Julian walked away, mumbling, "I'll do this alone."

* * * *

Mamie waited until Julian turned the corner. She spun to a pretty woman with crisp, short blond hair and round eyes. Her accent sounded German. "Who are you?"

"I'm Claudia, owner of Wanderlust Excursions. I hope your review won't be negatively affected by what Julian did."

"No! Of course it won't. I've had a wonderful tour. Julian does his job extremely well."

"You say that, but how can I be sure you mean it?"

Gary snorted. "Your credibility is sliding downhill fast."

Before Mamie could respond, Claudia turned to Gary. "You. I recognize your voice. You're the anonymous caller who told me about Julian dating a passenger. *Ja?*"

Gary shrugged, showing no outward concern he'd been caught. "So what if I did?"

Mamie couldn't believe this guy. But she needed to make sure Julian didn't get blamed for everything that went wrong. She turned to Claudia. "Julian pushed hard to keep me off this tour. Please, blame me for what he did. I pushed and he resisted."

"But in the end, he gave in to you?" Claudia raised a thin brow.

"Yes."

"You will write the report and all Julian's infractions will no doubt be reflected."

Mamie shook her head. "No. I told you before, I have nothing bad to say about your operation."

"I believe it when I see it in print."

Mamie's blood pressure rose. Claudia gave new meaning to the word stubborn. "There is one thing that could be a problem."

"Ah, see! What is it?"

"The total lack of flexibility from the main office."

Claudia's dark eyes opened wide, but Mamie swung around and faced Gary. "As far as you go, I can't believe you'd do all this just to get him to go back."

"Hey, a producer's got to do what he's got to do. I've got people breathing down my neck about Julian's return."

She shook her head. "I don't know how you can live with yourself."

Turning away from them both, she rushed toward the patio. As she rounded the corner, Julian stood with his back to the others, picking up the guitar leaning against a stone wall that Beppe's brother had let him borrow. Dread filled her heart as she approached him.

She came up from behind. "Julian, I wanted to tell you but—"

"Save it, Mamie. I can handle this number by myself. Now if you don't mind, I'm up."

He walked away from her and took a seat at one of two bar stools they'd requested on stage to do their song. Tuning the guitar, he ignored her.

He cleared his throat and the noise level died down. "I've never told any of you, but my dad went to Woodstock. He was twenty-one at the time. He also taught me how to play the guitar."

"Why, you rascal." Bob's face brightened. "Holding out on us?"

Julian smiled, but it lacked in his usual enthusiasm. "Guess I was."

She'd ruined everything. All the trust he'd handed her this morning meant very little if she couldn't reciprocate. Her eyes filled with tears.

She left the patio area just as Julian started to strum his guitar to the song they'd practiced multiple times. The idea he'd rejected her hurt too much for her to stay and listen. Not that it wasn't deserved. She'd betrayed him, although she never intended to hurt him by keeping her job secret.

She walked around the compound, dazed and upset, not really thinking about where she was going. Eventually she ended up outside Julian's apartment. The only place she really had to go.

She wandered to his bedroom and fell onto the bed, finally giving into the tears she'd fought. Everything about these past two weeks bombarded her like hard pellets. Nothing made sense. Her choices. His. The loyalty she clung to for her job, albeit a legal necessity but a rule. And yet, she so easily asked Julian to break the rules he'd been expected to follow. She'd never been more wrong but couldn't change it now. The myriad of thoughts inside her head made her temples throb, punishment for the mistake she'd made. She closed her eyes and took her punishment, drifting off with her regrets.

She woke shivering. The fog of a nap made it hard to open her eyes. As she turned her head to the side, she saw the time. Eleven p.m. Would he even return here tonight? She crawled under the covers and tried to get warm, knowing she needed to own one very real fact; Julian had every right to feel angry.

But she'd always be grateful to him. And while she might have owed him honesty, she gave him all she could within the legal restraints of her job. She'd tried to give him more of herself. Like stepping into the hot air balloon basket. Mostly so he could face his fears, but also to face her own. She cared about him, more than she could even comprehend in this short amount of time. Two weeks. Barely a blip on the radar of life.

Yet they were two weeks that had flipped her world right side up. She no longer wanted to hide in her apartment. She also didn't want Felix's job, but did believe she needed a change.

All she knew right now was that the gift of time had once again been bestowed upon her here in Tuscany, yielding some generous rewards.

New friends. Special moments shared with Julian. Good food and drink. Beautiful scenery. Every encounter presented a world filled with possibilities. A world she couldn't have imagined while sitting inside her apartment alone and sad.

Faith, love, and life. Three things she took for granted many years ago, but the possibility of them was restored. Maybe it had been the long talks with Julian or the magic of Tuscany. It didn't matter where it came from.

She'd changed and deep down, she'd always known all of this would have to come to an end.

She got up from the bed and took out her notebook with a pen. Propping a pillow against the teak headboard, she returned to the bed and opened the notebook onto her lap. Even if she had to leave, she couldn't do it without Julian knowing how much he mattered to her. Given his anger, she wouldn't be surprised if he didn't come back here tonight.

So she started to write...

Dear Julian,

I never meant to hurt you or lie. I'm sorry you had to learn about my real purpose on this trip the way you did...

Her lids got heavy but the pen kept moving. She struggled to fight sleep because she wanted Julian to understand the reasons behind everything she'd done.

Chapter 23

Julian opened Beppe's car door and laid the guitar case on the backseat. He walked around to the car's front and leaned on the hood. From here, he could see the bedroom light on in his villa. He wasn't ready to face her yet.

Damn her, stealing his trust while she walked around with a lie. Why had she done any of the things she did for him? Was it for her story, to give it a human element?

Doing his show had taught him that drama pulled in viewers. Maybe adding some color to her review about meeting an adventurer gone sour and her steps to save him would make for better sales. He'd been stupid. Real stupid. Or was he? Every second spent in that hot air balloon with her seemed so right, exactly where he'd been meant to be.

A twig snapped and Julian looked up. Beppe approached, walking toward the car in a path of light from a nearby lamppost. He took a bite of a cannoli. "The partygoers have all gone to bed."

"It was a fun show." Julian tried to sound normal.

"*Sì*. What happened earlier? And why was Claudia here?"

"She found out I let Mamie on the tour and, well, everything else. She pretty much fired me."

He nodded. "Maybe I can talk to her?"

"At this point, I'd appreciate any good words that might get her to change her mind. I also found out tonight Mamie has been lying to all of us."

"Mamie? How so?"

"She's reviewing the tour for a pretty big travel publication. People aren't always who you think they are."

Beppe remained quiet for a moment then said, "You know, my nonna used to say '*Accade di più in un'ora che in cent'anni*.'"

Julian considered the words. "'More happens in an hour than in a hundred years'?"

"*Sì.* Look at you. I have known you since were seven. You've gone through some big changes, but they all happened in an instant."

"It's true. Like my parents' death, or watching another man die?"

"Yes," Beppe spoke softly. "Or like meeting Mamie."

He crossed his arms over his chest. "Yes, well, she's on this tour under false pretenses. How can I trust anything between us now?"

"I see." He slowly finished off the cannoli then wiped his hands on the side of his pants. "Even if she is, I know her desire to get you on that hot air balloon came from a genuine place."

"How can you be sure?"

"Because we talked about her husband and child. When she asked me to get my cousin to do this, she told me how scared she was, but she knew her husband would want to see her do it. And she wanted to do it for you."

Julian didn't want to believe it, but the bond between them during that ride still carried undeniable power. "So you're saying I'm an ass for being mad?"

"I see a different man than the one that started this tour. A short time for such a transformation. It's either Mamie, or these Woodstock worshipers." Beppe laughed.

Julian couldn't stop a smile. "They are a fun group."

"Yes, but maybe not the reason you have changed."

"Maybe."

"Don't let her leave here believing you don't see that."

Julian looked away, feeling some shame over his prior behavior.

"Now you need to get off my car, so I can go home." Beppe put a hand on Julian's shoulder. "You know you are like a brother to me."

"And you to me."

Julian hugged Beppe, lucky to have found a brother in a friend.

Beppe got in the car and took off down the dark driveway. Julian headed to the villa. He entered, the place quiet and dark except for the bedroom light. Walking to a spot just outside the bedroom doorway, he saw Mamie curled on her side, asleep on the bed. The Yankee emblem on her T-shirt rose and fell with each long breath. He stepped closer.

A notebook lay on top of the blanket. He glanced at the open page and saw the words *"Dear Julian."*

He leaned closer to read the first lines.

I never meant to hurt you or lie. I'm sorry you learned about my real purpose on this trip the way you did. If it matters, the piece I planned to write contained nothing but good things. Because it is the truth.

I didn't share why I first came to Tuscany for one simple reason: my employer required me to sign a legally binding agreement not to make my identity known as part of this book series. Otherwise, I'd have told you, not at first but most definitely after these past days together.

It occurs to me as I sit here writing this that maybe us parting on not-so-great terms makes the end of our two weeks easier. The universe's forces might have known it wouldn't be easy if everything had remained so good.

We live in two different worlds. Your choices and mine don't follow the same path. And we both have choices to make about our careers at this junction.

For what it's worth, these two weeks have been the best I've had in a long time. This beautiful country will always live in my heart. And so will all the moments we have shared. I will never forget how you made me see beauty I might otherwise have missed.

I hope that

She must've fallen asleep. Julian swallowed the hard lump forming in his throat.

He studied her beautiful face, so peaceful in sleep, no longer showing the pain he'd seen when he'd turned his back on her on the patio a few hours ago. Now, slumber brought a pure and undisturbed expression. Not that of a woman who'd lost the people she loved most in the world, but somehow remained tough enough to keep going, board a plane alone and take on this trip when she still deeply missed her old life.

He rounded the bed and lay beside her, taking her in his arms and drawing her close.

She stirred and rolled to face him. "Hi. When did you come in?"

"A few minutes ago. I read the note you were writing me. Sorry."

"It's okay. I wasn't sure you'd come back tonight."

"I wasn't either. Beppe knocked some common sense into me."

The tense lines of her face softened with somber smile. "I know learning the truth about my work was a shock. I hope you understand I didn't like keeping it from you."

"I do. Coming from Gary, it had a little more punch." He reached up and traced her cheek with his finger, trying to accept the fact that he needed to let her go because it was what she needed. "The letter you wrote, you're right. We both do have to figure out our lives."

Tears welled in her eyes. "Trying to date on two different continents isn't a good way to start new lives."

"I guess it isn't." He wanted to believe they could, but also understood why Mamie needed to spread her wings after the loss of her husband.

"Doesn't mean we can't keep in touch," she said, a hopeful tone in her voice.

"Of course. Maybe someday our paths will cross again. Friends forever?"

Mamie nodded as a tear slid along her cheek. "Yes. Forever."

She buried her head against his chest and he held her tight, breathing in the scent of her hair, the softness of her skin. Little details he'd probably forget after she was gone. He closed his eyes and soon his mind drifted into a hazy state thinking about tomorrow and the trip to the airport. Although his heart ached just thinking about it, he understood they had no other choice.

He'd finally figured out his life, closed the door on a past that had haunted him since his boyhood.

And he had Mamie to thank.

Chapter 24

September

Julian looked at his watch. "You'll have an hour and a half to walk around on your own and have lunch. Then meet me back here at one."

A hand shot up from the back of the crowd.

"Yes, Mr. Levine?"

The tall, thin man pushed his wire frame glasses up his long nose. "Might I suggest we synchronize our watches? Yesterday a few people were two minutes late."

The group of actuaries from a firm in New York City had booked the "History Buff's Guide to Tuscany" tour and they had a yen for exactness even Julian couldn't quite compete with.

"Sure." He glanced at his watch. "I've got twelve-o-two?"

The others looked at their watches, with a few making adjustments. He tried not to laugh. No matter what group he traveled with, he wanted them feel comfortable.

Another hand shot up, this time Melinda Honeycutt, a sixty-something single traveler who wore pleated slacks and pearls every day. "Is it true you used to host an adventure show where you participated in some risky stunts?"

He smiled. "That was me."

Claudia may have only taken him back because she loved including in her marketing brochure that one of her Italian tour directors used to be a well-known travel show host.

Melinda shook her head, the way a mother might reprimand a child. "By my calculations, I'd say you're lucky to be alive."

"You may be right. Now that I'm older and wiser, I've learned that it's the ordinary things in life that can yield the sweetest rewards. No odds needed on that. Enjoy lunch and see you back here at one. Sharp."

He walked half a block to his favorite cafe in San Gimignano—not far from Paolo's restaurant—and ordered a pizza, then checked his email. Claudia had sent a message to all the tour directors, reminding them she needed to fill two new positions. Business was good.

He thought back to how he'd almost lost this job. Maybe it was the call Mamie's publisher made to Claudia two days after Mamie had boarded the plane to fly home. Claudia all but begged him to stay with the touring company, making it easier to send Gary on his way. Even if Julian hadn't stayed at Wanderlust Excursions, he wouldn't have gone to work for Gary again.

The simple blessings found in each day he spent taking tourists around Italy was all he needed or wanted. Well, almost.

His phone buzzed with a text message. He pushed the button and saw it was from Mamie.

Hey! Miss me still? Where are you today?

His heart filled with longing for her, overshadowed by a wave of sadness, their distance from each other too great. He typed back, *Yup, I miss you every single day. I'm in San Gimignano right now. Thinking of you.* He smiled with the thought. They texted almost daily.

San Gimignano! You know you're killing me, right?

He laughed and typed, *Same old, same old for me. Tell me about the first day at the new job. Do you like it?*

Thanks to Joel and his connections, Mamie found a new job at a small publishing house and moved from her condo in the New York City suburbs to upstate New York. A big step that made Julian so proud of her. She'd told him she loved living upstate because, in some ways, it reminded her of Tuscany. Since she'd left, each time they talked on Skype he couldn't miss how she possessed a new energy. At least compared to those early days on the trip with the Wanderers. It made him feel good to see her this way and he remained thankful to still have her in his life. Even if it was in such a remote way.

His phone pinged with her response.

So far so good. But it's only been four hours. Oh! I got an invitation to go to a Halloween party that the Wanderers are holding in Bethel, NY, where the Woodstock concert was held. It's close enough for me to drive. I can't wait to see them.

Fondness for the Wanderers settled in his chest. He'd never, ever forget that tour. He typed back, *They sent me one, too. I'm scheduled to guide a tour in southern Italy that week. Bummer.*

Big bummer. I'll be thinking of you. It may be a while before I can get a vacation with the new job. But you can always come here... Enjoy San Gimignano.

Julian's food arrived. He put away his phone, wishing more than anything he could see Mamie again.

* * * *

"So this is the spot?" Mamie took in the colorful, late October foliage surrounding a wide-open hillside at Bethel Woods. A modern-day homage to the concert that would never die in the minds of those who attended. Mamie tried to imagine the crowds, the music filling the air, and the general message of peace, love, and rock n' roll.

"This is it. People everywhere you can see and a large stage at the bottom of the hill," Bernie said, his voice soft and reminiscent. He glanced at Mamie. "You know I met Sandy here."

"I remember." Bernie had shared the story one night after dinner while they'd stayed at the villa.

"We were sitting over there." He motioned toward a large clump of tress. "It was during day two. Canned Heat was singing 'Going Up the Country' and this gorgeous blonde walked by." He paused for a second and a slow smiled grew on his face. "It was love at first sight."

Mamie's heart softened. After all these years, their love was still obvious. "That's sweet, Bernie."

Footsteps sounded on pavement near the grass's edge and Sandra appeared between them while tying the belt on a knee-length sweater. "It's chillier out here than I thought. Aren't you cold, Mamie, in that light blazer?"

"I'm good. Maybe living in Ithaca is toughening me up to the cold."

Sandra slipped her arm around Bernie's waist as she glanced to Mamie. "Do you like your new job?"

"I do. Being an acquiring editor is a bit more like what I used to do before the car accident."

Sandra nodded and frowned. "Then I'm glad you're happy. Joel said you work with his friend now?"

Joel and Tina. They had Mamie's back. On the flight back to New York, they'd sat a few rows back. During the flight, the two of them talked to her about having to leave Julian behind and her past. When Joel learned about her work background, he'd mentioned his friend who owned a small press.

Mamie smiled. "Yup. I can thank him for a new start in a new town."

Sandra rubbed Mamie's arm with motherly affection then scanned the empty hillside. "It really is pretty around here."

"I was just telling Mamie about the day we met." Bernie glanced down at his wife. "Remember, we were sitting over there?" He again pointed to the tree clump.

"No we weren't. We were on the other side."

"Are you sure?"

"Positive." Sandra shook her head. "You're getting more and more forgetful. Did you even remember Canned Heat was playing?"

"Of course." He furrowed his brows. "Right, Mamie?"

"Yup. He even called you a gorgeous blonde."

Sandra beamed. "Now I now he's losing it. You'd better get inside. Bob needs help setting something up. Mamie, don't rush. It's a beautiful day. Enjoy the view."

After they left, Mamie got out her phone and snapped a few pictures. She texted one to Julian.

I'm with the Wanderers! Here's the famous concert grounds.

Julian. God she missed him. He'd become her best friend. One who texted her every day and often was the last person she communicated with before bedtime. Once a week they'd Skype. She missed him and hated to admit it, but their closeness was forming a bond so similar to love, she had no other way to describe it.

When she accrued some vacation time in the spring, she'd consider a trip to Italy. But it seemed so far away.

She brushed aside the blue mood about to form. Life had been good lately. On her own, she'd managed to start a new life in a new place. She went to her office every day, had made friends in the upstate community. The colleges nearby kept the crowds young, and visitors passed through to sample vineyards on the Finger Lakes. When she'd described it that way to Julian, and shared that it reminded her of Tuscany, he'd said, "All that's missing is some Renaissance art and me."

She laughed along with him, but the part about him only reminded her how he was the one thing missing from the new picture of her life.

She snapped a few more photos, capturing the color palette of autumn found in the sienna, red, and yellow trees. Nature's renewal. Change, needed for the promise of spring growth. Like her, and the trip to Tuscany that changed her outlook on life.

Her phone pinged.

The famous Woodstock grounds, huh? Pretty place. What are you doing now?

She typed back, *Just enjoying the view.*
Seconds later, he replied.

Me too. Turn around.

Turn around?

She slowly turned. Julian stood, staring back with a huge smile. Since the last time they'd talked on Skype, he'd cut his hair shorter but he'd kept the tidy beard and mustache. "Hi, gorgeous."

"What are you...you didn't tell me—"

"Surprise!" He approached, arms opened. "How about a hug?"

Mamie rushed into his arms. As they closed around her, she absolutely knew there was no better place in the world than right here.

"Oh my God, Julian." Tears filled her eyes and she held him tight, not wanting to ever let him go again. "I can't believe you're here. Nobody told me."

As she blinked to clear her eyes, she spotted Sandra and Bernie near the main building, watching them. She leaned back, holding onto Julian's shoulders. "Did Sandra and Bernie know?"

Julian waved to the couple. "They all did. Sandra came and got Bernie when I arrived to give us time alone."

Mamie laughed. "Why those stinkers."

"Blame me. I wanted to surprise you. Then my flight into Stewart got in three hours late. I'd planned to be here when you arrived."

Mamie loved how being close to him felt so natural and right. "I can't believe it." The way they parted returned to her. Waking next to him the morning they had to leave. Her teary goodbye at the airport, both of them making promises to stay friends forever using today's technology. "I've missed you. A lot." A gust of wind blew a strand of her hair across her cheek.

"Me, too." He reached out and tucked the hair behind her ear then cupped her cheek with his palm. "I've missed everything about you."

"You know, when we were texting a few minutes ago, I was thinking how every feeling I've ever had for you just keeps getting stronger and stronger."

His eyes softened, like they had during their magical first kiss. "Yeah? Me, too." He softly pressed his lips to hers then leaned back. "Missed me like that?"

"Exactly like that. How long are you staying?"

"Two weeks. In fact"—he drew her close—"if you'll have me, I'd love to stay with you."

"You'd better!" Mamie slipped her hands around his neck, stretched up and kissed him deeply. She could sense the others watching and didn't care.

When the kiss ended, he smiled. "I've wanted to do that for months now."

"Guess I did, too. Technology is a wonderful thing, but it has limits."

He laughed. "Those limits. We'll have to figure that one out. You know, Claudia is thinking of branching out with some tours in the States. It could be an option career-wise for me."

Mamie couldn't believe how her day just changed on a dime. But wasn't that the way it worked?

He reached down and took her hand. "Every single day since you took off on that plane, it seems I can't go to sleep at night unless I've said good night to you."

"Same for me." She squeezed his hand tight and vowed not to let go until she had to.

He blinked out at the hillside. She turned to look at the view, too. The bright afternoon sun made the golden leaves blaze.

"Wow, this view, it's even more powerful in person. The sacred grounds my dad used to talk about."

"I'll bet he'd be thrilled you are here."

Julian nodded, his expression solemn.

"I know I am."

He turned to her and smiled, genuine and glowing. "Want to walk down there with me? I want to see the memorial thing at the bottom of the hill."

"Sure."

They started down the hill, hand in hand.

Mamie glanced his way, still not believing that he was really here. "I wish I'd known so I could take some time off work."

"Oh, your boss said he'd let you take what you need."

"My boss? You talked to my boss?"

"Joel helped me out. Said Dan was a friend of his and he'd explain what was going on. To show my thanks, Joel said I had to send his friend a signed publicity photo. My Eddie days are over, but I figured to get time with you, I'd do it."

She laughed. "Wait? So Dan knew about this and all the Wanderers? Only I was left out in the dark?"

"Yup. It was a two-continent conspiracy. Just so I could have this moment."

She couldn't believe how all the forces in her life had made this happen, while she happily went about her day oblivious to it. "I guess I'll forgive them."

Yes, she had no doubt she would. Too much of her life had been spent in real darkness, and the efforts of every single person to give her this surprise gift warmed her heart. Hand in hand, they continued down the hill. Happiness. She no longer took it lightly.

In case you missed it, here's an excerpt from the first book in the Blue Moon Lake series:

SHARE THE MOON

Sometimes trust is the toughest lesson to learn.

Sophie Shaw is days away from signing a contract that will fulfill her dream of owning a vineyard. For her, it's a chance to restart her life and put past tragedies to rest. But Duncan Jamieson's counter offer blows hers out to sea.

Duncan still finds Sophie as appealing as he had during boyhood vacations to the lake. Older and wiser now, he has his own reasons for wanting the land. His offer, however, hinges on a zoning change approval.

Bribery rumors threaten the deal and make Sophie wary of Duncan, yet she cannot deny his appeal. When her journalistic research uncovers a Jamieson family secret, trust becomes the hardest lesson for them both.

A Lyrical e-book on sale now.

Learn more about Sharon at
http://www.kensingtonbooks.com/author.aspx/31604

Chapter 1

New Moon: When the moon, positioned between the earth and sun, nearly disappears, leaving only darkness.

November

The sabotaged kayaks beckoned. Sophie Shaw trod a thin layer of ice pellets on the lawn as she headed to the lake's edge, where eight boats waited to be returned to the storage rack. The fickle New England weather had offered sleet-dropping clouds an hour earlier. Now, a wink from the sun reflected against Blue Moon Lake.

She dragged the first boat up a small incline, annoyed some bored teenagers had considered destruction of property entertainment. Growing up she and her friends had respected the local businesses.

A UPS truck screeched to a stop in front of a row of shops on Main Street. The driver hopped out and ran into Annabelle's Antiques with a box tucked under his arm. Sophie glanced both ways along the road for signs of Matt, whose new driver's license and clunker car played to every mother's fears. Fifteen minutes earlier, she'd texted him for help with the boat mess. He'd replied "k."

Sophie's flats glided along the slick lawn. She gripped the cord of a bright orange sea kayak and, using two hands, struggled backward up the slope. Her foot skidded. The heel of her shoe wobbled for security but instead, her toes lifted off the ground and flashed toward the clear sky. The burning skid of the cord ripped across her palms just as her other foot lifted and launched her airborne. *Thud!*

Air whooshed from her lungs. Pain coursed through her shoulder blades, neck, and spine. The ground's chilly dampness seeped into her cotton khaki pants, raising goose bumps on her skin. Seconds passed without breath before she managed to swallow a gulp.

Lying flat on her back, she stared at the cornflower blue sky and spotted a chalky slice of the moon. The night Henry died, a similar crescent had hung from the heavens, barely visible nestled among the glittering stars. She prepared for the scrape that threatened to tear the gouge of her scarred heart. Seven years. Seven painful years. She closed her eyes and after a few seconds, the weight of sadness lifted off her chest.

Tears gathered along her lower lashes. She pushed a strand of unruly long hair from her face. Footsteps crunched on the ice pellets and headed her way.

"Matthew Shaw…" Fury pooled in her jaw as she resisted the urge to yell at her son. "You'd better have a good excuse for taking so long."

A man with cinnamon hair, short on the sides with gentle waves on top, knelt at her side. She studied the strong outline of his cheeks and the slight bump on the bridge of his angular nose that gave him a rugged touch, but he wasn't familiar.

"Are you okay?" He searched her face.

The stranger hovered above. Tall treetops, clinging to the last of their earth-toned foliage, served as a backdrop to her view. A vertical crease separated his sandy brows. She couldn't pry herself from his vivid blue eyes, in part stunned from the fall, but also by her first responder.

For several long seconds she stared, and then mumbled, "I think so. Just a little shocked."

A whiff of his musk cologne revived her with the subtle charm of a southern preacher casting his congregation under his spell.

He frowned. "Does it hurt to move anything?"

"Sometimes it did before I fell."

The stranger's face softened and his lips curved upward. "A sense of humor, huh? That's a good sign."

"I suppose." His deep voice relaxed her like a cup of chamomile tea, the balanced and certain tone of his words easing her wounded spirit. Maybe this guy was a sign her rotten luck might change. "So, where's your white horse?"

"In the stable. Today I came in the white Camry." He motioned with a wave of his hand to a corner of the parking lot.

She pushed up on her elbow to look and a sharp pain jabbed her neck. "Ow!"

"Careful." His smile disappeared. "I was on my way over to help when you fell. You hit pretty hard."

The heat of embarrassment skittered up her cheeks. Not only had he witnessed her spastic aerobics, but she never played the distressed-damsel-on-the-dirty-ground card. A woman proficient at fly-fishing, who learned how to drive in a pickup truck and who, in her job as a journalist, had uncovered a corrupt politician, should be up and running by now.

"Go slow." His request suggested doling out orders came easy. "May I help?"

She nodded. He slipped a gentle hand into hers. The chill coating her skin melted against his warm touch. His well-groomed nails and thick fingers suggested he didn't work outdoors, rather the clean hands of a man who spent his days in an office. No wedding band either. He helped her sit and studied her as if a question perched on the edge of his thoughts.

"Can I call someone?" He blinked. "Your husband?"

"Oh, I'm not married." She caught the slight twitch of his mouth. "My son's supposed to be on his way to restack the boats."

Since her divorce from Mike, she'd concluded the available men in Northbridge were as predictable as the assortment at the dollar rental video store, filled with decade-old hits she'd seen so many times they held little interest. This man was a refreshing change.

"Ready to try to stand?" He took her by the elbow and she nodded.

Once on her feet, their hands remained together.

He glanced at them and let his drop. "You'll probably think this is crazy but—"

"Sophie?" The owner of Griswold's Café stood across the street and wiped his hands on a stained white apron. He'd placed the call to her father to alert them about the vandalism at Dad's boat shed. "You okay?"

"I'm fine." She waved. "Thanks."

She returned to the newcomer's gaze, as blue as the deep Caribbean Sea and as shiny as a starburst.

He raised his dirt-stained hands. "You might want to check yours."

Sure enough, her palms carried the same smudges from the impact of her fall. "Hold on. I have something to clean us off."

She trotted to her car, hoping the backside of her blazer covered any mess on the back of her pants.

After finding a package of wipes in the center console, she cleaned herself spotless and peeked in the rearview mirror. Her dark chocolate curls scattered with the freewill of a reckless perm. She neatened them with her fingertips then grabbed her cell and tried to call Matt but landed in his voice mail. The second she hung up, the phone rang. Bernadette's name showed on the display.

"Hey."

"Is your speech ready for tonight? You're our star speaker."

Bernadette always latched onto a crusade. The first was in third grade, a petition over the slaughter of baby seals for their skins. For tonight's public hearing, Bernadette had promised everyone the fight of her life. Her special interest group's concern about the large-scale development on Blue Moon Lake proposed by Resort Group International was a sore topic for many local residents, especially Sophie.

"Better find a new star speaker. There's a change of plans." Sophie readied herself for a negative reaction. "I'm covering the story for the paper now."

"You? Has Cliff lost his mind?"

"No. The other reporter can't do the assignment. Her father had a stroke earlier today. Cliff wanted to take the story himself, but I insisted he stick to his job as editor and let me do mine. I even made a five dollar bet I'd get a headline-worthy, bias-free quote from the company president."

"Do you think you can? I mean, RGI stole that land right out from under your nose. What was it…three days before signing the contract?"

Those were almost Cliff's exact words, along with some mumbling about how the paper's cheap new owner had cut his staff and he saw no other choice. "Two days."

"Honey, why would you want this story?"

"I have my reasons. This won't be the first time one of us needed to report on something close to us."

"Yeah, but wouldn't some public chastising against the corporate giant be good for your soul?"

"In a way." Sophie hesitated then decided to tell her best friend the truth. "Look, this is a chance to redeem myself. Prove to Cliff I really *can* stick to my journalist's creed after…well, you know, what happened with Ryan Malarkey."

"Mmm, forgot about him. He makes all us lawyers look bad." A long pause filled the air. "Guess that's a valid reason."

Sophie still harbored guilt from the last time a story got personal and she'd been fooled into violating her hallowed reporter vows. "Hey, on a lighter note, it's raining men over here at the lake."

Bernadette laughed. "What?"

"Some kids vandalized Dad's kayak shed. He asked for my help and this handsome guy appeared out of nowhere to help me. Fill you in later. He's waiting."

On her way back to the stranger, she studied his profile. Men this desirable didn't drop out of the sky around here. Why was he in town? Visitors to Northbridge weren't unusual in the summer, but not late fall. He faced the water, looking in the direction of the rolling hillside of Tate Farm, the property under discussion at tonight's controversial public hearing.

She neared the visitor and he turned around.

"Are you the owner of this place?" He pointed to the wood-sided shed with a sign reading "Bullhead Boat Rentals."

"No. My father runs it with my brother. Dad's too old to be walking around in this icy mess and my brother is gone for the day." She handed him a wipe. "They also operate the local tackle shop and Two Rivers Guided Tours, guided fly-fishing trips."

"I remember the tackle shop." He cleaned his hands and tucked the dirty wipe in his jacket pocket. "My family came here for a couple of summers. Close to thirty years ago."

Sophie studied him again. Summer vacationers passed through here with the blur of a relay race.

He brushed a dead leaf off the knee of his faded, well-pressed jeans. "Such a great little town." He scanned the main street, unhurried and relaxed, then took a deep breath, as if to savor a nostalgic moment. "Quintessential New England."

Although she'd lived all her forty-four years in Northbridge, she looked around with him. A few cars parked on the road near a long row of pre-WWI buildings, now housing retailers who had serviced the town's residents for countless decades, such as Handyman Hardware and Walker's Drugs. The retail stretch was sandwiched between her favorite place to eat, Sunny Side Up, a metal-sided, trolley car-shaped diner and the weathered façade of Griswold's Café. The popular hangout for waterfront meals had a karaoke night the locals rarely missed.

She examined his profile again. Surely she hadn't forgotten someone with such a sexy full lower lip and strong chin?

"I can't imagine anybody being unhappy here," he said, his tone quiet.

She held in the urge to retort with a cynical remark. Every time she stuck a foot out of town, circumstances jerked her back. "Too bad you picked today to return. Most of our visitors enjoy the warmer weather."

"I'm house hunting."

"Oh. Well, we have a lot of summer residents."

"I want a year-round place."

The absent wedding ring held renewed interest. "Where are you from?"

"Manhattan."

She adjusted her crooked scarf. "Living here will be a big change."

"I know. I've always loved this place, though." He reached out and tenderly brushed a leaf off Sophie's shoulder. His gaze flowed down her body like a slow trickle of water.

An unexpected burn raced up her cheeks.

He lifted his brows. "Hey, I never knew the lake went by another name. The town website said the original name came from an old Native American word."

She nodded. "Puttacawmaumschuckmaug Lake." The long name rolled off her tongue with ease, the pronunciation a rite of passage for anyone born and raised around the body of water. "It either means 'at the large fishing place near the rock' or 'huge rock on the border.'"

"What?" He chuckled. "Puttamaum…"

She shook her head and repeated the difficult word.

"Puttacawsch—"

"Nope. It's a toughie. That's why a reporter who visited here at the turn of the century suggested in his column we change the name. He said the water's beauty was as rare as a blue moon, and the phrase stuck."

He grinned, easy and confident. "My kids will love this place."

Kids? Sophie buried her disappointment. "Are you and your wife looking at the other towns bordering the water?"

"No. I like Northbridge. Oh, and I'm not married," he said matter-of-factly. His gaze arm-twisted her for a response.

She wanted to fan her hot cheeks but instead regrouped while pointing across the lake. "If you have a spare few hundred thousand and want to help the town out, take a look at Tate Farm. A developer wants to buy it to put up a large resort. Maybe you can outbid the guy."

"Oh?"

"Uh-huh. There's a public hearing tonight."

The hearing would be her first chance to meet the corporate vipers from Resort Group International face-to-face and she couldn't wait to hammer firm president, Duncan Jamieson, with some tough questions. With any luck the zoning board would vote down their request so the offer she'd made, along with her dad and brother, would be back in play.

The stranger's brows furrowed and he stroked his chin.

"Don't worry. I'm confident our zoning board will vote no on their proposal and keep the nasty developer away. By the way, I'm Sophie."

He dropped his gaze to the ground for a millisecond then looked back up. "I'm Carter."

If Nana were still alive, she'd have said in her thick Scottish brogue, "Verra good sign, Sophie. Carter comes from the word cart: someone who moves things." Nana held great stock in the art of name meanings.

He'd certainly moved Sophie.

Matt's rusty sedan whipped into the lot, ending the lusty thoughts. Her son hurried over, unease covering every corner of his face. "Sorry I'm late."

"What took you so long?"

"Grandpa called to make sure I helped you." He dragged his hand through his messy dirty-blond hair. "We were talkin'."

She had her suspicions about the topic but rather than ask, she introduced him to Carter.

He turned to Matt. "What do you say we let your mom take it easy and we'll finish this job?"

Matt nodded and trotted to the boats.

At her car, Carter opened the driver's door. "Better hop in." His tone lowered. "Your hands were cold before."

Sophie's knees softened and she tried to speak, but no sound came out. Turmoil reigned inside her body as he jogged away from her and caught up with Matt.

She tried to shake off the lost control caused by this stranger. This little incident had stolen some of her strength and lately every morsel was necessary to stay afloat. On the roller coaster of life, she had been taking a wild ride. First due to a chance to own the vineyards, giving her a helping hand from her inner grief and fulfilling a life-long dream. Then two weeks ago, RGI had barged into town and yanked her offer from the table.

Carter pointed to a kayak and said something. Matt laughed. The scene made her miss having a man in their household. Her heart softened, awed by the way this knight who'd arrived in a shiny white Camry galloped in and took charge...and how she'd simply let him. Was something good finally stepping into her life?

Disappointment skimmed her chest. Who was she kidding? Nothing would come of this.

Her cynical nature hadn't developed overnight. Rather, she had soured over time. Lost opportunities, gone due to circumstances beyond her control: Mom's cancer, Sophie's unplanned pregnancy, her subsequent marriage to Mike, even her lost bid on the land RGI now wanted.

Time to forget this guy and concentrate on her job. She'd have to work harder than ever to stick to her journalistic creed, but any teeny, albeit truthful, crumb of negative news about RGI or its president, Duncan Jamieson, could sway the scale on the zoning board vote. Then the greedy developer would disappear from Northbridge forever.

Her family wanted that land. Land their ancestors were the first to settle back in 1789. Land where the winery plans of their dreams could come to life. The most important reason, though, was protecting the sacred place where her firstborn son, Henry, had died.

Chapter 2

A long line of cars pulled into the well-lit high school parking lot, higher than usual volume for a public hearing. Sophie grabbed her bag and hurried toward the entrance, hoping she could still get a seat up front.

As she neared the large regional high school, she passed a noisy group standing in a circle at the front of the building, chanting the plea "Save our Lake." Their signs bore the acronym "S.O.L.E." stacked on the left and the words, "Save Our Lake's Environment" extending from each corresponding letter. Protestors weren't the norm at these types of events and their presence added a thick cloud of tension to the cool night air.

Bernadette marched with the vocal group. Nana had liked to remind everyone how Bernadette was living proof her name theory worked. "I canna think of a better name for that lassie. She's named to 'be brave like a bear' and sure acts the part." There were times Sophie found *any* explanation about people's behavior to offer a measure of peace. After all, a wise person took heed in all the messages around her and her name meant "wisdom."

She waved to Bernadette, who yelled with more exuberance than any other protestor. A rosy glow highlighted her full cheeks and her large green eyes burst with equal excitement. She shook a defiant fist in the air.

"Nice boots," Sophie yelled over their noise. Bernadette had tucked her jeans into new boots, with razor thin heels and pointy toes, which crossed the border into sexy. Opposite of the sensible heeled style Sophie wore. "You're Northbridge's own *Che Guevera* in her Jimmy Choo's."

"You'd better start reading *Vogue*. These are from Target." Bernadette pushed aside her sable brown bangs, which always seemed due for a trim. "Grab a sign."

"I'm working. Remember?" Any public appearance of bias while covering a story could get back to her editor.

"Yeah, yeah. Same old excuse." Bernadette punched a follow-up fist of solidarity at the sky and resumed her chant.

The details about Carter would have to wait until after the hearing. Since Sophie's chance meeting with the handsome visitor, she couldn't shake her craving to learn more about him, a sensation that left her liberated and scared at the same time. Talking to the stranger was easy and comfortable, the way sliding into a pair of well-worn slippers let her know she was home, safe and exactly where she belonged.

She turned toward the entrance and slammed into a stiff body, making her stumble back a step.

"'Scuz me." Otis Tate dipped his bushy eyebrows in annoyance, his Adam's apple jutting out just beneath the scruffy edge of his white beard. As usual, his younger brother, Elmer, lagged several steps behind, shoulders stooped and taking away the extra few inches of height he held over the senior of the two septuagenarians.

"Sorry. I didn't see you." A cold breeze sent a chill through Sophie's wool skirt and tights, numbing her immediate reaction to scream "traitor." The mere sight of them made her blood boil. After they'd accepted Resort Group International's offer, they didn't even have the decency to give her a phone call. Bernadette had learned about the deal at her law office and called Sophie, adding to her humiliation. They probably hadn't given any consideration to the deep ties she held to the land. With no wives or children, their only goal was to sell to the highest bidder and retire near some friends in Florida, a consideration no self-respecting New Englander would utter aloud.

Otis cleared his throat. "Listen, we want you to know this isn't personal."

"I'd suggest you look up what personal means."

Both his brows arched. "Listen Sophie, we hadn't signed anything with you yet. Business is business. You'll find another spot for your winery." He elbowed Elmer.

Elmer flinched but didn't respond. Instead, he stared at the protestors, his downturned mouth giving away his sadness.

Otis leaned close enough for her to catch the warmth of his breath. "I heard Cliff gave you this story last minute. I assume you'll give it fair coverage."

The comment struck Sophie as hard as a kidney jab.

Her tone downshifted to a harsh whisper. "Nana was a friend of your dad's. She told me his name meant honorable. I wonder what she'd say about his sons."

Otis' face turned beet red and Elmer's froze like ice, as if her words cast a voodoo hex, Nana-style.

She raised her voice. "You don't have to fret over my coverage. I'll report on this with the unbiased dedication of an attorney defending a murderer." She turned to walk away then stopped and glared at both men. "Correction. Alleged murderer."

Elmer dropped his chin to his chest and it touched the ends of his flannel shirt collar. Sophie didn't care if she'd shamed the nicer of the two brothers. He, of all people, understood why she didn't want the land in the hands of strangers.

Two weeks after her son died, Elmer had paid Sophie a visit. Several people in town wished to set up a memorial garden for Henry, right on the spot where he'd passed away on the Tates' land. Elmer had requested her permission, admitting he wanted the memorial too. Henry had worked their farm every summer since turning fifteen and had grown close to Elmer, often calling the gentle old man his surrogate granddad. She'd agreed to the garden.

Now the place was hallowed ground. She visited there every year on the anniversary of Henry's death, his birthday or any other time she needed a tangible reminder of his life.

"If you'll excuse me, I have to get inside." The thick lump settled in her throat and tears burned in the back of her eyes.

Once inside the auditorium, she managed to get one of the last seats in the front row. On stage, members of the Northbridge Zoning Board had already taken their places behind a dais of two old rectangular fold-up tables with several microphones spaced along the tops.

She took a breath to relax. Attitude accounted for ninety-nine percent of any situation and regret over her backlash at the Tate brothers moments ago hit hard and fast. The wall clock showed three minutes before seven, so she used the time to scribble more questions for RGI on her notepad. A minute later, the group of protestors noisily filled the empty row behind her, where they'd left a few belongings to save their seats.

"How'd we sound out there?" Bernadette craned her neck to examine the crowded auditorium and slipped off her coat to reveal a white tee shirt with green letters spelling out S.O.L.E. printed across the bust line.

"Menacing. Only a fool would face you guys."

Bernadette pointed with her chin to the back of the auditorium. "Speaking of fools, here they are now."

A group of five men in suits had entered. Amongst town officials, she recognized the lawyer from Hartford representing RGI, who dressed fancier than the locals in his expensive-looking suit. She studied the two men to the attorney's side and stifled a gasp. The pitter-patter of her heart picked up speed.

Bernadette tapped Sophie's arm. "There's the head fool himself. Duncan Jamieson, president of RGI."

"Which one?"

"The hot tamale on the end, with wavy hair and wearing a navy suit."

"Are you sure?"

A puzzled expression flitted across Bernadette's face. "Absolutely. He came into the office two days ago to schmooze with one of the senior partners."

Sophie's mouth went as dry as dust. Bernadette had just identified Duncan Jamieson, head of RGI, as none other than Carter.

His presence begged for attention and separated him from the other men. Besides the expensive shine to his suit, assuredness permeated from every pore. He surveyed the crowd then leaned close and said something to his attorney, who nodded.

The group of men walked toward the stage. As he neared Sophie's section, his gaze met hers then dropped to the press badge dangling from her neck. He looked at her again and blinked. She held her breath, as much afraid he'd remember her as he'd forgotten her. After a negligible pause, his lip curled into a smile of clear delight. Before she could react, he winked and sealed the acknowledgement.

Sophie's pulse pounded in her ears as she neared code red. His cozy wink not only told others they'd met but dredged forth the lusty awareness of him which had consumed her body earlier. A sharp poke jabbed her back.

"What the hell was that?" Bernadette whispered. "Do you know him?"

"In a manner of speaking." She refused to turn around.

Carter, a.k.a. Duncan Jamieson, took the steps up to the stage and sat behind the long table with the other men. That guy had played Sophie more smoothly than a winning hand of poker, but she wasn't about to take his lies in silence.

Meet the Author

Sharon Struth believes you're never too old to pursue a dream. The Hourglass, her debut novel, is a finalist in the National Readers' Choice Awards for Best first Book. When she's not working, she and her husband happily sip their way through the scenic towns of the Connecticut Wine Trail, travel the world, and enjoy spending time with their precious pets and two grown daughters. She writes from the friendliest place she's ever lived, Bethel, Connecticut. For more information please visit sharonstruth. com or visit her blog, Musings from the Middle Ages & More at www. sharonstruth.wordpress.com.

www.ingramcontent.com/pod-product-compliance
Lightning Source LLC
Chambersburg PA
CBHW031410250626
47155CB00004B/1490